What Matters Most

Georgia Beers

What Matters Most

This trade paperback original is published by Brisk Press, Brielle New Jersey, 08730

Edited by Lynda Sandoval
Copy Edited by Heather Flournoy
Cover design by Ann McMan
First printing: March 2017

ISBN-13: 978-099667749-3

By Georgia Beers

Novels

Finding Home

Mine

Fresh Tracks

Too Close to Touch

Thy Neighbor's Wife

Turning the Page

Starting From Scratch

96 Hours

Slices of Life

Snow Globe

Olive Oil and White Bread

Zero Visibility

A Little Bit of Spice

Rescued Heart

Run to You

Dare to Stay

What Matters Most

Anthologies

Outsiders

www.georgiabeers.com

Acknowledgement

Each book I write has a behind-the-scenes team that helps me make it the best book it can be. They deserve my gratitude every time. So thank you from the bottom of my heart to:

Lynda Sandoval and Heather Flournoy, my awesome editing team.

Carolyn and Susan, my amazing publishers at Brisk Press.

Ann McMan, my ridiculously talented cover artist.

Carleen Spry, my source for all things Chicago.

Rachel, Nikki, Melissa, and the Central NY Romance Writers, my cheerleading squad.

And you, the most wonderful readers a girl could ask for.

Dedication

To Debbie Metzger, my very own Favorite Cousin

CHAPTER ONE

"WELL, THE LAST GUY I had a date with smelled like an egg salad sandwich that had been left in the sun." The woman paused for dramatic effect, then added, "For days."

Kelsey Peterson's laugh burst out of her and seemed to surprise both of them. "Oh, no. Gross."

"So gross."

Kelsey was familiar with this woman. Well, not this exact woman, but this kind of woman. In her thirties, dating again—most likely after a divorce—and had probably seen way too many of her evenings taken up by unworthy men the online dating service said were "perfect matches" for her.

"The one good thing that came out of it is it made me understand how important it is to smell nice. What's that saying? 'You never get a second chance.'"

"To make a first impression," Kelsey finished. "And I'm right there with you about smell. If somebody smells bad—or even if they smell okay, but it's not a smell their date enjoys—it's hard to come back from that."

"You get me, Kelsey." The woman's smile was imperfect, her front teeth slightly overlapping, and Kelsey found it endearing. "I'm Jennifer, and I am open to suggestion." She held out her hand and Kelsey shook it. "What do you recommend?"

This was where Kelsey shined and she knew it. Smell was her thing. She had the uncanny ability to talk to somebody for a very short time, size them up visually, and pick the exact right scent for them. Nobody knew exactly how she did it—not even her—but customers routinely asked for her, going so far as to eschew all the other employees in her Common Scents store, willing to wait however long it took for Kelsey to get to them.

"You seem like a warm scent person to me," Kelsey said and led her to the opposite side of the store. "Many of your warmer scents lean toward food—vanilla, cinnamon, apple—but that's not necessarily a bad thing. Especially on a date."

"If I'm a warm scent person," Jennifer began, holding out her hand for Kelsey to squirt a small dot of Vanilla French Toast lotion onto it. "Are there cold scent people?"

Kelsey made a face and tilted her head from one side to the other, weighing the question. "I'd call them cool, but there aren't many. There are people who are more floral. Some are nature-scented people. Seasonal scented."

"How do you know?" Jennifer rubbed the lotion in and took a sniff. "Oh, my God, that smells awesome."

"I don't really know. It's just a hunch. A feeling that I go with." Kelsey gave a modest shrug. "It's just my thing."

"Well, your thing is right on the money because I love this." Jennifer held up her hand. "I have another date next weekend with a new guy. Let's see what he thinks of Vanilla French Toasted Jennifer." She took two bottles off the shelf, paused, then snagged a bottle of bubble bath as well. With a sheepish grin at Kelsey, she explained, "I like baths."

"Who doesn't?" Kelsey asked. "We've actually got some bath bombs back in that corner display." She pointed toward the back of the store. "There's a Vanilla French Toast one that just arrived last week."

"I need that."

"I thought you might." Kelsey watched for a moment as Jennifer moved away from her, and before she could turn to help one of the next three people waiting for her, her cell phone buzzed in her back pocket. She excused herself and stepped away and behind the counter to take a quick look. As she pulled it out and read the text, Jeanine, one of her two other employees working with her today, bumped her with a shoulder as she passed by, a basket of new stock in her hands.

"Let me guess. Hannah the Not-So-Secret Admirer?" She grinned to take away any sting the tease might have held.

Kelsey rolled her eyes good-naturedly and shook her head. "I keep telling you. We talked. She knows I don't feel that way about her."

"Which doesn't mean she doesn't feel that way about you." Jeanine braced the basket between her thigh and a nearby shelf and began stocking. "You know that."

Jeanine was right, but there really wasn't anything Kelsey could do about it. She and Hannah had met through an online gathering site for lesbians and lesbian events, and while they'd hit it off as friends, there was really no spark there for Kelsey at all. No chemistry. And that was okay. Being new to town, having only been there for two months, Kelsey could use all the friends she could get and Hannah was great for that. They had a lot in common and texted almost every day.

"I do know that." What else could she say? "There's a softball game tonight."

"Dig out your cheerleading outfit."

"I sometimes wish I played." With a wrinkle of her nose, she added, "But mostly not."

"That park is a haven for local lesbians. If meeting new people is what you're trying to do, that's a good place to be."

Jeanine was certainly right about that, which Kelsey found amusing, as Jeanine was straight. The park being a lesbian gathering place was the main reason Kelsey went pretty much every week to Hannah's game. Now that she'd opened and settled comfortably into running her store, she was ready to branch out, meet some new people, and begin to establish herself in Westland, lay down some roots. She planned to be here a while.

Sending back a quick text telling Hannah she'd see her there and no, she didn't need a ride (thereby avoiding any leading on of Hannah *and* forcing herself to drive around on her own—two birds, one stone), she slipped her phone back into her pocket and turned her attention to the sixtyish woman who needed a gift for her granddaughter.

"If I get her something I like, she'll end up smelling like her grandma and I'm pretty sure she doesn't want that." The woman grimaced and Kelsey squeezed her upper arm.

"No worries. We'll find something just for her," Kelsey said and led her toward the far wall. "Tell me a little about her."

Once the lunch hour died down, so did the influx of customers, and Kelsey was able to scoot to her office in the back and get some paperwork done. There were orders to be placed, sales reps to call back, and displays to open. As the owner and manager of the store, she didn't really need to be on the floor at all. She had employees to do the selling. But the truth was, not only did she enjoy helping people find the right scents for themselves or for loved ones, customers often requested her. In less than nine weeks in the Westland store in Pineview Plaza, she'd garnered herself a bit of a reputation, customers coming in and saying their friend/sister/cousin recommended they talk to "Kelsey, the Owner" to find just the right product for them. She was proud of that.

Just before five, Kelsey wandered back out into the store, knowing Jeanine had to leave for her night class. Jeremy, who covered the five-to-nine shift, was just walking through the front door.

"Ladies," he said as he gave a nod to Jeanine and a customer she was helping. Jeremy was super handsome, very put together, and totally gay. Which actually helped in the sales department, as straight women seemed to have tons of faith in the fashion suggestions and any makeup tips they could get from gay men. Apparently, scent was no different. With his dark, wavy hair and precisely trimmed beard, Jeremy looked like any one of the Prince Charmings from a Disney movie, and the women in the store often did double takes at him. "Boss," he said to Kelsey, as he went behind the counter and into the back area to drop off his stuff. Kelsey followed him so they could go over what she needed done during his shift, then they both headed back out into the store.

"Softball game tonight?" Jeremy asked as he rang up Jeanine's customer so she could get her stuff from the back and get to class on time.

"Yes, sir." Kelsey shouldered her messenger bag and her small purse. "The cheerleaders are important."

"Truer words were never spoken," he said with a wink as she headed toward the door. "Have fun."

As was her tradition, Kelsey always stopped at the Starbucks about a mile down the street from her shop on the way to a game. As was also her tradition, she felt a little guilty every time because, being a small business owner, she knew she should patronize other small businesses, not overcharging behemoths like Starbucks. But she could freely admit to an addiction. To their coffee (mostly the caramel macchiato). To their pastries (mostly the enormous Rice Krispies treats because she was too lazy to make them at home). And to the little pouches of dried fruit trail mix that she couldn't seem to find anywhere else. With limited funds, she couldn't afford to stop more than once or twice a week, but on softball nights, it was an indulgence she allowed herself.

The store was fairly busy, buzzing with an equal mix of young hipsters and business folk who were finishing up their days, grabbing a blast of caffeine to get them home. Kelsey placed her order for a grande caramel macchiato with whole milk, deciding to splurge and forego the skim milk this time. Five extra minutes on the bike would be her payment, she promised herself. She gave her name, grabbed a dried fruit trail mix pouch, paid, and moved to the end of the counter where six other people were waiting for their orders. She scanned her phone, checking for mail, texts, skimming Facebook, but was bored quickly and slipped the device back into her bag, choosing instead to people watch.

Always so much more interesting than Tumblr, she thought as she gazed around the group of waiting customers.

The woman caught her eye almost immediately, so stunning Kelsey had to make a conscious effort to pull her gaze away, afraid she'd be caught staring. No, not staring. *Ogling.* The woman was that attractive. And just like that, it was as if all the sound in the Starbucks simply faded away. There was no chatter, no other people. Only her and a beautiful woman she'd never met before.

Blond hair fell just past her shoulders, bouncy with a slight wave to it, several varying shades of gold shot through. Navy blue skirt and jacket, tailored to perfection, the sleeves pushed up to not quite her elbows. Conservative heels with no sign of a scuff anywhere. As she scrolled on her phone, Kelsey watched her hands, could see she had a ring on her right hand but not her left. The skin on her forearms looked smooth and creamy, the tone not really pale, but not quite tanned, falling somewhere in between. Kelsey found herself wondering would it be as soft as it looked if she were to run her fingertips over it. More importantly (the big question for Kelsey), what did she smell like? Was she warm? Did she smell like apples with a touch of clove? Warm chocolate? Lavender maybe? She wasn't quite close enough to find out, and when she finally pulled her eyes away from the bare forearms and shifted her gaze upward, the woman was looking directly at her, an amused smile on her face.

The world came screaming back.

"Shit," Kelsey muttered quietly as she looked away, her ears suddenly assaulted by all the noise around her which, in reality, had never actually dimmed. She yanked her phone back out and tried to look busy, to look like she was occupied, to look like anything other than a creepy pervert staring at the pretty girl in Starbucks.

"Grande caramel macchiatos, one whole, one soy," the barista called out. Kelsey stepped forward to grab hers.

So did the blonde.

They each took a cup and before Kelsey could even peek at hers, the blonde said, "Um...are you Shelley?"

Kelsey furrowed her brow and shook her head. The blonde turned her cup so Kelsey could see "Shelley" scrawled across it in black Sharpie. "Oh," Kelsey said, understanding. "No, I'm not Shelley." With a glance at her own cup, she added, "But I'm not Lisa, either."

With an understanding nod, the blonde held up a finger, then sipped the coffee in her hand. "Whole milk," she said and handed the cup to Kelsey. "Looks like you're Shelley after all." She took the other cup from Kelsey with a gentle smile.

"Well, then, it's nice to meet you, Lisa," Kelsey said, because something about that gentle smile told her it was safe to joke with this woman.

"Back atcha, Shelley," the woman said, held up her cup in a little salute, then went on her way, tickling Kelsey's senses with the scent of...cinnamon? Honey? She couldn't quite tell. Kelsey watched her walk toward the door, watched the easy sway of her hips in the skirt, listened to the click of her heels, couldn't pull her eyes from the toned calf muscles.

"Good God," she said under her breath. She brought the cup up to take a sip and noticed a very faint imprint of light pink lip gloss on the lid. Kelsey couldn't help the smile that broke out across her face.

The softball game went into extra innings, which was a bummer because nobody should be forced to sit on bleachers for any longer than they had to. Kelsey shifted for the twenty-seventh time and wrinkled her nose at Ree sitting next to her on a vinyl cushion.

"I need one of those," Kelsey said with a sad sigh.

"You say that at every single game," Ree responded, chuckling.

"That's because it's true every single game."

"Target. Sporting goods section. Nine ninety-nine." Ree's attention was hijacked by sight of the batter, her wife DJ. "Come on, baby! Base hit!"

The evening had grown muggy, causing Kelsey to question why she hadn't ordered her coffee iced. Each sip sent an uncomfortable wave of heat through her body and, much to her dismay, she was going to have to toss it. A glimpse down at the cup reminded her of the lip gloss print, and she smiled to herself as she recalled the visceral effect that blonde had had on her. Women caught Kelsey's eye often; she could admit that. She was an admirer of the female form in all its shapes, sizes, and colors, and she would never apologize for that. But this one...

"Hey, Ree?" she asked as she leaned to her left. "Can I ask you something?"

They weren't close, Kelsey and Ree. They were acquaintances at best. But they saw each other every week on these very bleachers, always sat next to each other, and for some reason, they felt safe with one another. Ree always smelled like baby powder and and that made Kelsey feel totally comfortable with her. They'd talked about racism, sex toys, and politics—among other things—at various times during various games.

"Sure." Ree kept her eyes on the game, as she always did, but Kelsey knew she was listening. Her dark hair was spiked pretty dramatically today, and her earrings were bright green cupcakes with tiny red cherries on top.

"Have you ever met somebody..." Her voice trailed off as she looked for the right words.

"I've met several people, believe it or not."

"Ha ha. You're hilarious." Kelsey pushed playfully at her. "No, I mean, have you ever met somebody you found so immediately attractive and so *intensely* attractive that you felt like the world stopped around you?"

Ree faced her then, and Kelsey took another sip of the heatstroke-inducing coffee just to do something with her hands. "That's how it was when I met DJ," Ree said kindly.

Kelsey met her gaze, saw the softening in her light eyes. "Yeah?"

"Definitely." Ree turned back to the game, but kept talking. "I'd been dating on and off. A handful of women, but nobody really clicked. You know? I liked most of them quite a bit, but that...spark? Not there. When I met her, though?" With a jerk of her chin, she indicated her spouse, who was now on second base. "It was like I was suddenly under water." She turned to Kelsey, her eye contact penetrating. "You know what I mean? Like, I could still hear stuff, but it was muffled. Muted. There was nothing but her." The smile that broke out then was so tender and loving that, had she not started the conversation herself, Kelsey would have felt like she was intruding on something very personal.

"Wow." It was all she could think of to say.

Ree flushed a pretty pink. "Yeah." She nodded, returned her focus to the field. "So, I totally get what you're talking about. Why?"

Kelsey shook her head with a shrug. "No reason. Just curious."

Ree studied her, knew she was lying, but thankfully didn't push. She simply ended the conversation with, "Believe me, it doesn't happen often. We should all take note when it does."

The batter hit a pop fly then, which was caught and effectively ended the game.

"Thank God," Kelsey muttered as she rubbed the small of her back, and Ree chuckled in agreement. They collected their things, as did the rest of the spectators, and made their way down to the players.

"Hey, you." Hannah Keene wore a huge smile on her face, showing off a mouth full of artificially straightened teeth and a dimple on her chin. Her unique green eyes sparkled, as they always seemed to when she was around Kelsey, and she ran a hand through her short brown hair, scratched at her scalp. Face glistening with perspiration, she reached out and wrapped an arm around Kelsey's shoulders, gave her a squeeze. "I'm so glad you're here. Would have been nice to win for you."

"You played well," Kelsey said.

"They played better."

"That happens sometimes."

Kelsey said hello to several of Hannah's teammates, waved here, nodded there, smiled and laughed and congratulated. It was a really nice group of people that Kelsey was slowly getting to know. When she'd decided to make the move nearly nine hundred miles from home, it hadn't occurred to her that making friends in her thirties might not be as easy as it had been when she was in college. It took much more effort, first of all. Because she didn't work in an office setting, she didn't find herself surrounded by new people, possible friends. And because she was the boss at her shop, she wasn't comfortable hanging with her employees during personal time. That felt somehow inappropriate. So she'd had to do some creative research and come up with her own way of finding like-minded people. Thank God for the Internet. She'd found Lesbian Link-Ups. She'd found the softball league. She'd found Hannah.

Half an hour later, Kelsey sat at a round table in Point Blank, the local bar that sponsored Hannah's team. Ree sat on her left and a woman named Barb was on her right. Barb was a big girl. Not fat, just big. Broad shoulders, huge hands and feet, and a frame that had to surpass six feet. Her wife was Carla, the team's pitcher, and she came to every game just like Ree did. As she settled herself into her chair, she gave Kelsey's shoulder a squeeze. Kelsey smelled the scent of sandalwood that always seemed to accompany Barb.

"Hey there, Kels. How's life as a small business owner in the suburbs of Chicago?"

Kelsey grinned, as Barb asked her the exact same question every time they saw each other. It was a running joke now. "Not bad, Barb. I'm surviving." That was about all she was doing, but she wasn't close enough to Barb to get into such specifics, so she simply smiled.

As if choreographed, three drinks were set in front of the three of them all at once. A beer for Ree, a club soda for Barb, and a glass of white wine for Kelsey. The three of them thanked their suppliers all at once: DJ, Carla, and Hannah. Kelsey felt Hannah's hand brush the back of her head as she headed toward the pool table to take on one of her teammates.

"You sure you two aren't a couple?" Ree teased.

"I'm sure," Kelsey replied, not for the first time.

"Maybe you need to tell Hannah that," Barb commented before squeezing the wedge of lime into her club soda.

"Oh, I have. Believe me." This subject made Kelsey a little uncomfortable, despite the fact that it wasn't the first time it had been broached. These were Hannah's friends. They'd known her a long time, much longer than they'd known Kelsey or than Kelsey had known Hannah. They wanted her to be happy and Kelsey understood that, but she always felt like she had to tread carefully.

"Hey, Kels." Hannah's voice rang out from across the small bar. "Come over here and be my good luck charm." She was bent over the pool table, cue in hand, looking over her shoulder at Kelsey. "I can't make this shot without a little help."

Kelsey bit down on her bottom lip as Barb sipped her club soda and hummed an, "Mm-hmm," quietly.

The other six people around the pool table were looking her way, and the last thing Kelsey wanted to do was embarrass Hannah in front of her softball buddies, so she sighed softly and pushed her chair back from the table. Wine in hand—she was going to need it—she walked over to the pool table, trying not to notice the obvious happiness that colored Hannah's expression as she struck with the cue and sank the intended ball. A combination of cheers and groans went up around the table as Hannah stood, grabbed Kelsey, and kissed her on the cheek. Her usual scent was musky and Kelsey got a big dose of it with Hannah so close.

"Thank you, sweetheart," Hannah said.

"I didn't do anything," Kelsey replied, trying to downplay with a shrug. "I just stood here." She took a sip of her wine. Hannah's grin was lopsided and happy. And sweet and adorable, Kelsey had to admit.

"You're here," Hannah said, the grin hanging on. "That's all I need."

CHAPTER TWO

FRIDAYS TENDED TO BE good, business-wise. People took the day off for a long weekend or they took half the day and came in to shop on their lunch hour, knowing they didn't have to go back to work. Plus, Friday was a good day. People were happy on Fridays, and happy people spent more money.

Kelsey sat in the back in her office doing paperwork. The end of July was around the corner and that's when most of the bills were due. She'd put in her orders now, but she'd get billed for them within the next two weeks. Most of the invoices were Net 30, meaning she had thirty days to pay. Finally. Establishing credit took time, and even though she'd run a similar shop back home in Charlotte, it had been one shop in a large company of shops and the credit wasn't based solely on her. Here in Westland, it was.

A glance at the security monitors on her screen told her there were five customers milling about. Jeanine was helping one, talking animatedly with her hands as she did, and Kelsey smiled fondly. She'd specifically picked Westland. She'd needed a change. She'd been to Chicago on several occasions for long weekends and a business trip or two and liked it very much. Research told her Westland was an up-and-coming suburb and that, despite the currently high cost associated with renting a business location, costs would come down over the next few years. It had taken a ton of studying, some gloves-off business talk with her father, the corporate businessman, and a very big small business loan that still made her nervous. But she'd finally found a spot and been able to open Common Scents.

She liked it here.

The town was charming. The people were nice. She wasn't sure she was ready for the winter, but she was trying to think of it as an adventure. Her small apartment was less than five miles away, and she was getting to know some of the local residents.

Slowly but surely.

Her computer beeped an incoming e-mail. A supplier letting her in on a new scent of lotion that sounded promising. A new blend of their pumpkin spice. As Kelsey realized she'd have to get ready for fall scents, a glance at the monitor told her Jeanine was still helping a customer and there was another waiting at the counter. She made her way out on the floor to ring out.

A few minutes later, as the third person took her bag from Kelsey with a grateful smile, Hannah popped into view.

"Hey there," she said with a grin. No matter what, she always seemed happy. That was one of the things Kelsey liked most about her.

"Is it colorful balloon day?" Kelsey said, with a nod to the balloon-covered scrub shirt Hannah wore with her navy pants. "Nobody told me."

"One of the many joys of working in a pediatrician's office," Hannah said. "Teddy bear day is the best, though."

"I bet." Kelsey leaned on the counter. "What brings you by?"

"I thought I'd take you to lunch with me." Hannah's green eyes sparkled. "I only have forty-five minutes, so I'm going to my usual haunt and thought maybe you'd keep me company."

Hannah's "usual haunt" was Marco's Deli, which just so happened to be down the mall a bit from Common Scents and had the best broccoli and cheese soup Kelsey had ever tasted. They also made amazing sandwiches. Kelsey would go once or twice a week. It was that good.

"Looked like you had a nice handful of customers in there when I stopped by," Hannah said later, taking a big bite of her ham and Swiss. "That's good, yes?"

Kelsey nodded, spooned in some soup, chewed. "It is. I'd like it to be busier. I'm thinking of running another sale soon, try to bring in more people."

Hannah shook her head. "I don't know how you do it. I couldn't deal with people all day."

Kelsey gave a snort. "You *do* deal with people all day."

"Yeah, but they're patients, not customers. The phrase isn't 'the patient is always right.'"

"True."

"You actually like people. I can't stand them."

"I don't believe that," Kelsey said with a chuckle. "I've seen you around people lots of times."

"People I like, yes. Not strangers. Not crowds. I'd much rather be with a small group of people I know than a large group at a party or something." She chewed as she gazed out the window at the comings and goings in the parking lot. Turning back to Kelsey, she said, "I only have a small handful of people I consider close to me, but those people mean a lot."

Kelsey smiled. "My mom's like you."

"Well, your mom is obviously awesome."

"She is. I miss her." The last line was said more wistfully than Kelsey had intended, but Hannah picked up on it.

"Yeah, you're kind of far from home, aren't you?"

"Kind of."

"How come? You've never told me." Hannah chewed and watched Kelsey with those intense green eyes.

Kelsey shrugged. "I needed to get away."

Hannah stopped chewing and gave her a look. "Really? That's all you're going to give me? Away from what?"

Kelsey grimaced. "My ex?"

Hannah immediately squealed like a delighted small child. "I knew you had layers, Peterson. I *knew* it. Details, please."

With a glance at her watch, Kelsey arched an eyebrow evilly. "Sorry, Charlie, you have to get back to work."

"No!" Hannah grabbed Kelsey's wrist and turned it so she could read the time. "Damn it!" She crumpled up the paper from her lunch, finished her water, then said, "Don't think I'm not going to follow up on this later." She pointed a finger at Kelsey. "I want all the juicy dirt."

Kelsey couldn't help but laugh at the excitement her friend exhibited. "It's really not all that juicy, I promise."

"Still." They stood up at the same time. "Drinks tomorrow at Boomer's?"

"I'm at the shop all day tomorrow."

"After that." One corner of Hannah's mouth quirked up. "You'll be ready for a drink after twelve hours at work."

Kelsey nodded. "That is true. Okay. I'll meet you there at nine thirty?"

"Perfect." Hannah gave her a kiss on the cheek once they hit the sidewalk and parted ways, Hannah toward her car and Kelsey back to the shop. "See you tomorrow." Hannah waved.

Kelsey was surprised to find she was actually looking forward to the next night. She hadn't really shared much personal detail with Hannah since they'd met. She'd mostly stuck to superficial or work-oriented things, though she wasn't sure why. She'd kept her issues with Janice, her ex, buried pretty deep.

Maybe it was time to open up a little bit.

Saturday morning had been slow, but the afternoon picked up, and by three, Common Scents was fairly full of customers smelling, spraying, and rubbing lotion on their hands. The new Salt Air body spray was a hit, and Kelsey had to break into the spare box in the back room to restock the shelf. As she did so, a customer next to her was spraying fragrances into the air, then sticking her face into the mist to smell. When she caught Kelsey's eye, she made a sheepish expression and said, "I can't decide."

"Maybe I can help." Kelsey set the box on the floor and stood next to the woman, who was in her late forties and dressed in denim capris and a navy-and-white-striped top. She studied her, squinted, inhaled quietly. "You seem a bit floral to me. More nature scented." Kelsey moved down the aisle about two feet and pulled a Spring Lilac body spray tester off the shelf. She sprayed it into the air, smelled it herself, then gave one nod. "Try this one."

The woman did as Kelsey had, and her eyes widened. "Wow. I love that." She repeated the gesture, sniffed again, and smiled. "That's the one. Thank you!"

"You're very welcome." Kelsey smiled and emptied the box of the last four bottles when Jeremy came up to her.

"There's a woman here to see you," he said quietly near her ear.

Kelsey followed his gaze to the counter where a heavyset woman stood looking out of place and irritated about it. "I'll be right there."

Managing to avoid eye contact with a handful of customers as she walked by, Kelsey returned the box to behind the counter, then turned to the woman, whose brown hair had a prominent line of gray along her part. Her face was slightly pinched, like she'd just seen something unpleasant, and she smelled strongly of cigarettes. "How can I help you?"

"I'm Betsy Siegler." She stated it as fact—which Kelsey assumed it was—but also as something Kelsey maybe should have known already. She did not offer her hand.

"I'm sorry, do I know you?"

Betsy Siegler sighed loudly. "My mother owns this building. She's your landlady."

"Oh! Of course." How Kelsey was expected to know that Martha Jenkins had a daughter named Betsy Siegler, she had no idea, but she did her best to remain friendly and open. "Let's go into my office so we have some privacy," she suggested, gesturing for the woman to follow her. Mostly, she wanted to free up the space for the customers who'd begun to stack up. Once in the small room, Kelsey indicated the seat in front of the desk and she took the one behind it. "How can I help? Is Mrs. Jenkins all right?"

"Well, she's ninety-three," Betsy said with a snort, as if that explained everything.

"Okay." Kelsey raised her eyebrows in expectation.

"She's going into a nursing home." The sentence was blurted in an almost disgusted tone, as if it was Martha Jenkins's failure that she couldn't live alone at ninety-three years old.

"I'm sorry to hear that."

"Yeah, well. It's been a long time coming."

It had only been a couple months since Kelsey had seen her landlady and she'd seemed fairly coherent then. The rent was paid through an agency, so Kelsey didn't have much need to see Mrs. Jenkins in person, but it hadn't seemed like it was "a long time coming" for her to go into a home. Somehow, though, she was pretty sure Betsy Siegler wouldn't appreciate being contradicted. "And what can I do to help you, Mrs. Siegler?"

"I'll need to be raising your rent," she blurted.

And there it was.

They sat there, the two of them, Betsy Siegler looking satisfied, and Kelsey probably looking as blindsided as she felt. She took a moment to breathe, to get her bearings, to measure her own voice so she wouldn't yell.

"I have a lease that's good through next spring." Kelsey's voice was calm. Professional. Much to her own surprise.

"Yeah, I know. But if I buy the building and it's put in my name, that can be changed easily." So she'd looked into this before dropping her bomb.

"My store's only been open for two months. Barely. I'm still paying back start-up costs. A rent increase this soon was not something I planned on, Mrs. Siegler. Surely, you can understand that."

"Of course I can," Betsy said and picked at something on her pant leg. "But I'm sure you can understand that—not to be blunt—it's not my problem."

"Right." It was about all Kelsey could think of to say. She stood, needing this woman out of her office. Thank God, Betsy got the hint and also stood.

"I don't know when this will happen, but my lawyer will be in touch." With that, she turned and left. Again, she didn't shake Kelsey's hand. She didn't wait for her. She just...left.

Kelsey waited until she saw Betsy Siegler on the security monitor heading for the front door before she let herself drop back into her chair. "I can't afford more rent," she mumbled out loud to the empty office. "I'm stretched too thin as it is." She tapped a fingernail on the surface of her desk. "I'll have to fight it. Can I? Can I fight it? I'd need a lawyer, which I also can't afford. Oh, for God's sake." Dropping her head into her hands, Kelsey willed herself not to cry. There had to be something she could do. She just needed time to think.

But first, she needed some air.

The security monitors showed the crowd had died down somewhat, so she didn't feel guilty leaving Jeremy on his own so she could grab a short break. She suddenly felt so tired, like her legs were made of canvas bags filled with sand and she was barely able to drag them along. Funds be damned, she decided a blast of caffeine might help and found herself at Starbucks without really remembering how she got there.

Late afternoons on Saturday didn't have a lot of people looking for coffee, apparently, as there were only two other people in line when Kelsey entered and took her place. She waited patiently, studying the menu board and trying to concentrate hard on it so her brain wouldn't be dragged back to the Land of Financial Ruin. She placed her order for an iced mocha latte, paid, and moved down the counter. She was checking her phone when a voice nearby said, "It's nice to see you again, Shelley."

Because that wasn't her name, it took Kelsey a beat or two before she absorbed the words, unscrambled them, and realized who was talking. She whipped her head around and met the gaze of some stunningly blue eyes. "Well, hello there, Lisa. It's nice to see you again as well."

Lisa's lovely mouth curved into a gentle smile. "A Saturday afternoon, huh?"

"I needed a little help getting through the rest of my work day."

"Oh, you're working on the weekend. Me, too." She held up a hand before Kelsey could speak. "Let me guess." She tapped a long finger against her lips as she thought, and Kelsey had a flash of the lip gloss print on her last cup of coffee. It made her stomach tense up. In that good kind of way. "You're a hair stylist and Saturdays are your biggest day."

I can play this game, Kelsey thought as something deliciously sensual passed through her. "Exactly right. And you..." She looked at Lisa's outfit, a black pantsuit just as perfect and professional as the last time. "You're a lawyer. For the DA's office. You have to get your coffee and get back in time for the interrogation that's about to happen, um, downtown."

Lisa threw her head back and laughed, a big, hearty laugh that wasn't at all what Kelsey would've expected hers to sound like. "Perfect. I love it. I'm keeping that."

"Me, too."

Their coffees were announced, Lisa getting the same caramel macchiato with soy milk as last time. "You changed yours up," she commented as Kelsey's latte slid across the counter.

"I like to keep the baristas on their toes."

"Understandably." Lisa sipped her drink. "Well, I need to head back to the, um, prison. Next time I see you, I want to hear all about your wackiest client that day. Deal?"

"Only if you fill me in on your latest murder case."

"You got it." With a wave, Lisa said, "Catch you next time, Shelley."

And for the second time in a week, Kelsey found herself watching this beautiful blonde walk out of her life, watching her legs, her hips, her amazing ass, and not knowing if she'd ever see her again.

The little thrill of excitement it gave her was the first she'd felt in a very, very long time.

Boomer's was a small sports bar about halfway between Kelsey's apartment and the building where Hannah worked. They'd met up there a couple of times after work, but never on a weekend. It wasn't often that Kelsey saw Hannah in anything other than her work scrubs or her softball uniform, but tonight, she looked like a regular human in jeans, a red V-neck tank top, and red Chucks on her feet. She sat at the bar with a beer in front of her and looked over at the door when Kelsey opened it.

"Hey, you," she said, her face lighting up. She slid off her barstool and held out an arm. Hannah was the queen of the one-armed hug, and as always, Kelsey slipped under it and let Hannah squeeze her shoulders. "How was work?"

Kelsey groaned to illustrate her point as she took a seat. The bartender was a broad-shouldered man in his fifties who looked like he'd seen a thing or two in his time behind the bar. But his eyes were kind and crinkled a little when he smiled and asked Kelsey what he could get for her.

"Do you have any white wine?" she asked him.

"I've got a Chardonnay and a Pinot Grigio. Oh, and a Reisling."

"The Pinot, please."

"You got it."

As he left to pour her wine, Hannah said, "So?"

Kelsey raised her eyebrows. "So what?"

"Why the groan? Unruly customer today?"

"Oh, that." Kelsey shook her head as she recalled the superior attitude of Betsy Siegler, her utter lack of compassion for the position she was putting Kelsey in. "Unruly daughter of my landlady is more like it."

"Explain." Hannah made a motion for the bartender to put Kelsey's wine on her tab. He gave a nod and set the glass down on the bar.

"You don't have to buy that," Kelsey protested.

"I know that. I want to. You can get the next round." Hannah sipped her beer. "Tell me what happened."

With a deep sigh, Kelsey told the story, how Betsy Siegler had basically come into the store, dropped a bomb Kelsey was pretty sure she couldn't avoid, and left. "I was just kind of...stunned."

"It sucks, absolutely. Maybe she won't raise it a lot?" Hannah shrugged and her expression was hopeful.

"I can't afford for her to raise it at all," Kelsey told her. "I am budgeted down to the penny. When I signed the lease, I was under the impression I'd have a full year at that cost, so that's what I used to base all my other costs on. This will throw everything off, no matter how small the raise is." She didn't get into the fact that she'd really cut things closer than she should have, but she was sure her father would remind her of that. The little strip mall that housed Common Scents had the lowest rent she could find in the area. She'd counted on it staying that way for a good twelve months.

"You can't let it stress you out, though. That doesn't do you any good."

Kelsey pressed her lips together to keep from biting out a sarcastic comment. Hannah was trying to be supportive. She knew that. But Hannah was twenty-five and still lived with her parents. She was saving money so she could get her own place, but still. She didn't have bills like Kelsey did. She didn't really get the challenges of being on her own financially, let alone owning her own business. Kelsey just nodded. "That's true." She sipped her wine. "Can we talk about something else?"

"Sure." Hannah finished her beer and gestured for another.

"I've got that one," Kelsey told the bartender.

"So." Hannah put her forearms on the bar and scrutinized Kelsey. "Tell me about the ex."

Fabulous. Another subject she preferred to ignore.

"There's not a lot to tell," she said in an obvious attempt to deflect.

"Well, you told me you left the entire state of North Carolina to get away from her, so I'm thinking there might be a little to tell." Hannah held her thumb and forefinger very close together.

"Well. To get away from her and a lot of other people."

Hannah propped her head on her hand, elbow on the bar, and waited.

"God, you're relentless," Kelsey muttered. "Fine." She took a sip of wine. "Janice and I were together for five years. She's older than me by eight years, so most of our friends were her friends first. She was pretty well into her career as a bank manager. I was twenty-five with a business degree, and I was working for a shop similar to mine, but part of a big chain. I was moving up, but hating the politics of it."

Hannah nodded for her to continue.

"So, about three and a half years in, I start to feel a bit of distance between us. She's working later, going to 'work functions.'" Kelsey made air quotes. "We're not talking like we used to. We're spending less and less time together."

"Uh oh." Hannah grimaced. "Affair?"

"That's what I thought at first. All the signs were there." Kelsey recalled how she felt during that time...sad, alone, out-of-the-loop, and most of all, stupid. "I started paying more attention, asked her if everything was okay. She always laughed it off, made me feel like I was being some neurotic worrier. Finally, I got tired of wondering."

"Tell me you followed her. Please tell me you followed her."

Kelsey blushed a tiny bit, but Hannah's obvious excitement kept the shame at bay. "I followed her."

"Yes!" Hannah gave a fist pump. "I have this vision of you, all Olivia Benson-like, slinking down in the driver's seat of your car as you sit on a stakeout."

"Trust me," Kelsey said with a chuckle. "It was far less glamorous."

"Was it an affair?"

"No. It was a night class."

"What?" Hannah's brow furrowed. "A night class?"

Kelsey gave a slow nod and took a sip of her wine. She set the glass back down, spun it slowly by the stem. "She was taking classes to help with a promotion the bank had offered her. In Asheville."

Hannah blinked at her. "So, wait. She was taking night classes she didn't tell you about so that she could take a promotion she didn't tell you about in a city you didn't live in? And that she didn't tell you about?"

"Exactly."

"WTF?"

"Exactly." Kelsey finished off her wine, signaled for another.

"Wow. That's cold."

"We had talked about moving to Asheville down the line. I never expected her to just...go without me. To this day, I'm not a hundred percent sure what happened, but I suspect there was somebody else. Somebody she met at work. I've checked her Facebook page and she's been 'in a relationship' with some chick since about a week after she moved there, so..."

"Wow," Hannah said again. "I'm sorry, Kels."

"Thanks. It was hard because our friends were her friends first, so I lost most of them in the split. That's when I decided to get away. Far away."

Hannah raised her glass. "To far away." Kelsey touched hers to it and they sipped. Hannah looked at her intently for several moments before saying softly, "That sucks."

"It did. But it's over. I'm past it. I'm just kind of sensitive to secrets now, you know?"

"I bet you are. I totally get it."

"Anyway." Kelsey shrugged. "That's my story. Sad but true."

"For what it's worth, I think your ex is an idiot." Hannah smiled tenderly at her.

"So do I."

They clinked glasses again and Kelsey actually found herself feeling a little bit lighter. She hadn't told anybody that story since she moved. Since before she moved, really. The truth of the matter was, she'd abandoned a lot of her old friends when she'd moved in with Janice, so when they split, Kelsey found herself alone in more ways than one. This move had been a big deal for her. A huge deal. And it wasn't easy. Moving away from her family, from everything she was familiar with, so that she could start all over again at thirty-one was stressful. It was frightening. It was hard. But she'd done it and for that, she was proud of herself.

She could only pray that Betsy Siegler wasn't about to take it all away.

CHAPTER THREE

IT HAD BEEN NEARLY a week since the bomb-dropping visit of Betsy Siegler to Common Scents, and Kelsey could feel herself relaxing even as she tried not to let her guard down. There was no way somebody as singularly focused as Mrs. Siegler would warn Kelsey she'd be contacted by her lawyer and then just disappear, never to be heard from again. The world was not that kind. Kelsey was pretty certain of it.

Still. Every day that went by with no phone call, no visit from a slick-looking guy in an Armani suit, no reminder of what had happened the previous Saturday, saw Kelsey's stress levels reducing, saw her breathing just a tiny bit easier, despite her own internal promise to be ready at all costs.

Jeremy had things under control at the shop—Thursday nights weren't historically busy—so Kelsey had headed home and found herself in her small but charming apartment by six, which was nearly unheard of.

After enjoying a leisurely dinner of eggs over easy, bacon, and toast, she collapsed onto her well-used couch, pulled out her laptop, and surfed Netflix to decide on something to watch. It wasn't often she had free time like this, and she knew she should probably do a little cleaning, but the idea of vegging on her couch with a glass of wine and a cheesy horror movie was way more appealing than scrubbing the toilet or dusting her dresser.

She was twenty minutes into *You're Next* when her phone buzzed, signaling an incoming text. A glance told her it was her cousin Chris, and Kelsey gave a little squeal of delight.

You up for some FT? the text read.

Kelsey didn't even respond. She simply hit the FaceTime icon on her laptop, and in a few seconds she could see Chris's smiling face filling her screen.

"Well, hello there, favorite cousin of mine," Chris said with her usual lopsided grin.

"Boy, are you a sight for sore eyes. Hi."

Chris's mom and Kelsey's mom were very tight sisters. When they had babies less than a year apart, it only stood to reason that they'd be tight as well. Chris was older—a fact she liked to hold over Kelsey's head often when they were growing up—but they'd always been incredibly close. They'd attended the same college. They spoke at least once a week, if not more often. They could read each other like books. When something was bothering Kelsey, Chris always knew, sometimes simply by looking at her cousin's face.

"What's going on, Kelderama?" Chris asked, the squinting of her brown eyes visible on the screen as she used one of the umpteen childhood nicknames Kelsey couldn't seem to shake. "You've got the Worry Divot going in a big way." She indicated the spot above her own nose where Kelsey always got a crease from scowling with worry.

Neither of them had siblings, so they filled that role for each other, acting more like sisters than cousins. They also enjoyed using the fact that they were both gay as a way to endlessly tease their mothers, blaming their genes and letting their fathers off the hook.

"First, tell me how Boston is." Chris had moved there from Charlotte about six months before Kelsey had moved to Westland, to take a job at an international marketing firm.

"It's okay. It's a really cool city. Lots to do and see."

"That should sound great, but your tone is unconvincing."

Chris made a sound of frustration and tucked some of her sandy hair behind an ear. "I know. It's just...I'm working so much. Which isn't a surprise. I mean, they told me during my interview that it'd be a bitch of a first year, but..." Her voice trailed off and her eyes looked away from the camera.

"You don't have any time to meet people." Kelsey understood completely, despite the difference in their jobs.

"Yes! That's exactly it. I work a seventy- or eighty-hour week and then all I want to do when I'm not in the office is sleep. I've got, like, zero extra time. As you can see," she held her phone farther from her face to reveal the background: an office. "I'm still at work."

"You're an hour ahead of me," Kelsey said with a glance at the clock. "It's after eight there. Go home."

"It's only five thirty on the west coast."

Kelsey grimaced. "I'm sorry, Chrissy. I know what you're going through. I mean, my hours aren't as brutal as yours—"

"And you're the boss," Chris interjected.

"And I'm the boss. But I know exactly what you're going through. Meeting people is tough, especially if your time is limited."

"You've done a commendable job, if your Instagram is any indication. Are you and Hannah official yet?" Chris waggled her eyebrows in a ridiculous gesture that made Kelsey laugh.

"No, we're not, and we won't ever be. I told you, she's sweet, and I like her a lot, but it's not there for me."

"Still? I mean, she's seriously cute."

"You think so? Well, fly out here and I'll introduce you."

"I just might do that."

"Promises, promises," Kelsey said with a snort.

"So talk to me. What's going on that has you looking so stressed?"

Kelsey took a deep breath and launched into the entire story of Betsy Siegler, her mother, and her threats, ending with how she hadn't heard anything since, and it was freaking her out a little bit because her heart wanted to pretend nothing was going to happen and everything was fine, even though she knew better.

"Maybe you're overthinking it," Chris offered with a shrug. "Maybe it will be fine."

Kelsey fiddled with the ring on her left forefinger, spinning it with her other hand in a nervous gesture. "I suppose anything is possible. But I just don't see Betsy Siegler as a woman who's going to raise my rent by twenty bucks. More likely, it'll be a few hundred. Or more. It's an up-and-coming area, and property values are going no place but up."

"Have you talked to your dad?" Chris asked the question quietly, obviously knowing how it would make Kelsey bristle.

"No."

"Maybe you should?" When Kelsey looked away, Chris went on. "He's a good businessman, Kels. He knows his stuff."

"Yeah, he also told me opening my shop was...let me think. How did he say it?" She rubbed her chin in a gesture of thinking, but she didn't need to. She remembered *exactly* how he'd said it. "Oh, right. 'Short-sighted, wishful thinking.' That's how he viewed my hopes for success."

Chris sighed. "I'm sorry. I know he's tough on you." They were quiet for a beat or two. "What are you going to do?" Chris finally asked.

"I don't know yet." Kelsey shook her head. "The only thing I can do right now is wait until the axe falls. See what kind of damage I'm in for and go from there."

"I'd tell you not to stress about it until you have to, but I've met you." Chris's grin was tender and Kelsey felt her heart warm.

"Yeah, well."

They chatted for a few more minutes about their parents and other things before bidding each other goodbye. Kelsey sat in the silence of her small apartment for several long moments and tried to focus on her breathing, to just get herself to stop worrying so much.

I'm going to give myself an ulcer, she thought, not for the first time.

Chris was right about one thing: she shouldn't let herself go into full-blown panic mode until she had to, and she was skirting dangerously close to it as it was. She was fine right now. The shop was fine in this moment. She remembered one of the women she'd met through the softball team telling her all we have is this moment. There is no future. There is no past. There is only now. And while she'd smiled politely but had internally rolled her eyes at such hippie-Karma-silliness, she understood now that there was something to it. Maybe she would die in her sleep tonight; she had no way of knowing. And then none of her current worries would matter. She'd have spent time freaking out for nothing. All she had was right this very moment. The present. The now.

What did she want to do with *right now*?

With a nod, she refreshed her screen and went back to Netflix to watch the final girl outwit the bad guys. It wasn't a bad way to spend the moment.

Friday dawned hot, and the brightness of the day got Kelsey moving early. She made sure her outfit consisted of layers. While the heat could get surprisingly heavy given how far north it was, it was the air conditioning inside that messed with her body temperature. It was difficult to fathom how it could be ninety-five degrees outside, but she could be looking out the window from her shop with goose bumps on her arms. She had to be careful adjusting the temperature, though, because her customers never seemed to be as chilly as she was.

The morning sunshine had a joyful effect on Kelsey as she drove, sunglasses on, radio turned up loud. Her talk with Chris the previous night had helped her to relax. Whatever was going to happen was going to happen, with or without her incessant worrying. That was fact. When she'd opened her eyes this morning, she'd been pleasantly surprised to feel that lightness still holding on, keeping the worry at bay. It was a nice change of pace.

"I do believe a Frappaccino is in order on this beautiful morning," she said aloud to the empty car as she steered it into the Starbucks parking lot. It was earlier than she was usually there on the occasional mornings she stopped in, but she also had over an hour before she needed to get the shop opened, so she wasn't worried.

To the shock of no one, the place was packed, a good fifteen people waiting in line to place their orders. What did shock Kelsey was the mane of wavy blond hair on the head of the woman at the end of the line. Funny that she'd recognized it from the back. It made her mentally chuckle as she took her place behind Lisa and said quietly, "Big case today?"

Turning to face Kelsey, Lisa's face flushed just a little bit and a grin split across it, revealing perfect teeth. "Shelley, hey. Yes. Huge case today. How'd you know?"

"The suit," Kelsey said, waving one finger up and down. Not only had she noticed the smart cut of the suit itself, but she'd also noticed how well it was filled out. Especially the backside of the pants... "You look really sharp. Perfect for chowing down on a measly public defender."

"My favorite midmorning snack." They each shuffled forward a few inches. Kelsey could smell that usual Lisa scent: cinnamon, honey, some kind of subtle fruit—cranberry? "What about you? You're in early. Let me guess: a weekly hair appointment with an elderly woman."

"I wouldn't call her elderly, but she's older, definitely. Yes. She needs, um, a set and a blow dry." Kelsey laughed at her own attempt to wing some hairdresser speak. "Good guess."

"Most people—and by 'most people,' I mean people who aren't my grandmother—don't want to roll out of bed directly into the salon." Lisa furrowed her brow. "Though I guess that'd be a great way to have terrific hair for the day."

Kelsey laughed as they approached the cash register. Lisa put in her order for her usual, then said, "And whatever this lovely lady is having this morning," as she gestured to Kelsey.

"Oh," Kelsey said, caught off guard. "Really?"

"Absolutely. My treat."

Kelsey ordered her Frappaccino, then turned to Lisa. "You didn't have to do that."

"I don't have to do anything." Lisa handed her Starbucks card over to the cashier and gave him their names as Shelley and Lisa, making Kelsey chuckle.

"Thank you." Kelsey took a chance by reaching out, touching Lisa's arm lightly, then dropping her hand back down.

"You're very welcome." Lisa's smile was wide, seemingly genuine, as she put her card back in her wallet, her wallet into her purse. They slid down the counter to stand at the end with the handful of others who were waiting on their caffeinated beverages.

"So, tell me about the case."

"Oh, it's a good one." Lisa lowered her voice to a whisper. "Murder."

"Ooohhhhh," Kelsey said, her voice just as quiet. "Listen, if you have a suspect that looks anything like Shirley Knight, she's guilty. Just sayin'."

Lisa barked out a laugh and it seemed startlingly loud on the heels of their whispers. "I'm pretty sure we have a placard of some sort in the office that says as much."

"It's probably in Jack McCoy's office."

"I bet you're right."

"Good. It's very important information to have."

Their drinks were called and set on the counter. Shockingly, their fake names were spelled correctly—though they were on the wrong drinks. They laughed and switched cups. Lisa held hers up and touched it to Kelsey's.

"Have a great day, Shelley. I must go protect and serve."

"Do it well. And thanks for the Frap." Kelsey was getting used to the view as Lisa walked away from her.

It was a nice one.

A very nice one.

CHAPTER FOUR

REE AND DJ LIVED in a cute bungalow about half an hour from Kelsey's apartment in a little gem of a neighborhood Kelsey hadn't discovered yet. She was nervous, though she wasn't sure why. Much of the softball team would be at this party, so it wasn't like she'd be walking into a den of strangers. Hannah had said there'd also be some faces that were new to Kelsey, and she was looking forward to that. For now, though, the butterflies had kicked up their speed and felt like they were dive-bombing into the sides of her stomach.

It was three houses up before she found an open spot to park, did so, and pulled out the bowl of spinach artichoke dip she'd made for the occasion. She'd dressed in denim shorts and a pink-and-black-striped tank, sandals on her feet, and for about the twenty-third time that day, she wondered if she should have worn something else. What, she had no idea. It was an afternoon outdoor picnic party. Shorts and a tank seemed perfect attire.

"Too late to do anything about it now anyway," she muttered as she glanced around. She spotted Hannah's car down the block as well as a couple belonging to softball players.

Okay. I got this.

As she approached the front door, Kelsey realized the party sounds—laughter, the buzz of conversation, music from Pink—were coming from behind the house, so she detoured to the back where she found a gate in the chain-link fence that surrounded the yard.

"Kelsey!" a familiar voice called out, followed by a few more, and Kelsey felt herself grin at being so happily greeted.

"You made it," Hannah said, opening the gate latch for her and ushering her into the yard. Ree waved from the deck where she was setting a plate of something on a table. DJ called to Kelsey from within the above-ground pool and waved a wet, beefy hand.

There were maybe fifteen people milling around the yard, and the party had only just begun, so Kelsey expected more would turn up. A foursome was playing a game where they threw two balls connected by a string at a ladder-shaped thing about twenty feet away. A few people splashed around in the pool and the remainder sat in chairs on the small deck. Kelsey felt Hannah's hand in the small of her back, directing her toward the back door.

Ree reached out and hugged her. "We're so glad you're here," she said when she pulled back, and the smile in her eyes was warm and kind. She went around the deck, pointing a finger at each person Kelsey might not have known, introducing them. Kelsey did her best to remember the names, knew she'd most likely fail miserably, but smiled in greeting anyway. "Kelsey is a fellow requisite cheerleader at the games. She keeps me company in the stands."

"I brought a dip," Kelsey said, holding out the dish. "It needs to go into the oven for about a half hour."

"Follow me," Ree said, and Kelsey did, feeling Hannah right behind her as they went through the back door into Ree's kitchen.

"Did you have any trouble finding it?" Hannah asked.

"None at all," Kelsey told her with a smile. Hannah had wanted to pick her up, but Kelsey felt it was safer if she had her own wheels. That way, she could leave when she wanted and wasn't tied to somebody else's schedule. Since Ree's remark a couple weeks ago about Hannah thinking they were a couple, Kelsey had attempted to step more carefully, texting less, taking a longer time between responses. She felt awful because she suspected Hannah felt the shift, but it was definitely the best course of action.

"What are you drinking?" Hannah asked.

"What are my options?"

Hannah laughed and looked at Ree, who was putting Kelsey's dip in the oven. "She's clearly never been to your house before."

"Right?" Ree laughed.

Turning back to Kelsey, Hannah said, "Basically, whatever you want."

"Wow. That gives me a lot of options." Kelsey chuckled as Ree threw her a wink. "You know what? I'll just have a beer."

"Cool. What kind?"

Kelsey's eyebrows raised. "I have options there, too?"

"We don't mess around," Ree informed her.

"Apparently not," Kelsey said.

Hannah simply grinned, took Kelsey's hand, and led her back outside, down the deck steps and around to the side of it.

Three large coolers were lined up, end to end. Hannah flicked the tops open on each of them and Kelsey saw more brands of beer than she could count.

"Wow," she said again. "You guys *don't* mess around."

"Nope."

Kelsey pointed. "I'll have the shandy."

Hannah grabbed it before Kelsey could move, popped the top with the opener on a long chain around her neck, and handed it over.

"Nice bling," Kelsey laughed, pointing at the opener.

"Preparation is everything."

Kelsey was given a chair at the table on the deck where she participated peripherally in a few conversations, but mostly listened. The woman to her right (Kay?) was a physician's assistant and the woman on Kelsey's left (Amy, maybe?) was a pediatric nurse. This meant Kelsey spent a lot of her time doing her impression of a tennis match spectator, turning her head from one side to the other to follow the conversation (which was very interesting, despite her not being a part of it). She watched the party guests come and go, some having other places to be, some having had earlier obligations, so arriving later. Hannah bounced around, checking in on her regularly, which Kelsey found simultaneously sweet and irritating, as the impression she was giving to those around them was pretty obvious.

"So...Kelsey is it?" Kelsey's attention was snagged by the woman directly across from her. She had short, chestnut hair and warm brown eyes. At Kelsey's nod, she asked, "What do you do?" The others at the table turned their gazes her way.

"I own a scent shop," Kelsey said.

"A scent shop?"

"That great little place in Pineview Plaza," Hannah piped in, seeming to materialize out of thin air. "She sells lotions and body sprays and stuff. Smells amazing in there."

Kelsey smiled, again feeling a sprinkle of gratitude and a prickle of annoyance.

"Oh," the woman said with recognition. "Common Scents?" At Kelsey's nod, she added, "I love that store."

"I'm glad," Kelsey said with a nod and smile.

"You just opened it recently, right?"

"About two and a half months ago, yes."

"Are you from here?"

Kelsey shook her head and took a sip of the beer she was nursing. "Charlotte."

"North Carolina?" At Kelsey's confirmation, the woman gave a knowing smile. "Well, winter oughta be new for you."

Chuckles went around the table and Hannah offered, "I'm going to take her shopping for boots, a coat, gloves, all that good stuff."

You are? Kelsey thought, but let it slide rather than embarrass Hannah in front of her friends. Instead she simply smiled and asked where the restroom was.

"I'll show you," Hannah said.

As gently as she could, Kelsey said, "That's okay. Just tell me."

To Hannah's credit, she did.

Inside the house—and once out of the kitchen—it was peaceful and quiet. The small powder room off the hallway smelled pleasantly of jasmine and there were three framed photos on the wall. All were of Ree and DJ, and all were taken someplace other than Westland. One showed them posing on some red rock—maybe Utah or Arizona? In another, they both sported Mickey Mouse ears and huge grins. The third, they stood huddled in front of Niagara Falls, looking like they were being pelted with gray rain, but smiling widely anyway. In each photo, they gave the impression of complete happiness, arms around each other, teeth gleaming from inside enormous grins. Kelsey couldn't help but smile, and then she felt a slight pang in her chest.

What's that about?

Silly question. She knew. She knew exactly what it was about. And while it was an uncomfortable feeling that made her the tiniest bit sad, she also knew it was a good thing. For the first time since pulling herself together after Janice's abrupt, shocking, and painful departure, Kelsey was actually feeling a little...lonely. She'd honestly wondered if she'd ever feel that way again, ever find herself ready to try something, someone, new.

Was it time?

Her thoughts immediately went to Lisa, from Starbucks, which was silly, as she knew nothing about her and suspected there was probably a handsome and devastatingly fit man waiting for her at home. Still, she was the first woman to snag Kelsey's undivided attention in a long time. It only made sense her brain would head there first.

And thinking of Lisa made her smile. Nothing wrong with that.

She glanced at the photo from Disney World again, ran her fingertips over the smiles on Ree's and DJ's faces, smiled herself at how ridiculously happy they looked just to be standing there next to each other.

Yeah. She wanted that again.

One day.

One day soon.

Kelsey stayed at the party until about six o'clock, but claimed she had some paperwork to get done before the shop opened at nine in the morning Monday. Not exactly a lie, but not the whole truth. In actuality, Sundays were her only full day off and she had to do some fun and exciting things in her apartment...like clean the bathroom and mop the kitchen floor.

She did neither of those things, though. Instead, she turned on the TV, plopped on the couch with her laptop, and looked up the lesbian dating site she'd overheard a couple women discussing at the party.

It was time.

To be honest, she hated the idea of online dating. It seemed to her there was no way to tell if you had that spark with somebody, that all-important chemistry, just from reading their words on a page. For example, she knew that if she'd been virtually paired by a computer dating service with Hannah, she'd have definitely gone on a date, as they looked great on paper, had a lot in common. Hannah was cute, she was smart, she was funny, but that instant attraction just wasn't there for Kelsey and the date would have led them to exactly where they were now: friendship.

"Which isn't really a bad thing," Kelsey said aloud. "Can't have too many friends, especially in a new town."

There was a long span of time that simply consisted of her staring at the home page, at the little red box that cheerfully shouted *Sign Up Here!* Her attention shifted between the *NCIS* rerun on the television and her computer screen, back and forth, back and forth, before she finally blew out a breath and clicked the box, muttering, "Damn it," under her breath.

It didn't take long. There was a list of twenty questions about personality, likes, dislikes, all of which seemed reasonable, some credit card info, and a place to upload a photo. That turned out to be the most difficult aspect of the whole thing for Kelsey: choosing a photo. There was a handful on her computer and she pared it down to three. One was a shot of her on a hike with Chris the last time they'd been together. Kelsey had her hand on the trunk of a tree and was looking up at the branches. She liked that one. Another was a photo of her and Janice. She could easily crop her ex out, and had, but she kept it because she herself had been having a really good hair day that day. The third was a shot Hannah had taken of her only a couple weeks ago while messing with Kelsey's iPhone (unbeknownst to her). It was startlingly flattering, a close-up of her smiling, looking away from the camera, squinting in the sun. She'd been surprised when she'd discovered it the following day; she'd laughed at Hannah's antics, but hadn't been able to bring herself to delete the shot. It seemed to capture her perfectly.

Yeah. That was the one.

She posted it, finalized her account, and abruptly shut the laptop. *Now*, she would clean the bathroom.

Monday brought her a ton of things to be done at Common Scents, which was a good thing, as she was having major buyer's remorse about the dating site. So much so that she'd texted Chris in a full-blown panic at six that morning.

You need to chill. This is a good thing, Chris had typed much later, when Kelsey was in her office at work.

Freaking out is a good thing? Kelsey had fired back. *Explain.*

No, creating an account is a good thing, Chris had clarified. *I'm proud of you.*

Oh, good. Kelsey knew her sarcasm was most likely lost in text. She had barricaded herself in her office, too uncertain to deal with customers. *Still freaking out over here.*

Deep breaths. And then check and see if you got any matches!

Kelsey stared at the screen on her phone and chewed on the inside of her cheek for several seconds before responding. *I'm afraid.*

You're silly.

Her intercom crackled to life then, and Jeanine told her the sales rep from the cruelty-free lotion manufacturer had arrived. Thank God.

Duty calls, she typed to Chris. *Back later.*

Stephanie Bradley from Earthly Products looked the part of a woman selling cruelty-free cosmetics. Her blond hair was cut short and stylishly, longer in the front than in the back, swooped to the side and tucked behind an ear. Hammered silver disks dangled from her ears and her makeup was very simple—just mascara, lip gloss, and a touch of blush—and effective. Her skirt was long and flowing, her sandals simple, and her toes polished a bright blue. She was exactly what she needed to be to sell her product: earthy, approachable, and not at all pushy. If there was one thing Kelsey couldn't stand it was the hard sell, and she refused to be bullied into buying anything. Stephanie did it right. She talked about her products, about the making of them and how they were made with no animal by-products and were never tested on animals, and she handed several samples over to Kelsey. Then she let Kelsey make her own determinations.

The lotions were silky and absorbed quickly into her skin. Kelsey liked that and knew her customers would as well. The Orchid Breeze had a lovely, very subtly floral scent. Not too heavy, not too cloying. It just tickled her nostrils.

The fragrances were similar in characteristics. Kelsey spritzed the Mint Julep body spray into the air near her, then took a sniff. Same thing: subtle, gentle scent, just a tease.

This went on for a good seven or eight minutes as Kelsey opened, sniffed, and sampled just about everything Stephanie had to offer. Stephanie sat quietly, observing, answering any questions Kelsey had, but otherwise letting her product sell itself.

It did.

"I really wish I had ten suppliers like Earthly," Kelsey said with a grin. "The whole cruelty-free thing is a very big selling point for a big chunk of my customers, but there aren't enough of you guys to go around."

"Yet," Stephanie said, returning the smile. "We're getting more and more requests, which means our competitors must be as well. I think it won't be long before we see some of the larger manufacturers extending their lines to include cruelty-free. That may help to bring costs down."

"It was a big sticking point at my last store," Kelsey confided.

"Cost?"

"No, cruelty-free products. I used to work for a big chain store that shall remain nameless, but my manager refused to even consider entertaining some of the cruelty-free stuff out there. They cost more and that's all she needed to see: her profits dwindling. Didn't matter that the dwindling was minimal."

"Studies show that a large percentage of people—women in particular—are perfectly willing to pay a little more for products that are cruelty-free. And that number grows every year."

"And that's why I'm going to place an order with you."

"Fantastic." Stephanie clapped her hands together once, then pulled out a sheet detailing all the available products and handed it to Kelsey.

"I'm going to start small, see how things go."

"Absolutely." Stephanie woke up her iPad and they got to work choosing products and scents, discussing the benefits and sales potential of different items in this particular market. It was nearly an hour later that they completed their business. Stephanie stood and shook hands with Kelsey. "You're going to be so pleased with our products. I promise you."

"I believe that."

Kelsey walked Stephanie out through the shop where a handful of customers browsed and held the door for her. With a wave, she headed into the parking lot, and Kelsey took a moment to breathe in the fresh air, feel the sun on her face. Which only lasted a moment before it became too hot. With a shake of her head she went back inside and busied herself with a couple of customers until her stomach growled loudly, reminding her it was nearly time for lunch.

Back in her office, she glanced at her phone to see a text from Chris. In all caps, it said simply, *AND???*

Kelsey sighed loudly and dropped into her chair. "I will never hear the end of it if I don't take care of this," she said to the empty office. "Fine."

On her laptop, she signed into the dating site and was startled to see she had twelve responses waiting for her. "Wow." She sat and stared for a moment before lifting one shoulder in a half shrug and saying, "Okay. Let's see what we've got."

Of the twelve, six of them had photos of women who, if they didn't look like serial killers, at least appeared to have been on an episode or two of *Hoarders*. She deleted them immediately, pulled out her peanut butter and jelly sandwich, and set to reading up on the remaining six.

Half an hour later, she was left with two serious possibilities.

The first was a chiropractor in her early forties. A bit older than Kelsey had considered originally, but the profile photograph was nice. Her name was Donna. She had dark hair cut in a straight, sleek style that ended just above her shoulders, kind eyes, and a warm smile. Some of her likes included reading (which Kelsey loved), kayaking (which Kelsey had never done but was willing to try), and sports (okay, two out of three wasn't bad). She responded to the initial contact, agreeing to a date.

The second one was very cute, according to her photograph. Reddish-brown hair in a ponytail, wispy bangs brushing across green eyes and lightly freckled skin. She was Julie, she was thirty-five, and she was a bank manager. She liked independent films (Kelsey was willing), nature hikes (Kelsey loved those), and baking (Kelsey was happy to reap the benefits). Julie also received an e-mail.

When she was finished, she picked up her phone, scrolled to Chris's last text, and typed, *Mission accomplished.*

CHAPTER FIVE

THE BAR WAS CALLED Planter's, but Kelsey had no idea why. It was a sports bar, clean and neat enough, with lots of TVs showing soccer, baseball, and golf, none of which Kelsey cared about even a teeny bit. Oh, well. She ordered herself a light beer, preferring to keep a fairly clear head, found a small table not too far from the door, and waited for Donna, her online date.

Kelsey was early. That was her usual MO, but today, she wished it wasn't. Sitting there with time to kill only made her rethink this whole online dating thing and wonder if she had lost her mind completely. What was she thinking? Why would she want to put herself through this? Those questions pinballed around her head for a while before calm rationality kicked in and reminded her that this could be fun. This could be awesome. Donna could end up being the love of her life. She had no way of knowing.

She sipped her beer and told her brain to shut the hell up and stop torturing her.

The bar's patrons consisted mostly of men who were mostly loud, shouting at the TVs and at each other, but they were amusing. Kelsey was almost done with her beer when she felt a tap on her shoulder and a voice asked, "Kelsey?"

She turned to meet a steady brown gaze that belonged to a woman Kelsey had never seen before. Like, ever. Not in person. And not in a photo. Short salt-and-pepper hair topped a head with a ruddy face and crinkles around the eyes, her complexion telling Kelsey she was outdoors a lot. She was stocky, bulky but not fat, more muscled than anything else. Clad in cargo shorts with more pockets than Kelsey could count and a navy blue T-shirt, she smiled and held out her hand.

"I'm Donna."

"*You're* Donna?" Kelsey asked, shaking the hand but confused.

"I am."

"You don't look anything like your profile photo." *Like, it can't even be an old picture of you because it's* not *you.* She didn't say those words, but they flew through her head and announced themselves on a megaphone.

Donna chuckled and sat down. "Yeah, I know."

"Like, it's not even you."

"True." Donna offered no explanation, just ordered herself a beer from the waitress, then lifted her glass in a salute. "So. You're super cute."

Kelsey squinted at her and held up a hand. "Wait. That's it? You use a photo that's not you and I'm just supposed to shrug and be fine with that?"

"Everything else in the profile is true, so you really did pick me." Donna was infuriatingly nonchalant about what she'd done.

"But...you're catfishing me."

Donna squinted and cocked her head. "Nah."

"Um, yeah. You are. That's pretty much the definition, you know? I've set up a date with somebody who is not what she told me she is."

Finally, Donna shifted in what seemed to be discomfort—maybe? Kelsey didn't know her well enough to be sure. "It's just a picture. That's the only thing I told a little white lie about."

"Yeah, see, telling me you look like one person when you actually look completely different isn't a little white lie. Not in the grand scheme of dating."

"You got a problem with the way I look?" Donna's eyes had hardened and Kelsey realized this was a no-win.

"Not even close to being my point," she said, pushing herself to her feet as she felt her anger rise.

"What is your point?"

Could she really be this obtuse? Bracing her hands on the table, Kelsey leaned forward. "My point is, if our very first date is predicated on a lie, what else would you lie about down the road?" There was no way Kelsey would get into her last relationship and how the lies had compounded the hurt. She owed nothing to Donna. Glad she'd already paid for her beer, she grabbed her purse and left the bar, feeling more annoyed than she expected...which annoyed her more.

Once in her car, she pulled out her phone, plugged it in, and dialed Chris.

"Yo," came her cousin's voice through the speaker above the car's windshield.

Kelsey didn't give her time to say more. "Strike one."

"Already? Wasn't your date, like, ten minutes ago?"

"She catfished me." Kelsey said it through gritted teeth, surprised at how mad she was.

"How?" Then Chris gasped. "Was she a guy?"

"No, but she wasn't the person in her profile pic either."

"She used a fake picture? Oh, that's not cool."

"That's what I told her."

"You did? Go you."

"I thought she needed to know. I'm not starting any relationship off with a lie. I'm just not. I've had enough of that."

Chris shifted gears then. Kelsey could hear it in her voice. "I'm sorry, Kels. Just shake it off. You've got a coffee date with the other chick tomorrow, right? Maybe she'll be better."

"Maybe." Kelsey sighed as she pulled into the lot of her apartment complex. "I will say this: if she doesn't look a thing like her photo, I'm not saying a word. I'm just leaving."

"I don't blame you." Shifting again, Chris cleared her throat and asked, "Hey, you up for a visit from your favorite cousin?"

Kelsey gave a little squeal of delight, her mood instantly lighter. "When would I *not* be up for that? Yes! When? Say tomorrow."

Chris's hearty laugh came over the line. "No, not tomorrow. But in the next few weeks maybe? Would that work for you?"

"Any time, any day of the week. You are always welcome to stay with me whenever. You know that."

"Okay. Good. I'll keep you posted."

They signed off, and Kelsey turned off her car and headed inside.

Her small apartment was starting to feel like home. It had been important to her from the beginning to make it so, but having lived with Janice for a few years, there was a lot she didn't want to haul to Illinois with her. Memories she didn't want to bring to her new life. Mainly dishes and bedding, everyday things. She'd spent more than she'd intended, but every time she pulled out her brightly colored plates or snuggled under her duvet with the purple and pink stripes, she was glad she had.

Happy she hadn't wasted an entire Sunday with the online date that wasn't, she settled down with a book, snuggled into her couch. She'd read for a while, then take a walk in the sunshine, enjoy some fresh air. She had to be in early tomorrow. Mondays were always busy for her at work with bill paying and order writing, so she liked to use her Sundays for relaxation. Plus, tomorrow was her coffee date with Online Date Number Two, which, given how things had gone today, she was not looking forward to in the slightest.

Shaking her head with a sigh, she opened her book and let herself be whisked away. At least for a little while.

Monday morning brought with it gray and rain and the occasional rumble of thunder. It had also flown by for Kelsey, who'd spent much of it on the phone trying to fix a botched order that had been delivered. Her supplier had argued with her over responsibility for much longer than they should have before realizing their own error and apologizing up and down in an attempt to fix things. Though it wasn't easy, Kelsey managed not to say, "I told you so," and instead graciously accepted their offer to overnight the correct stock and have the incorrect delivery picked up, all at their own expense.

A glance at her phone showed her two things: Hannah had texted twice, and it was very close to the time she was scheduled to meet Online Date Number Two.

Kelsey's cheeks puffed as she blew out a breath. She hadn't told Hannah about the online stuff, didn't feel it was any of her business. At the same, she felt like maybe she should tell her, that it might help set the record straight, so to speak, regarding how Kelsey felt about her. She also thought that might just be mean, so she was torn. And thereby, did nothing.

Shaking it off, she grabbed up her purse and headed out of the office and into the store, which was quiet.

"I'll be back in about an hour," Kelsey said to Jeanine, squeezing her shoulder.

"Good luck," Jeanine said with a wink.

Because of the unfamiliarity of Planter's, Kelsey was glad she'd chosen her Starbucks this time. She knew the location, knew the layout, felt comfortable there. Plus, it was during the lunch hour, so there'd be no stretching this date beyond an hour...and she could cut it shorter than that if need be.

Julie was easy to find because she looked exactly like her profile photo, right down to the ponytail. "Thank God," Kelsey muttered as she approached the table for two. "Hi," she said, ducking to catch the woman's eyes. They were green and warm and her smile grew when she met Kelsey's gaze.

"Yes. Hi. You must be Kelsey."

They shook hands. Julie's grip was firm, and Kelsey imagined as a bank manager, she must shake hands all day long. "I am. It's nice to meet you."

"Same here."

"Let me just grab a cup of coffee and I'll be right back, okay?"

Julie nodded and Kelsey hopped in a line she wished was shorter. Julie's profile was to her, and she was able to study her emerald green suit, sensible pumps, a purse that was small but functional. She had both hands around her cup on the table and was slowly turning it in a circle—a slightly nervous tic, maybe? The line moved along at a fairly quick pace and soon Kelsey had her Frappuccino in hand and returned to Julie.

"I'm a little nervous," Julie admitted, once Kelsey was settled in her seat and had taken a taste of her drink. "I've never done this before."

"Online dating in general? Or meeting somebody cold like this?"

"Well, both. Neither. I mean, I've never done the online dating thing." Julie's soft chuckle was uncertain, and Kelsey felt a pang of sympathy for her.

"If it makes you feel any better, neither have I."

Her smile was pretty, even if it came and went kind of quickly. "It does, actually."

"Good." Kelsey sipped again, realizing she was going to have to take the lead here. "So, tell me about yourself. I mean, I know from your profile that you work in a bank, that you like indie films and hikes. What else should I know about you?"

Julie caught her bottom lip between her teeth and nibbled on it as she looked over Kelsey's shoulder. "Um...hmm. Let me see..."

After a moment or two went by with nothing forthcoming, Kelsey tried to help. "Well, I can tell you that I'm somewhat new to town. I've been here about three months, and while I've met some people, I haven't been able to find somebody who interests me that way, you know? So I went online last week." She sipped her drink. "How about you? What made you try online dating?" Then she watched with increasing horror as Julie's eyes welled with tears.

"My wife of twelve years left me right after Christmas," she managed to squeak out before a quiet sob escaped her lips.

Oh, my God. What the hell? Kelsey blinked at Julie for a beat before handing over her napkin in a feeble attempt at help. "I'm so sorry," she said, not knowing what else she could possibly offer.

Julie took the napkin and blotted the corners of her eyes with it, then sniffled loudly. "I'm sorry," she said, glanced at Kelsey, then looked away again. "I just...I don't know what happened." And she dissolved into tears once more. "Twelve years. *Twelve years*. And that's it? Just like that? She just...goes?" She blew her nose with a honk that had three people in line turning to find the source of the sound. "I mean, what is *wrong* with women these days? That they think it's okay to just *do* that?" And finally, she made direct, intense eye contact with Kelsey, who then realized Julie expected an answer.

"Um, yeah. You're right. Totally. Women suck."

"*They so do*." Julie reached across the table and closed her hand over Kelsey's wrist, held it in a grip that was almost painful. "You get it, don't you?"

"I...guess?"

"I knew it." Julie leaned forward to she was almost lying across the table. "I knew the second you introduced yourself that you'd get it."

"Oh. Good." *What is happening?* Kelsey wanted to look around for help, but was afraid of breaking eye contact with Julie and sending her off into another sobfest.

For the next twenty minutes, Julie went on about her ex (Meg; a tall, handsome contractor; her likes included Delmonico steak, chicken wings—the hotter the better—and brandy; she was a Pisces and very good with her hands). Kelsey sat quietly, nodded where she felt it was expected, grunted here and there, and mostly struggled to keep from looking at her phone to see what time it was. *How the hell did I end up in this situation?*

When it was Julie who finally glanced at her own phone and commented on where the time could have possibly gone, it took everything Kelsey had not to sob with relief.

"I'm so glad we met," Julie said as she gathered up her things. "I think this is going to be good." She waved a finger between the two of them. "I've got your number, so I'll give you a call later, okay?" She was all smiles now, the tears long gone.

All Kelsey could do was nod, as there wasn't a way to take back her phone number. At least she'd be able to screen the calls. Before she had the time to dodge it, Julie bent toward her and kissed her on the cheek. With a tender smile and a little wave, she headed toward the door, dropped her trash in the receptacle next to it, and left. Kelsey watched her go, afraid to move until she was sure Julie was totally gone. It wasn't until she actually saw her drive out of the parking lot that she let out the breath she'd been holding, her entire body deflating like a balloon with a slow leak, until her forehead rested on her fists on the table in front of her. She groaned.

"Poor Shelley. That looked like all kinds of fun." The voice was familiar and friendly and warm, despite the teasing tone. Kelsey looked up and into the eyes of Lisa.

"How much did you hear?" Kelsey asked.

"I was right there doing some work." She pointed to a table not far from Kelsey, but behind her, so it was no wonder she hadn't seen her. There was a laptop and a purse sitting there. "I saw the first tears come."

"Terrific."

"Blind date?"

"Online. So, just as bad."

Lisa took Julie's vacated seat, set her coffee cup down, and smiled at Kelsey. She looked gorgeous, as always, waves of blond falling around her shoulders, her blue eyes kind and smiling. "I bet you can't wait until she calls."

Kelsey couldn't help but laugh at Lisa's feigned excitement; it was contagious. "I wish she'd call *right now*." She picked up her phone, frowned at it. "Not yet. Darn it."

They chuckled together for a moment. Then Lisa grew a bit more serious. "You okay?"

Kelsey sighed as she nodded. "Yeah, I'm fine. Just wondering why I put myself through this at all. It's gone exactly the way I anticipated it would."

"Poorly?"

"Yeah, you could say that."

"How many dates?"

For some reason, it felt a little...weird...to be telling Lisa this stuff. "Just two."

"So far." Lisa's eyebrows went up. "Right?"

"I think two was enough."

"I didn't peg you for somebody who gives up so easily."

Kelsey narrowed her eyes at her and was hit with an inexplicable blast of fortitude. "Well I wouldn't have to online date at all if you'd go out with me instead." *Oh, my God! What?*

"I wish you could see the look on your face right now." Lisa laughed heartily while Kelsey sat still and felt herself blush. After a moment, Lisa's face went back to serious and she said, very quietly, "You have to actually ask me."

And just like that, the rest of the coffee shop fell away. The hum of conversation faded. The smell of coffee and pastries became muted. There was nothing in Kelsey's world at that moment except for the woman across from her. The creamy skin, the deep blue of her eyes, the halo of blond hair, and a dangerously sexy smile. It was just like Ree had described it when she'd met DJ. That feeling of being underwater. When Lisa quirked one eyebrow, Kelsey had no choice but to pose the question.

"Have coffee with me?"

Lisa sipped from her cup, held Kelsey's gaze. "I'm having coffee with you right now."

Kelsey cocked her head and grinned. "Have coffee with me another time. When it's just the two of us and we can talk. Like, really."

"Like, really talk? I don't know. That seems to be asking a lot..." Lisa looked off into the distance, but the ghost of a grin told Kelsey she was teasing.

"You're killing me here."

"I know," Lisa said with a chuckle, then reached across to close a hand over Kelsey's forearm. It amazed her how completely different her hand felt than Julie's had not that long ago. This grip was warm and soft and held the promise of possibility. "I'm sorry. I would love to have coffee with you."

"Good. How about Friday at noon? Right here."

Lisa gave a nod and her smile grew. "That sounds terrific. I'll meet you here?"

"Perfect." Kelsey looked down at Lisa's hand on her arm again and noticed her watch, the time. "Crap. I need to get back to work."

"Me, too," Lisa said, and they both stood. There was a moment of quiet, a beat of silence where they simply held each other's gaze before moving into action again.

"I'll see you on Friday," Kelsey said as she moved toward the door.

Lisa smiled softly and gave her a nod. "You will."

Back at the shop, Kelsey finally understood what it meant when somebody said they were walking on air. She felt like her feet barely touched the ground as she moved around the floor. She helped a woman decide on Nutmeg and Cookies lotion. She directed another to the Lavender Spring body spray. When a third asked about more cruelty-free products, Kelsey happily told her about the recent meeting she'd had with Stephanie Bradley and all the new stuff that would be in soon. The afternoon flew by, and Kelsey couldn't remember the last time she'd been so incredibly satisfied with her choice of career as a small business owner. Funny how one small thing could alter her entire attitude.

What Matters Most

Friday couldn't arrive fast enough.

CHAPTER SIX

KELSEY HADN'T REALLY BEEN up for going out Thursday night with the team. Her original plan had been to bow out gracefully and leave the game a bit early so she didn't have to explain to Hannah or anybody else why she wasn't going. But the game had been a nail-biter and Kelsey really wanted to see how it ended. Hannah's team won by one run and the mood was happily celebratory. There was no way Kelsey could sneak away...and she didn't want to by then.

Point Blank was packed. Hannah's team's opponents were all friends—and all lesbians from what Kelsey could gather—so they came to the bar, too. Along with the regular Thursday night crowd, the bar was standing room only. Normally, one of the two regular bartenders was struggling to find something to do; Kelsey had watched him mop the floor, scrub empty tables, and replenish the beer cooler. Not so tonight. Tonight, both he and his female partner behind the bar were running their asses off trying to keep their customers' glasses filled.

The tables had all been full when they'd arrived, so both teams were standing along the bar, and the decibel level was high. Kelsey stood and quietly sipped her beer, people watching and eavesdropping on various conversations. Ree was suddenly next to her and bumped her with a shoulder.

"I thought you were gonna scoot early," she said, a clear drink in her hand.

"I was. I changed my mind."

"Couldn't bear a Thursday evening without us, could you?" Ree winked and sipped from her glass.

"That's exactly it. You're onto me already."

"You're pretty easy to read." She ducked close to Kelsey's ear. "Here comes your girlfriend," she whispered.

"Stop that," Kelsey said in reply, giving Ree a playful swat as her eyes landed on Hannah pushing and sidestepping her way through the crowd.

"So," Hannah said as she stopped next to Kelsey. The person near her at the bar decided to leave, and Hannah found herself with some space, so she backed against the bar and put her elbows on it.

"So," Kelsey replied and took a sip of her beer. Hannah had played well and was painted with the dirt to prove it. Her short, dark hair was finally drying around the ends where it had been plastered to her face and neck by sweat. Her normal musky scent was amplified, but Kelsey didn't mind because Hannah hadn't stopped smiling since the game ended, her flushed cheeks adding to her youthful appearance. She was a lot of fun to be around tonight, so Kelsey was glad she'd come after all.

"What are your plans for Saturday?"

Kelsey squinched up her face to think, then lifted her beer high in the air as somebody brushed too closely past her. "Whoa," she muttered, then refocused her attention on Hannah. "Saturday?" she asked, louder this time, so she was sure Hannah could hear. "I have to work for a while, but other than that, I think nothing. Why?"

"My folks are having their annual barbecue. They have one at the end of every August. It's fun. Tons of people there. Some from the neighborhood. Some family. A few of my softball friends. You should come, too."

A few weeks ago, there would have been no question. Kelsey would have declined. But she'd been growing more comfortable with her new life over the past few weeks and found herself relishing opportunities to meet new people. And a barbecue sounded like a fun summer thing to do. It was already late August and, from what people had told her, summer would finish up and disappear before she knew it. While there was a distinctive change of seasons at home in North Carolina, she knew it was nothing like what she'd get in the suburbs of Chicago.

"Does it matter if I show up later in the day?"

"Come any time you want. There will be food and beer all day long."

"I think that sounds fun," Kelsey said with a smile, and her response made Hannah's grin widen. "I'd love to come."

"Excellent! I'll text you directions." Her excitement was kind of adorable and Kelsey smiled as Hannah punched information into her phone.

"There," she said when she finished, and her green eyes sparkled when they met Kelsey's.

"What can I bring?"

"Oh, my God, nothing. There will be so much food. My mom always overdoes it. Every year. Just bring your smiling face."

"I can do that."

Hannah touched her beer bottle to Kelsey's and lifted her shoulders as she smiled. "I'm so glad you're coming. You're gonna love my parents."

Kelsey felt a little bump on her arm and remembered that Ree was still standing next to her. She was carrying on a conversation with somebody Kelsey didn't know, but she was pretty sure Ree'd been able to hear her entire exchange with Hannah.

Hannah drained her beer and set the bottle on the bar. "Gotta hit the little girls' room." She touched a hand to Kelsey's cheek, winked, and disappeared into the crowd.

"Big step, meeting the parents," Ree said, and Kelsey couldn't quite tell from her tone if she was kidding or serious. Maybe a little of both.

"Yeah, I didn't really think that through, did I?" Kelsey gave a half-hearted chuckle as she set her beer down next to Hannah's empty one and toyed with the ring on her forefinger. She looked at Ree and said quietly, "I'm going to have to tell her directly again at some point, aren't I?"

Ree grimaced, tilted her head one way, then the other, as if weighing pros and cons. Finally, she gave one nod and said, "Yeah, I think it might be best. Whatever hints you gave her, she's not taking them. I mean, you don't have to crush her or anything, but maybe some clarification would help a little bit."

Nibbling on the inside of her cheek, Kelsey wondered what the gentlest way was to say, "Hey, I like you but I don't *like you* like you." She wrinkled her nose. She'd been pretty clear...or so she'd thought. She'd met Hannah and had kept her at arms' length, strictly in the friend zone ever since, despite the clues Hannah had dropped making it clear she'd like more.

"There's not really a good way to do it," Kelsey said, more to herself than to Ree.

"I know. Just...keep it light. Friendly. You know?"

"Well, we *are* friends, so..." Kelsey shrugged. "Okay. I need to go anyway. This is a good time for an escape."

Ree laughed, then laid a hand on her shoulder. "Relax. It'll be fine."

Kelsey nodded. "Thanks, Ree."

"Sure."

Back at her apartment, Kelsey wasn't sure what to do with herself. It was too early to go to bed—and she was too wired to sleep anyway—but she couldn't find anything to occupy her mind and keep her from anticipating her coffee date tomorrow. The uncomfortable situation with Hannah didn't seem like such a big deal when she thought about where she'd be tomorrow at noon. One corner of her mouth quirked up as she flashed back, could hear Lisa's voice in her head saying, *"You have to actually ask me."* God, it was a simple, innocent sentence, so why did it feel so indescribably sexy? Every time she thought about it she got butterflies in her stomach, and now that it was so close, they wouldn't stop flying around. She was in a constant state of happy anticipation.

"Clothes," she said out loud to the empty living room. "I can figure out what I'm going to wear."

In her bedroom, she opened the small closet (her next place would have a giant walk-in, she'd decided after one week in this place) to scan her options. Just as she reached for a purple top, her cell rang. Chris, FaceTiming.

Kelsey hit the Answer button and propped the phone on her dresser so she could talk to Chris and still do what she was doing. "Let me guess: you're still at work."

"You know me so well, Kettle Corn. Waiting on a west coast client to send me an e-mail."

"You're the most important person I know," Kelsey said, wide-eyed for the camera, teasing her cousin.

"Shut up," Chris said with a laugh. "You have no idea how important I am."

"Probably true."

"What's new, K-Pete?"

Kelsey laughed at the new nickname. After a brief internal debate, she decided to spill. "I have a...sort of...a date tomorrow."

"What?" Chris's voice went up several octaves. "With who? Hannah the cutie pie?"

"No, not with Hannah the cutie pie."

"With another online match?"

"Nope."

"Oh, my God," Chris whined. "Just tell me already."

It was interesting in that moment as Kelsey realized she hadn't mentioned Lisa to Chris at all. She hadn't talked about her in detail to anybody except Ree, and that was only a vague mention in passing. She wondered why. Did she want to keep Lisa for herself? Was she afraid it was too good to be true and she should simply keep her as a fantasy? And now an actual date with her had altered things dramatically? *I mean, it's been made quite clear she plays on my team by the fact that she pretty much asked me to ask her on a date. Right?*

Filling her lungs with a deep breath, Kelsey slowly let it out and launched into the story for Chris. "I met this woman at Starbucks."

"When?"

"A month and a half ago, maybe?"

"I'm going to ignore the fact that you're just telling me now," Chris said, her eyebrows furrowed sternly as she glared at the screen. "But I reserve the right to revisit it. Go on."

"At first, I just saw her. Like, from across the room." Kelsey remember the first time she'd laid eyes on Lisa, how drawn to her she'd been. "She was gorgeous, all blond and business-y, checking her phone. And then she caught me looking."

Chris whooped with delight. "She busted you?"

"She did. I was looking at her legs, I think, and when I brought my eyes up, she was looking right at me."

"That's embarrassing."

"Totally. Anyway, we'd ended up ordering the same thing, so when our drinks came and our names on the cups were both wrong—"

"Of course they were. Because Starbucks."

"Exactly. She'd ordered soy milk, so she drank from her cup, figured out it was mine, and we switched. And called each other by the wrong names." Kelsey grinned at the memory.

"Which were?"

"Shelley and Lisa."

"Kelsey. Shelley. I can almost let it slide."

"Right? Anyway, that was the end of the first meeting."

"How many have there been?"

"Three."

Chris nodded. "Continue."

"The second time was a Saturday, right after my landlady's bossy daughter came to visit. I was in need of something nice, so decided to get a coffee and Lisa was there."

"You call her Lisa?"

"And she calls me Shelley."

"What's her real name?"

Kelsey bit her lip and hesitated before responding. "I don't actually know."

Chris said nothing, simply looked into her phone and raised one eyebrow.

"I know, I know," Kelsey said with a laugh. "Can I go on with my story?"

Chris made a rolling gesture with her hand.

"She was there and she said hi and we tried to guess why each of us was working on a Saturday. She guessed that I was a hairdresser and Saturday was my busiest day. I guessed that she worked in the DA's office like on *Law & Order*. And we just sort of ran with that."

Chris opened her mouth, closed it again, and gazed off into the distance. Then she looked back at the screen and said, "Okay, so let me get this straight. You don't know her real name. You don't know her real job. Which essentially means you know nothing about her except that she's hot. And you've got a date with her?"

"Well, when you put it like that..." Kelsey made a face that was half-grin, half-grimace.

"Where's the date?"

"Starbucks. Duh. Tomorrow at noon."

"Oh!" Chris sat back in her chair. "Okay, that's fine then. I was worried you were going someplace at night, to a seedy bar or something to meet this woman you know nothing about, never to be seen again."

"Lunchtime coffee. Perfectly safe."

"Thank God. You had me worried."

"No need, favorite cousin of mine. I'll be fine." Kelsey loved Chris's concern, even if she thought it was a little silly. To change the subject, she asked, "So when are you coming to visit me?"

"Possibly in a couple weeks. I haven't ironed it out yet." Chris glanced down as an electronic beeping sounded, then back up. "There's my call. Gotta run. I expect a date report tomorrow!"

"Wait! I need help figuring out"—Chris disappeared from the screen—"what to wear," she finished, to no avail. Kelsey sighed and dropped the phone onto the bed, then went back to perusing her closet. Dressing for a first date was like walking a fine line. She didn't want to go overboard and dress so far away from how she usually did that every time Lisa saw her after that would be a disappointment. She didn't want to dress too casual, though, for fear of seeming to have made too little effort. Finding the middle was hard.

Twenty minutes later, there were three pairs of pants and six shirts tossed into a haphazard pile on the bed, and Kelsey stood in front of the mirror surveying her handiwork. Black capris that fit as though they were tailored for her rear end (they were not), a sleeveless top in a deep turquoise that helped accent the deep blue of her eyes, a chunky silver necklace, and black sandals. She turned to her left, then her right, stood looking straight on for a beat, then finally gave one nod of approval.

It would have to do.

Was Lisa going through the same issues? she wondered as she took the clothes off and put them neatly back on hangers—no way was she going to iron in the morning. Probably not. She liked to imagine Lisa being slightly less of a freak than Kelsey herself, and the thought made her grin. She changed into yoga pants and a baggy T-shirt, then settled on the couch to watch TV. A glance at the wall clock made her sigh.

Why wasn't it tomorrow at noon yet?

CHAPTER SEVEN

IT WAS A TYPICAL FRIDAY at Common Scents, and for that, Kelsey was grateful. Busy mornings tended to fly by, and this one had. When she glanced at her watch and saw that it was 11:40, she gasped aloud, causing the customer she was helping to look at her with alarm.

"Everything okay?" the middle-aged brunette asked, rubbing Put the Lime in the Coconut lotion into her hands.

Kelsey smiled. "I am. Just lost track of time, and I have an appointment. Anything else I can help you with before I scoot?"

The woman smiled. "Nope. This is perfect." She picked up the bottle of lotion and grabbed a second one. "You've been a huge help."

Kelsey smiled, then headed back to her office. It took massive amounts of effort not to sprint, but she managed to get there while still appearing somewhat professional. All she really wanted to do was giggle and squeal like a five-year-old girl, but she kept control of herself.

Ten minutes later, she slid her car into the last available parking spot at Starbucks. "Wow," she whispered to the empty interior of her vehicle. "Busy today."

Inside, the line was long, and a glance around did not show her any beautiful blond women who might be waiting for her. Okay. She was here first. That was good. It would allow her to get her bearings, her coffee, and to relax a bit.

Just breathe.

Such a simple command could seem almost impossible when nerves were factored in, but Kelsey closed her eyes and inhaled slowly. She looked good. She'd switched out the turquoise top for a similar black one because she thought it made her look slimmer. Bringing a hand to her necklace, she felt the clasp in the front and twisted it back to behind her neck. With nervous fingers, she tucked some of her dark hair behind an ear, then ran a hand over the rest as she subtly glanced at her reflection in the glass of the pastry case. She made for an acceptably presentable silhouette, she decided, and tried to focus on something else.

She loved the smell of Starbucks. Coffee, pastries, sweetness. Some days—well, most days—the coffee was the strongest of the aromas. Obviously. That only made sense for a coffee shop. But sometimes, the croissants stood out. Or fresh cranberry bread. She loved to close her eyes, take in the smells, then look at the pastry case and see if her nose got it right. Some days, it was chocolate. Others, cranberry or lemon. Today, it was vanilla hazelnut coffee.

The line moved slowly. She briefly entertained the idea of getting Lisa's caramel macchiato for her, then decided she would. The less time Lisa had to stand in line, the more time she'd have to hang and talk with Kelsey.

It was nearly 12:10 by the time she got to the front of the line. Still no sign of Lisa, so she ordered the caramel macchiato with soy milk and a vanilla Frappuccino for herself, then moved on down the counter to wait. She craned her neck to see over the crowd of people in dire need of caffeine or sugar or both, but didn't see any familiar blond head.

"Grande caramel macchiato with soy. Grande vanilla Frappuccino for Kelly." The barista slid the cups along the counter and went on to his next order. Kelsey grabbed both drinks and looked for a table, scanning the faces crowding the shop as she went. Still no sign of Lisa.

The only empty table was outside on the Starbucks patio, but it was a gorgeous day, not too hot or humid, so Kelsey set up shop there, setting both cups on the table, taking a sip of hers, and pulling out her phone so she could at least pretend to be occupied by something other than waiting for her date. She checked her e-mail, gave a quick glance at Facebook, and then scrolled through today's top news stories.

By twelve thirty, her stomach had started to churn sourly, and her Frappuccino was not sitting well in it. At twelve forty-five, she wasn't looking at her phone at all. She stared off into the parking lot instead, not really focused on anything. The caramel macchiato with soy milk sat untouched, now cold, no lip gloss print on its pristine white plastic lid. Being stood up had never even crossed Kelsey's mind. Maybe that's why it stung so badly. She wanted to give Lisa the benefit of the doubt, but first, she needed to just be angry.

And she tried that.

But all she could manage was a profound sadness. A glance at her phone told her it was one o'clock and she needed to get back to the shop. She took a deep breath of fresh air and held it in her lungs before blowing it out. She kept trying to paint a self-confident picture on the whole thing, told herself it was Lisa's loss, while in the back of her mind, the owner of that little voice was shaking its head back and forth and whispering, "No. It's yours."

Tossing her half-empty cup and Lisa's full one into the trash, and feeling more disappointed than she ever thought possible, Kelsey headed back to work.

The disappointment hung on for the rest of the day. Kelsey did her best to focus on the store, assisted several customers, and threw herself into paperwork and orders. It worked for a while. At five, she got a FaceTime request from Chris, but ignored it, not yet ready to admit she'd been stood up.

A gentle knock had her looking up and into the kind green eyes of Hannah, who was standing in the doorway.

"Hi, you. Jeremy said you were back here and wouldn't mind if I popped in to say hi. Wanna grab something quick for dinner before you head home?" Hannah's smile was so sweet and her voice was so kind that Kelsey felt tears well in her eyes for a quick moment. Hannah's smile faded, and her expression changed to one of concern. "Hey. Are you okay? What's going on?" She looked over her shoulder, shut the door, and sat in the chair across from Kelsey's desk. "Talk to me," she said gently.

Kelsey sighed. She hadn't told Hannah about Lisa for obvious reasons, but maybe now was the time. And God knew, she needed to get it off her chest, how angry she was. Decision made, she filled Hannah in on Lisa, how they'd met, the setup of the date, and how Lisa had been a no-show.

Hannah's expression changed little by little as Kelsey told her story. She could see it, watched it happen, the subtle direction change of the corners of her mouth from up to down, the dampening of the sparkle in her eyes. Kelsey felt terrible, but knew this had to be done. Hannah deserved to know that Kelsey didn't look at her that way. That she, in fact, was actively looking elsewhere. She ended her story by reaching across the desk to grasp Hannah's hand and saying, "So, yes. I would love to go grab some dinner with you, because I could really use a smiling face in my corner."

They were the right words, apparently, and Kelsey breathed a quiet sigh of relief as Hannah's face broke into a smile. It wasn't as brilliant as her usual one, but it was there, and Kelsey decided she'd take it. Hannah stood, still holding Kelsey's hand and said, "For the record, Lisa is an idiot. Let's get dinner."

The evening had ended up being unexpectedly pleasant. Hannah seemed to be doing all right with the news that Kelsey was dating. Or trying to. They talked and joked and laughed and it all seemed perfectly normal, like always. That was a relief.

Back at home, Kelsey flopped onto her couch and was planning to surf YouTube for a little while when her phone rang. A glance told her it was her mother.

"Hi, Mom," she said when she answered. "Whatcha doing on this lovely Friday?"

"Just wondering how my baby's doing in a different time zone."

Kelsey chuckled. "Yeah, you're calling kind of late, aren't you?"

"We had dinner with the Smiths and just got home. We got talking about you, so it made me want to call. I miss you." Her mother's voice was sweet and wistful, and just dreamy enough to let Kelsey know she'd probably had a glass of wine or two.

"I miss you, too," Kelsey said, and it was the truth. Leaving her father behind hadn't been as painful; their relationship was rocky anyway. But leaving her mother had been harder than Kelsey had even prepared for. The day she'd set off on the eleven-and-a-half-hour drive from Charlotte to the suburbs of Chicago, she'd held it together admirably as they'd hugged their goodbyes, but then had cried openly from Charlotte almost all the way to Roanoke.

"What's new there? How's business?"

For a split second, Kelsey considered telling her mother about Betsy Siegler and her nerve-wracking visit. But her mother would go right to her father to tell him. Then she'd get the not-so-subtle "I told you that shop was a bad idea" speech, and she didn't think she could take that right now. "Good. Really good," she said instead. It wasn't a lie. Business *was* good. Not through-the-roof, I'll-be-rich-soon good. But it was okay. She was paying her bills. She was paying her employees. She was even paying herself. Not bad for a fledgling store in a new town.

"That's great. Making any new friends? You know I worry about you being lonely. Are you still going to the baseball games and hanging out with the team?"

Yeah, her mom was kind of adorable.

"It's softball, Mom. And yes, I'm still going. I've made several friends. I'm not lonely. You don't have to worry about me."

"Are you dating? Trying to date? Thinking about dating?"

Kelsey laughed. "Covering all the bases, are you?"

"Trying to."

"I'm thinking about dating." The image of Lisa's beautiful face flashed into her mind, but she didn't share the story with her mother.

"All right. I'll accept that. For now." She emphasized the last two words, her tone good-natured.

"I think Chris is going to come visit soon," Kelsey said, smoothly changing the subject.

"I heard. That'll be fun. She needs it. That girl is working way too many hours."

"I know." And they commiserated on that for a while.

By the time Kelsey hit the End button about twenty minutes later, she felt the same way she always felt after talking to her mother: homesick. She should have told her about Betsy Siegler. Her mom wouldn't be able to help, but she could give her a little pep talk, make her feel the tiniest bit better about it. Because, though she hadn't heard back from Betsy since her initial visit, the whole thing still sat in the back of Kelsey's mind, like the scary monster in a haunted house, hidden behind a door or in a closet, just waiting until you least expected it before he jumped into the open with a roar and scared the living shit out of you.

On the bright side, the homesickness wasn't nearly as intense as it had been her first few weeks here. So it was definitely fading, and that was a good thing.

Not wanting to think about the potential trouble her business could find itself in, Kelsey refocused on her laptop, looking for something fun to watch. Maybe some puppy or kitten videos were the way to go tonight. Anything to keep her mind off the two women who'd made her miserable over the past couple of weeks: Betsy Siegler and Lisa Whatever-Her-Real-Name-Was. It was time to wipe them both from her brain, at least temporarily, and focus on her weekend. Tomorrow, the store was running a sale, so business should be good. Busy meant it would go by quickly, and then she'd head to Hannah's family's barbecue.

She was surprised to find herself looking forward to that.

CHAPTER EIGHT

HANNAH WASN'T KIDDING WHEN she said there were tons of people at her parents' barbecue; Kelsey had trouble finding a place to park. The double-wide driveway was full, and parked cars lined each side of the street like rows of Oreos in a package, one after another after another. Luckily, an older couple was getting into theirs when Kelsey approached, so she stopped, put on her turn signal, and waited for them to pull away…which seemed to take an hour, but finally they left, and Kelsey parallel parked like a pro. Her driver's ed teacher would have been seriously impressed.

Going from the air conditioning of Common Scents to the heat and humidity of the late August afternoon had been a bit of a shock, as if Kelsey was suddenly moving through molasses and breathing through wet gauze. She used a finger to wipe the light sheen of sweat from her upper lip, shouldered her bag, grabbed the bottle of wine she'd bought on her way, and locked her car. It wasn't hard to tell which house was having the party, as the crowd in the backyard spilled out onto the side yard along the attached garage, guests with red Solo cups and paper plates in hand. The smells of chicken, hamburgers, and hot dogs wafted through the air and down the street, hooking Kelsey by the nose and drawing her along to where the action was.

Entering a party when she didn't know a lot of people was never a big deal for Kelsey. But when she entered the gate in the backyard fence, she realized this was *a lot* of people. For a moment, she simply stood inside the fenced backyard and looked around, her head turning, her eyes scanning, searching for any face that seemed even vaguely familiar.

"Well, don't you look like a deer in headlights," a friendly voice said.

Kelsey turned to meet the smiling gaze of a woman with the exact same eyes as Hannah and dark hair pulled back into a French braid. Her mother? An aunt? "Hi there," she said. "I'm Kelsey Peterson. A friend of Hannah's. She said there'd be tons of people, so I can only assume I'm in the right place."

The woman laughed, a gentle tinkling sound, pretty and delicate. "You are definitely in the right place." She held out a hand. "I'm Liz Keene. It's nice to meet you, Kelsey Peterson. Come with me and we'll find my daughter."

Liz Keene smelled pleasantly of lilacs, and she smiled, waved, and greeted people as they moved along through the large square backyard. There was an above-ground pool filled with kids splashing and screaming with delight. Two grills were pumping out steam, a large man in a red Kiss the Cook apron using his long-handled spatula like he was born to do so, flipping burgers with precision. In his other hand was a set of long-handled tongs, and with those he turned the chicken.

"Wow," Kelsey commented and Liz followed her eyes.

"That's my husband Jeffrey. He lives to grill."

"Kelsey!" Hannah's voice rang out over the crowd, causing several people to turn to look at the object of her shout. Hannah bounded down the stairs of the deck and threw her arms around Kelsey like she hadn't seen her in years. "I'm so glad you came," she said, quieter this time. When she pulled back, her smile was huge and her eyes just a tiny bit glassy. “Yes, I may have had a beer or two,” she said, at Kelsey’s scrutiny. “Or five. The party started hours ago!” She put an arm around Kelsey’s shoulder and squeezed. “I see you’ve met my gorgeous mother.”

“I have,” Kelsey said with a nod and a grin, then handed over the bottle of wine. “Thank you for having me. This is for you.”

Liz took the wine and touched Kelsey’s upper arm. “You didn’t have to do that, but thank you. This is lovely.”

“Come with me,” Hannah said, leading Kelsey away. “I’ll bring you to where there are people you know.” She slipped her hand down Kelsey’s arm and clasped her hand.

The crowd was very diverse in age, Kelsey noticed, as they passed different groupings here and there in the yard. Some were Hannah’s parents’ age. Some were a bit younger, probably parents of the kids in the pool...maybe neighbors? Around a table situated under a small tent, a handful of elderly folks sat talking and laughing in the coolness of the shade. In the very back corner of the yard, under another tent, sat a picnic table and a handful of people Kelsey’s age, a few of whom she recognized from softball games, either players or spectators.

“Gang, this is my friend, Kelsey. Kels, this is the gang.” Hannah went around the table and introduced everybody—their names left Kelsey’s head almost instantly, much to her dismay—and then asked her what she wanted to drink.

For the next hour, wine in hand, Kelsey sat at the table with Hannah and her friends and listened to them talk about any number of subjects. Movies. Politics. Food. She jumped in here and there, but had more fun just observing. They were a nice group of people, and Kelsey decided she was glad she'd come.

"Hey, where's the little girls' room?" she asked quietly as she leaned toward Hannah.

"Come with me." Hannah stood and led the way across the yard and into the house. Kelsey was surprised to note that the crowd hadn't seemed to have dissipated at all. The house was cute, not too large and not too small, and Kelsey realized that she knew very little about Hannah's home life, other than she still lived here at twenty-five years old and was saving as much as she could so she could get her own place. She didn't know what Hannah's parents did for a living. She didn't know if there were siblings. As she looked around the house, Kelsey suddenly felt like a terrible friend.

"Right here," Hannah said, as they stopped in front of a closed door in the hall. "Somebody's in there, so just hang." She glanced at Kelsey's near empty cup. "More wine?"

"That'd be great," Kelsey said, handing the cup to her.

"Be right back."

Kelsey leaned back against the wall, keeping herself out of the way as best she could of people moving through the hall, which connected the kitchen to the front foyer of the house. The wall was a pleasing shade of light mauve, and Liz Keene had a good eye for décor. There was some art on the wall, all with matching frames, all of various kinds of flowers. Each painting had at least a touch of the light mauve from the wall, tying it all nicely together. She was squinting to read the artist's name at the bottom of one of the paintings when the lock on the powder room knob clicked and the door swung open. Kelsey stepped back and out of the way of it, but then her breath caught in her throat as the pair of gorgeous blue eyes widened in shock.

"Here you go," Hannah said just then as she came around the corner with a red Solo cup half full of Pinot Grigio.

"Shelley," the woman coming out of the bathroom whispered in what could only be disbelief, and her face broke into a huge smile.

"No, goof," Hannah said with a laugh. "This is Kelsey. Kelsey, this is my half-sister Theresa."

"Kelsey," the woman said softly, as if trying out the name, seeing how it felt on her tongue.

Theresa. Lisa. Made sense.

But Kelsey couldn't move. She simply stood and stared and let Hannah continue to hold out the cup while she continued to not take it.

Lisa—er—*Theresa* didn't move either. The two of them simply stood there, overwhelmed by the shock of seeing each other someplace so utterly unexpected.

"You didn't show up," Kelsey said quietly. Finally.

Theresa looked chagrined and glanced down at her feet while her face tinted a pretty pink. "I know. I'm so sorry. I got stuck in a meeting and when I went to call you and tell you, I realized...I don't have your number." She cocked her head and made an expression that said, "Duh."

Of course! How could Kelsey be so stupid? They didn't have each other's numbers. The weight of disappointment that had been pushing down on her shoulders since yesterday suddenly evaporated, and she felt infinitely lighter. Happier. Shocked.

"Um...what's going on?" Hannah said, her eyes darting from Theresa to Kelsey and back. "Somebody wanna clue me in?"

This is my half-sister, Theresa.

Hannah's earlier words hit Kelsey like a board to the head. The object of Kelsey's desire was Hannah's sister! Oh, shit. Not good. Not good at all.

Theresa, obviously unaware of any tension, chuckled. "I met...Kelsey here—" She stopped and her face was bright, happy. "Not used to that name yet. I met Kelsey here at Starbucks a couple weeks ago." She told the whole story to Hannah, unaware that Kelsey had told the exact same story to her the day before. And while Kelsey wanted to watch Hannah, gauge her reaction and jump in if necessary, she had a hard time pulling her eyes away from Theresa.

Theresa.

Her name is Theresa.

There was a beat of silence as Kelsey realized Theresa had finished her story, but Hannah had yet to comment. Hannah's face was alarmingly neutral, like she was working very hard at keeping it that way, and Kelsey felt the sudden urge to lighten the mood. Change the subject. Something. Anything.

"So...you guys are sisters?" Kelsey made sure her confusion was apparent so she didn't have to say things like, *There's a pretty big age difference between you* or *But you look nothing alike...at all.*

"We have the same father," Theresa said, and a shadow passed so quickly across her face, Kelsey wondered if maybe she'd imagined it. "But, I look like my mom and Hannah looks like hers."

“Right,” Hannah said, and pushed the Solo cup toward Kelsey. “Here you go, Kels.”

“Oh. Thanks.” Kelsey took the cup and lifted it a bit in a salute of sorts, which was completely lame, she realized, as she did it.

“I’m gonna go back out,” Hannah said with an expression that said she needed to get out of that tiny hallway ASAP.

“Okay.” Kelsey didn’t know what else to say, so she and Theresa stood there and watched her walk away. “That wasn’t at all awkward,” she muttered after a couple seconds.

“Yeah,” Theresa said, sort of drawing the word out. She turned to look at Kelsey, normally smooth brow furrowed. “Why was it?”

Kelsey sighed, glanced back in the direction Hannah had gone. “It’s complicated.”

“So uncomplicate it for me.” Theresa’s voice was matter-of-fact. “Let’s get me a drink and we’ll sit down and you can fill me in.”

As if there was any way in hell Kelsey would say no to this woman. “Lead the way.”

Rather than back into the kitchen, Theresa led Kelsey toward the front foyer, which opened up to a large living room/dining room that took up one side of the house. The walls went from an earthy green in the living room to a muted, autumn-like orange in the dining room. Neither color was one Kelsey would pick individually, but in tandem, they worked remarkably well. That space was warm and inviting. Along a wall in the dining room ran a sideboard that was set up as a bar—and a shockingly well-appointed one at that. A quick scan showed

Kelsey four vodkas in various flavors, gin, three rums, vermouth, whiskey, bourbon, and several more bottles of which she couldn't see the labels.

"Wow. Somebody here knows their booze," Kelsey said with a chuckle.

"Yeah, that'd be my dad." Theresa grabbed a cup and filled it with ice from the bucket on the end of the bar. "You good on wine?"

Kelsey held up the cup she had yet to sip from. "All set." She tried not to enjoy the view too much as Theresa made herself a rum and Coke using the Myer's Dark. She wore denim shorts today—not an article of clothing Kelsey had seen her in yet, but now hoped to see her in more because her ass was...almost unbelievably perfect. Kelsey clutched her cup with both hands to keep from doing what she really wanted to do: slide her hands into the back pockets of those shorts and prop her chin on Theresa's shoulder from behind.

Theresa turned around to face her. "Follow me."

Kelsey snapped back to attention. Again, instead of going the expected way (out back to the party), Theresa led her through the front door to a tiny concrete slab of a porch with two white wicker chairs and a small table in between them. The cushions were a festive, summery lime green, and their location under the front door awning kept them cool in the shade.

Theresa made herself comfortable, crossing her ridiculous legs, and leaning back in her chair. She took a sip of her drink as she studied Kelsey, who tried her best not to squirm. And to ignore the ache growing low in her body. "So."

"So." Kelsey sipped her wine, more for something to do with her hands than from an actual urge to drink it.

"How do you know Hannah?"

"First of all, I had no idea she was your sister."

"Half-sister." The way Theresa said it made it feel like an important distinction.

"Half-sister. Okay." Kelsey sipped again. "Well, I'm fairly new to town. Once I got settled, I decided to make the effort to find some friends since they, shockingly, were not falling into my lap out of the blue."

Theresa laughed and Kelsey basked in the sound of it. "Imagine that."

"Right? So I went online, did a little searching, and found a lesbian website that had a bunch of local events listed. I went to a softball game, met Hannah, and we became fast friends."

"And more?" Theresa asked over the rim of her cup. All Kelsey could see was those eyes, and she couldn't look away.

"No," Kelsey said quietly. "We're just friends."

"You sure? Because she seemed a little...possessive of you in there."

Kelsey blew out a breath. "Yeah."

"Let me guess." Theresa sat forward, elbow on her knee, chin propped in her hand. "She wants more from this friendship than you do."

Kelsey pressed her lips together and waited a beat before giving a nod. "Yeah."

Theresa shook her head and sat back again. "Typical Hannah."

"What do you mean?"

"Nothing." Theresa took another sip of her rum and Coke and gazed off into the distance, watching a couple come out from along the side of the house. They waved to her as they headed to their car and she waved back.

"Did you grow up here? With Hannah?"

"No. I mean, yes, I grew up in Westland, but not with Hannah. My parents split when I was eight. My mom and I got an apartment on the other side of town. I didn't see much of my dad. He was always...busy. He eventually married Liz and they had Hannah when I was fourteen."

"That had to be tough on you. Fourteen's rough enough as it is."

Theresa sighed, and again looked off into the distance at something Kelsey couldn't see. "Yeah, I guess it was. Hannah and I were never close. I always felt like she got the parts of my dad I didn't. Like she was his new family." She shook her head then, as if trying to wake herself up. "Wow, that got maudlin fast, didn't it? Sorry about that." With a laugh, she reached over and squeezed Kelsey's knee. "Tell me about you. You said you're new to town. How long have you been here?"

Kelsey had to admit this was a much more comfortable subject. She felt a little...disloyal talking about Hannah like that. "A few months. I moved here in April."

"Wow, you are new. And what brought you here? A job?"

There was something exciting and sexy about having Theresa's full attention. She sat forward again, elbow on her knee, those intense blue eyes focused on Kelsey. "You could say that. I opened my own scent shop. We sell lotions, body scrubs, bubble bath, that kind of thing. Much of it is cruelty-free and a lot is handmade."

Theresa's face initially registered surprise, which smoothly morphed into slight awe as Kelsey explained her products. "Wow. That's impressive. You're a business owner."

"I am." Theresa's approval made Kelsey blush, and she liked it.

"Do you enjoy it? I mean, I assume you do or you wouldn't be doing it, right?"

"I do enjoy it. I like people, talking to them to find out what works for them as far as products, what scents they'd like best." She nodded. "It's good."

"That's pretty cool." Theresa looked like she meant it, and that made Kelsey grin like a fool. "And where are you new from? Where is home?"

"Charlotte, North Carolina."

"Wow. Winter will be interesting for you." Theresa's grin was teasing.

"People keep telling me that," Kelsey said, also smiling.

"Are you prepared? Like, do you have the right clothes? For snow and wind, I mean?"

Kelsey pursed her lips. "Not yet."

"Okay, well, I'd be happy to help you with that. I know a terrific store and I can help you pick out exactly what you'll need." Theresa said it like it wasn't an offer or a suggestion, it was simply fact. She would take Kelsey shopping for winter attire.

"I'd like that very much," Kelsey said, feeling that tightening in her abdomen. There was something incredibly sexy about

Theresa wanting to help her find clothes. "What about you?" she asked then, needing a change of subject. "What do you do?"

"Well, I don't run my own business, that's for sure. I'm not nearly as hip as you." Theresa finished off her drink. "I'm in real estate."

"That's pretty awesome."

"I think so. It can be boring to a lot of people, but I like it."

"And how long have you been in real estate?"

"Let's see." Theresa tapped a forefinger against her lips as she thought. Kelsey tried not to stare. "I started with my company at their home office in New Jersey eight years ago. I just got transferred about six months ago."

"Back to your hometown. That's kind of cool."

"Yeah, well, I wasn't sure I wanted to come back here." She glanced back at the house behind them. "Not all my memories are great, you know?"

"That makes sense." Kelsey wanted so badly to pry, to dig deeper, to know more about this breathtaking woman, but she also knew it was too soon. The last thing she wanted was to make herself look like some creeper asking questions that were *way* too personal. She managed to rein herself in. "But you made the move anyway."

"My mom talked me into it." Theresa gave a small laugh. "She can be kind of insistent."

"Mine, too. Moms can be like that."

"Right?"

They sat quietly for long moments. Not uncomfortably. In fact, it felt right sitting there on the porch in a wicker chair on a sunny summer day with Theresa next to her. It felt oddly perfect, and Kelsey let herself bask in it for an extra moment before sighing.

"I should probably find Hannah."

"Yeah," Theresa agreed as she looked out toward the quiet street, but her tone was less than convincing. "I'm going to take off, I think."

"Listen, can I actually get your number this time?" Theresa turned those gorgeous eyes on her and Kelsey felt her stomach flip-flop inside her rib cage. "Because I'd really like to see you again. For longer than fifteen minutes."

Theresa held her gaze for a delicious few seconds before saying softly, "I'd like that, too."

Kelsey pulled out her phone, scrolled to the contacts, and made a new entry. Then she handed it to Theresa so she could punch in the number. When she handed it back, Kelsey hit the Call button and Theresa's phone vibrated in her pocket. "Now you have mine, too," Kelsey said with satisfied expression.

"I do."

Again, their eyes held deliciously, and Kelsey tried in vain to recall ever having such intense eye contact with anybody else in her life. "I'll call you later." Kelsey stood up, cup in hand, and pocketed her phone.

"I look forward to that." Theresa held out her hand as if she was going to shake Kelsey's, but when Kelsey grasped it, Theresa just held it for a soft, warm moment. "See you soon, Kelsey."

Not trusting herself with the difficult task of actually making words, Kelsey gave a quick nod and reluctantly let go, then headed inside to find Hannah.

The house was still full of people Kelsey didn't recognize, but she smiled and nodded greetings to anybody who looked in her direction as she made her way through to the back door and then out onto the deck. She spotted Hannah in the back corner with the same group of people she'd initially led Kelsey to: her friends at her mother's party. Two had left and had been replaced by two more Kelsey didn't know. Then her eyes fell on Ree and DJ and she felt a quick blast of relief at seeing other friendly faces.

"I'm back," Kelsey said as she took a seat next to Ree, then turned to her. "Hi there. Good to see you guys." Ree squeezed her arm and DJ gave her a wave and a wink. Hannah didn't look at her, which Kelsey noticed and tried not to let sting. After Kelsey surmised that Hannah wasn't going to introduce her to the new members of the group, Kelsey half stood and held out her hand to them. "Hi. I'm Kelsey."

"Bev," the older of the two said as she enclosed Kelsey's hand in her beefy, much larger one. "This is my wife, Sue." She gestured to the very petite woman sitting next to her, who shook Kelsey's hand with unexpected gusto as she smiled.

"It's nice to meet you." Kelsey sat back down and took a sip of her wine, which was now lukewarm. She grimaced into the cup and when she looked up, she locked eyes with Hannah, who quickly looked away.

Kelsey opened her mouth to say something, but decided in front of a group of strangers was probably not the best place, and she closed it again. Instead, she focused on the people around her, did her best to participate in the conversations that were happening. Occasionally, she could feel Hannah's eyes on her, but she did her best to smile, laugh, and chat as if they weren't.

"I need a refill," Ree said to her. "Come with me."

It wasn't quite an order, but it was firm and Kelsey stood without question. "Okay. I could use one, too." She avoided looking at Hannah, simply following Ree into the house. The crowd inside had finally seemed to thin a bit, only a few people milled around the kitchen and bar. Once they reached the alcohol, Ree went to work mixing herself a gin and tonic. Kelsey watched in silence, waiting.

"What's going on with you two?" Ree finally asked, turning to look at Kelsey. She took a sip of her cocktail, her eyes never leaving Kelsey's.

Not bothering to feign confusion, Kelsey sighed heavily and found a bottle of wine. Not what she'd been drinking—this one was a red blend—but she poured it anyway. "It's a long story. Well. Long-ish."

"I've got nowhere to be," Ree said, leaning an elbow on the makeshift bar and raising an expectant eyebrow.

Resigned to her fate, Kelsey mimicked Ree's position and said, "Okay. Remember a couple weeks ago when I asked you about meeting somebody and feeling...alarmingly drawn to her? Like, physically?"

Ree gave a nod. "Of course. That was a fun conversation. Brought up some great memories for me."

"Well, I'd met somebody who had that effect on me."

"I gathered as much."

"We'd met a couple more times, but only in passing and we never really had much chance to talk. One of us was always on her way someplace else. But we finally made plans to sit and have coffee."

Ree's smile was genuine and she grasped Kelsey's upper arm, giving it a friendly squeeze. "That's great."

"It was. Except she didn't show."

"Oh. Damn."

"Yeah. And I was bummed. Like, more than I expected I'd be. And I saw Hannah that night, and she knew something was bothering me, so I thought maybe it was a good time to tell her."

"That you'd been looking to date others. Yeah, she needed to hear that, I think. Good call. How'd she take it?"

Kelsey bobbed her head from side to side. "She actually did okay. I mean, I could tell she wasn't happy about it, but she did okay. She was supportive and made me laugh and it was a good time. We talked over dinner and it was good."

"Okay." Ree drew the word out, knowing there was more to come.

Kelsey took a too-large gulp of her wine, then had a hard time swallowing it down. A quick glance around told her nobody was within earshot. "That woman was here today."

Ree's brows furrowed as she processed the information, then shot up toward her hairline as she comprehended it. "She was?"

Kelsey nodded, sipped again.

"Is she still here?" Ree said in a stage whisper this time as she craned her neck one way, then the other.

Kelsey laughed quietly. "No. She went home."

Ree gave a nod of understanding, then asked, "So…why is Hannah so bent out of shape?"

"It's her sister." Kelsey tried to hide behind her cup, but watched Ree with wary eyes.

"Her sister...?" Ree scrunched up her face like she was thinking and a beat later, her eyes flew open wide. Like, really wide. "*Theresa?*"

"Shhh!" Kelsey said, using her open hand to try to quiet her friend.

Ree clamped a hand over her mouth and took a moment to collect herself. "Sorry," she said in a whisper. "I'm just surprised is all."

Kelsey made a face of agreement. "Yeah. Me, too."

"You had no idea?"

"I didn't know Hannah had a sister. Let alone, that one."

Ree nodded. "Yeah, Theresa's...hot. Super hot. Definitely. I've only met her a couple of times. She and Hannah don't get along."

"I got that impression, though I didn't want to pry."

Ree shrugged. "I don't have a ton of details. Theresa's quite a bit older and they have different mothers. I think they each resent the other for whatever reason." She took a sip of her drink and seemed to contemplate the situation. "So, what happened? How did Hannah find out?"

Kelsey told her the story of the powder room, of Theresa astonishing Kelsey by simply...appearing.

"Okay, well, if that's not a sign, I don't know what is." Ree looked a bit incredulous as she took in the details of the story. "You were obviously meant to meet up with her at some point. Did you find out why she stood you up?"

Kelsey grinned. "Yeah. We didn't have each other's numbers. She got stuck in a meeting at work, but had no way to call me or text me or anything to let me know. She didn't even know my real name, and I didn't know hers."

Ree shook her head as she chuckled. "That is just bizarre."

"I know, right?"

"What happens now? Please tell me you got her number before she left today."

"I did. And I told her I'd call her. I mean, I *really* want to call her, but..." Kelsey made a face of confused uncertainty.

"But...?"

"Hello? She's Hannah's sister. Stay with me here, Ree." Kelsey playfully pushed at her.

"Oh! Right. Duh." Ree scratched her forehead.

"I'm not sure what to do." She sipped her wine, then sidestepped out of the way when a man approached. Kelsey smiled at him, watched as he mixed himself a vodka and Seven, then gave her a nod before heading into the kitchen. Kelsey picked up where she'd left off. "I mean, isn't there some unwritten rule about dating your friends' siblings or something?"

Ree took a moment and gazed off into the distance, looking like she was mulling it over. After several long moments, she said, "I think that's about dating your ex's sibling. I'm not sure it carries over to just friends' siblings." When Kelsey opened her mouth to reply, Ree held up a hand. "However, Hannah thinks of you as more than a friend, even if you don't think about her the same way, so this could get a little dicey."

Kelsey groaned. "That's what I'm afraid of." She swallowed, chewed on the inside of her cheek. "Ree, this girl. She's..."

Kelsey gazed off for a moment as she tried to find the words. "I wasn't kidding when I said I've never been drawn to somebody like this. It's a little unnerving."

Ree's expression softened and she closed her hand over Kelsey's forearm. "I know. I can see it on your face."

"Right? So just writing her off because of feelings that Hannah has, but I don't...I don't know if I can do that. I mean, should I have to?"

"Are you willing to give up Hannah's friendship?" Ree raised her eyebrows in question.

Kelsey blew out a breath, unsurprised by the question. "I don't know."

"Because it might come to that. I'm not saying it's fair, but I've known Hannah for a while now, and I'm not sure how well she'll take the object of her affection dating not just her sister, but her sister that she doesn't like very much. Put yourself in her shoes."

"I know. I know. You're right. I just..." Kelsey shook her head. "I guess I need to think about it, make a decision."

Ree nodded. "Should we head back out?"

Kelsey wrinkled her nose. "I think I'm gonna just head home. I have no desire to deal with the dagger eyes from across the table anymore, you know?"

"I get it." Ree gave her a hug. "I'll give her a little crap about it, don't you worry." She turned to head through the kitchen to the back door when Kelsey stopped her.

"Hey, Ree?"

Ree turned back, eyebrows up, friendly expression on her face, as always.

"Thanks. For listening. For the advice. For everything."

With a quick nod, Ree said, "You're welcome. Keep me posted."

"I will." Kelsey watched through the window as Ree headed back to the table and took her seat. Hannah bent toward her, obviously asked her something, then looked up at the house. Kelsey took that as her cue, found her purse, and was in her car in under a minute.

Home and quiet sounded perfect right about now. Home, quiet, and some serious brain racking.

Because right now? She was at a loss.

Darkness had fallen by the time Kelsey reached her apartment. She battled guilt over not having said goodbye to Hannah before she left, but honestly? She had no idea what to say to her. And if she was going all in with the truthfulness, she had to admit she was a little bit annoyed with her. It wasn't Kelsey's fault Hannah had feelings for her, was it? Kelsey had been up front about where she stood. Maybe not from the very beginning, but she'd never led Hannah on. So Hannah being angry at her now seemed...misguided? Unfounded? Not fair?

The night was humid, even for Kelsey's southern blood, and she was thankful her apartment had air conditioning. Annoyed she hadn't turned it on before she'd left for work that morning, she hit the button the second she walked in. It wasn't central air; it was a unit built into the wall and was louder than she would've liked, but it did the trick, and within a half hour, her little abode was comfortable enough that she stopped sweating.

Laptop in hand, she flopped onto her deep green suede couch, situated the throw pillows around her, and propped her feet up on the trunk that doubled as a coffee table. She had a few e-mails she'd left unanswered so she could make Hannah's barbecue before it got dark, and now seemed as good a time as any to take care of those. Plus, she hoped doing some work would keep her mind off Lisa/Theresa.

Which turned out to be a very silly assumption.

The instant she stopped typing her e-mail response and gazed up into the empty room, Kelsey's mind was filled with the breathtaking image of blue eyes, blond waves, and that killer half-smile. Then there was the voice. And that laugh!

Don't get me started on that laugh and how badly I want to hear it again, how badly I want to be the cause of it...

And that was the last of the e-mailing because it was replaced by remembering.

And daydreaming.

And wishing.

And desire.

Kelsey inhaled a full breath and let it out very slowly.

Theresa had said so much that Kelsey wanted to explore, to delve into. Why didn't she and Hannah get along? When she'd guessed that Hannah wanted more from Kelsey than friendship, Theresa had said, "Typical Hannah."

What did that mean?

Was she close to her mother? Did she get along with her father? What had made her move to New Jersey, and why had she chosen to return?

There was so much. Kelsey wanted to know all of it. Everything. And more.

She picked up her phone, scrolled to Theresa's number, added her last name. Typing "Keene," the same last name as Hannah's, was...odd, and she stared at it on the screen for several moments.

"Theresa Keene." Kelsey wet her lips. "Theresa Keene." She let it roll around her tongue, tasted how the name felt in her mouth, and immediately wondered what Theresa's middle name was. Then she laughed out loud at herself.

She had it bad.

"Screw it," she said, and hit Send. The phone rang three times before it was answered.

"You called," Theresa said quietly and, if Kelsey was reading her tone correctly, with pleasure.

"I said I would."

"True."

"I almost didn't," Kelsey said, the words out before she even realized she was about to say them.

"Yeah? How come?"

"I was torn." Kelsey's own honesty surprised her.

"Between?"

"My loyalty to Hannah and..." She hesitated only a second before continuing. "My desire to talk to you."

"And desire won, I see." Theresa sounded pleased.

Kelsey could hear the smile in her voice. "It almost always does."

"Hang on," Theresa said, "while I jot that down for future reference."

Kelsey chuckled and then there was a span of silence—not uncomfortable, which amazed her.

"I was hoping you'd call," Theresa said finally, and her tone was low and husky. Sexy.

"Inevitable, since I can't seem to get you out of my head."

"Good."

"What happens now?" Kelsey asked. At this point, she was reasonably sure Theresa was on the same page as her, but she needed her to make the next move. Kelsey had made the phone call. Now it was Theresa's turn.

"Well," she said calmly, slowly, as if she was purposely dragging it out. In a good way. "Now, I think we go on a date. Yes?"

Kelsey felt one corner of her mouth quirk up at the same time a delicious tightening happened low in her abdomen. "Are you asking me on one?"

"I'm getting there." At Kelsey's laugh, Theresa went on. "I was thinking more than coffee. Dinner. A nice dinner. What do you say?"

"I don't know," Kelsey said, taking her turn to drag it out. "I mean, are you going to actually show up?"

"Oh!" Theresa said, as if she'd been stabbed, then broke into that wonderful laugh. "I will never live that down, will I?"

"Not if I have any say, no."

Their laughter died down and Theresa said seriously, "I will absolutely show up. I promise."

"Then yes. I would love to have dinner with you."

"Fantastic. How's Tuesday? I have to work late Monday."

Kelsey clicked to the calendar on her laptop, saw she had a meeting in the afternoon, but that was it. "I can do Tuesday. Where?"

"I have a place in mind, but let me call and see if we can get in. Can I let you know on Monday?"

"Ooh, a secret location," Kelsey said with delight.

"How do you feel about Italian?"

"I feel very, very fondly about Italian. Doesn't everybody?"

"You haven't had Italian until you've had *this* Italian."

"I don't know...you're really cranking up my expectations. Dangerous." Kelsey heard the flirtatious tone without realizing she'd used it.

"You don't scare me," Theresa said, and her flirtatious tone put Kelsey's to shame.

And just like that, I'm wet, Kelsey thought, bringing a hand to her mouth in aroused surprise. *God, this woman.*

"All right, let me make some calls and I'll text you the name and address of the place. Sound good?"

"Sounds perfect," Kelsey replied.

"I'm really looking forward to it." Theresa's voice was quiet now. Serious.

"Me, too."

They said their goodbyes and disconnected, and Kelsey sat for long moments with the phone resting against her chin and a big, silly grin on her face. She only had one question.

How in the world was she going to make it through the next forty-eight hours?

CHAPTER NINE

IF IT WASN'T FOR the promise of the evening, Kelsey would have gladly crawled into bed, under the covers, and avoided the remainder of Tuesday, written it off as a horrible, useless day and waited patiently for Wednesday to come along and save her from the hideousness and frustration.

There were bad days. That was life. That was also retail. A career, a livelihood that depended on customers was always hit or miss. Kelsey knew this. She'd been in retail all of her adult life and some of her teenage years. Customers could be unreasonable assholes and you had to sit there and take it, the majority of the time, if you wanted your business to maintain a good reputation. In the age of social media, it only took one or two tweets from an angry customer to completely derail your sales. People tended to believe everything they read on the Internet, so one impossible-to-satisfy client could completely unravel your success. Horrific, but true.

Kelsey had become a pro at steeling herself, at smiling and nodding and not retaliating at all when a customer told her that a product sucked or that her store sucked or that she sucked. Offering them free stuff tended to head that irrational anger off at the pass, and on this particular Tuesday, Kelsey found herself offering free stuff to four customers. *Four!* Exorbitant and unprecedented.

She was shaking her head as she walked toward the back of the store, having sent Disgruntled Customer Number Four away with no less than twenty dollars' worth of free lotion to replace the "defective" lotion she bought last week.

"Customers," Jeanine whispered, as Kelsey passed. "Aren't they awesome?"

"No, they suck," Kelsey said just as quietly, because the last thing she needed was some other customer tweeting that the owner of Common Scents thinks her customers suck in general.

It was close to four o'clock when Kelsey dropped herself into her chair in the office and blew out a huge, overworked breath. Overall, she loved her job. Adored it. Was intensely proud of being a small business owner. But on days like today, with four unsatisfied customers and the letter that had arrived in the mail, she wondered if she shouldn't just throw in the towel and find herself a simple desk job. Something where she answered phones and filed papers and didn't worry about paying her bills and didn't take any of it home with her at the end of the day.

The letter in question was still sitting on her desk where she'd left it—okay, crumpled it up and threw it—after she'd read it earlier this morning. Its envelope was on the desk as well, the return address touting it being from Stone & Jeffers, Attorneys at Law.

The letter detailed that one Mrs. Betsy Siegler had purchased the building at Kelsey's address from her mother, effective two weeks from today's date. More information would be forthcoming.

Betsy Siegler had struck after all.

"I would like *no* more information to forthcome," Kelsey muttered to the empty office. "I would like Mrs. Betsy Siegler to fall off the face of the earth and leave me and my shop alone." With a huge sigh, Kelsey watched the security monitors, observed as one customer sprayed a body mist into the air and sniffed, as another rubbed lotion from a tester into her hands and held it up to her companion to smell, saw Jeanine restocking the foaming hand soap. Unexpectedly, her eyes welled with tears as she thought about how hard she'd worked on getting the shop up and running, and how alarmingly possible it was that she'd have to shut it down inside of six months because the rent was too much for her to afford.

Again, she thought about how her father would have a loud "I told you so" ready and waiting, and he'd deliver it with pleasure and gusto. She was sure of it. And she dreaded it.

Spinning her chair around so it was once again facing front, she rubbed her forehead and willed herself to stop worrying about something she couldn't control. She'd worry when she had to...which would probably happen soon enough. Until then, she should focus on sales.

The ding of her phone pulled her back to the present, indicating a text. It was from Theresa and couldn't have come at a better time. Kelsey smiled as she picked it up.

The name Rinaldi's and an address were staring at her. She was about to punch it into her Maps when a second text came through.

Meet me there at seven. It's very near my house, so maybe we'll go back there afterward for a nightcap, yeah? Bring your bathing suit.

Kelsey's eyebrows raised up into her hairline at the same time her thighs clenched all on their own and she realized exactly how much power this woman had over her. So much, so soon. It was frightening and exhilarating at the same time.

"Bring my bathing suit, huh? Well, that's ballsy, assuming I'd just automatically wear a bathing suit in front of you. Which, of course, I would." She glanced at the security monitor then, just to make sure Jeanine wasn't near enough to hear her.

I'll be there, she texted back. *Can't say I've ever had a nightcap in my bathing suit, but I'm willing to try anything once.*

Theresa's text came back almost immediately. *I am jotting more notes.*

Kelsey laughed. *See you tonight. Hope you actually show up.*

Theresa ended with, *Haha. Can't wait.*

Rinaldi's wasn't quite into the city. Rather, just on the outskirts, which was a relief, because Chicago traffic was an absolute nightmare of epic proportions. Driving didn't intimidate Kelsey. In fact, she enjoyed it. But just one Chicago rush hour traffic jam was all she needed to know she would avoid driving anywhere near the city at that time of day if at all possible for the rest of her life.

It was 7:08 when she approached the hostess desk and gave her Theresa's name. Being tardy was not something she enjoyed or did often, but there'd been a sudden surge of business at the shop and she didn't feel right leaving Jeremy all by himself. So she'd helped him ring out, leaving nearly twenty minutes later than she'd intended.

The hostess was a very pretty, very tall woman with sleekly straight dark hair and no curves to speak of in her black dress. She told Kelsey her party was already here and to follow her please, which Kelsey obeyed.

Down an aisle, around a corner, down another aisle in the deceptively large restaurant, and Kelsey's gaze finally landed on Theresa, sitting at a small corner table and scrolling on her phone. Kelsey took the short blip of time that Theresa wasn't looking to study her, to take her in.

She must have either gone home to change or had decided against wearing a suit today, which disappointed Kelsey momentarily, as she found the business suit unbelievably sexy. Instead, Theresa wore black slacks and a shimmering silver top with short sleeves. As Kelsey looked at her, Theresa lifted a hand and absently tucked some blond hair behind one ear, revealing a diamond earring that caught the candlelight from the table and tossed it toward Kelsey. The top had a scooped neck, leaving the skin of Theresa's throat bare and much of her collarbone visible. Kelsey had a sudden flash of herself kissing along that stretch to the center, running her tongue down to—

"Hey, you made it."

Kelsey's dirty train of thought was derailed by Theresa's cheerful greeting, and she had to make a conscious effort not to literally shake her head free of the fantasy. "It's funny that you sound so surprised, since I should be the one surprised that you made it." She grinned to make sure Theresa knew she was teasing.

"I will never live that down," Theresa said as she stood and gave Kelsey an unexpected kiss on the cheek.

"I told you. Not if I have anything to say about it."

They took their seats, the hostess handed them menus, and told them their server would be right with them. Then she was gone, and Kelsey was alone with Theresa. And just like at Hannah's house, she suddenly felt calm, relaxed, and aroused all at once. She couldn't remember ever feeling that particular combination around anybody else, not even Janice. It was comforting, and more than a little bit unnerving.

Theresa hadn't opened her menu. She simply placed her elbows on the table, propped her chin in her hands, and said, "So. Hi."

The smile on Kelsey's face widened on its own at those intense blue eyes focused on her. "Hi."

"How was work?"

And the smile dimmed a few watts. Putting her own menu down and mirroring Theresa's position, Kelsey said, "You know what? I had a terrible day at work and I don't want to talk about it. So how about we talk about anything else? Is that okay?"

"Of course it is." Theresa reached across and touched Kelsey's arm. "I'm sorry you had a bad day, though."

"For what it's worth, it just got a whole lot better."

The gentle coloring of Theresa's cheeks made Kelsey's entire day, right there.

"Good evening, ladies. I'm Mark and I'll be your server tonight. Can I start you off with something to drink?"

Theresa raised her eyebrows as she looked in Kelsey's direction. "Wine?"

"Yes, absolutely. You choose."

"Red?"

At Kelsey's nod, Theresa conversed with Mark about various brands. Kelsey didn't really listen because she was too busy watching Theresa's mouth move, watching the sparkle of the glossed lips and the occasional peeks of white teeth. Thick, dark lashes framed her blue eyes, just enough eyeliner to accentuate them. When she handed Mark the wine list, Kelsey's gaze fell to her hands, long fingers, neatly filed nails, delicate wrists covered by creamy skin...

"Kelsey?"

Kelsey blinked rapidly several times as if coming out of a trance. Theresa was looking at her, amusement clear on her face. Mark was gone. "I'm sorry?"

"I asked you if Pinot Noir was okay with you, but you seemed a bit preoccupied with...something." She arched one eyebrow knowingly.

It was Kelsey's turn to blush and she did so ferociously, feeling the heat rise up her neck and not stop until it reached her hairline.

Theresa simply picked up her water glass and took a sip, her eyes never leaving Kelsey's.

Already? Already she's got me like this?

Kelsey mentally shook her head in wonder. She'd been alone with Theresa exactly once, not counting right now. Aside from that, she'd spent a total of what? Fifteen minutes with her? Twenty? And already, Theresa affected her so deeply on such a...primal level. It was almost embarrassing.

Mark returned with the wine, thank God. He chatted with Theresa as he used his wine key, opened the bottle, and poured her a small amount to taste. Kelsey watched her sip, watched her blink slowly as she looked at Kelsey over the rim of the glass. Then she nodded to Mark, who poured two glasses, recited the specials, and gave them more time.

Theresa held up her glass and said, "To new cities, new friends, and new possibilities."

Kelsey smiled tenderly and touched her glass to Theresa's. They sipped and Kelsey let the wine roll around her tongue, coat her mouth before she swallowed it. "Oh, that's delicious."

"Yeah? I was hoping you'd like it."

The beginning of dinner went on like this, each of them catching the other's gaze, each gaze heated and almost smoldering. They managed to steer clear of work talk, which wasn't hard for Kelsey, as she was happy listening to Theresa talk about almost anything. Mark stopped by to occasionally top off their wine glasses, but they barely noticed, so absorbed were they in each other.

"Tell me about you and Hannah," Kelsey said finally, as she really wanted to know the details. She scooped a forkful of mashed potatoes into her mouth, chewed, then said, "I get the impression you're not fans of one another." She left out the part about Ree telling her exactly that.

"I did tell you. At the barbecue."

"No, you gave me the short version. Give me the long one."

Theresa took in a deep breath and let it out slowly. "Hannah and I..." She let her voice trail off and her mouth pulled to one side as she obviously looked for the right place to start. "My parents split up when I was eight. It was ugly. Yelling and screaming. Lots of tears from my mom. Constant arguments. My mom and I moved to the other side of the city, which doesn't sound that far, but was. And my dad used his freedom to act like he was twenty again. Drinking a lot, sleeping around, living the typical bachelor life. He had a one-bedroom apartment, which was always part of his excuse for not having me overnight. I may have been young, but even an eight-year-old knows when she's not wanted. I'm sure I cramped his bachelor lifestyle."

"You poor thing. That's horrible," Kelsey said, then took a sip of her wine. She couldn't imagine not wanting to spend time with your kid, and she wanted to scoop little eight-year-old Theresa up and hug her tight. She and her dad had their issues and their differences, but he would never have treated her like that. Ever.

"It was rough. It made me sad and angry at the same time. I started to lash out any time he called—which was by no means on a regular basis—because I was so hurt that he didn't want me. You know?" Theresa's eyes shimmered in the candlelight, and Kelsey again wanted to hold her, wrap her up in her arms, and tell her nothing would ever hurt her again.

"That makes perfect sense."

"That lasted the first year and a half of the split." Theresa ate a bite of chicken, gazed off into the restaurant as she chewed. "After that, he seemed to calm down, make more of an effort. Of course, by that time, I sort of hated him. At least the kind of hate that an eleven-year-old can have. Pained and misguided."

Kelsey nodded, fascinated by the story.

"Then he met Liz, and she reined him in the rest of the way. They bought a house, and when I was fourteen, they had Hannah."

Kelsey waited, sensing there was more, but that Theresa was building up to it.

"I know this is still teenage-me talking, but it felt a lot like my dad gave up on me at that point because he had this new daughter, and he would get it right this time." She sighed, stared off into space with her empty fork in her hand. When her gaze returned, it bored into Kelsey. "I tried, Kels. I really did. I wanted so badly to be part of that family. But he did everything with Hannah that he'd never done with me. Went to every parent-teacher meeting, every dance recital, every basketball game and softball game. He even chaperoned three of her field trips. I mean, actually took the day off from work to do that. He *never* did any of that stuff with me. He made exactly one of my volleyball games, and he had to leave early because Hannah had something going on."

"Wow." Kelsey's heart ached for teenage Theresa.

"So I started to insulate myself." Theresa shrugged, went back to her dinner. "I began to step back. From him. From Liz. And especially from Hannah. She got all the parts of my dad that I'd missed out on, and I really hated her for that for a long time." She looked up from her plate and made a face that said she knew how misguided that was. "It wasn't her fault. I know that now. But as a kid? All I knew was that she was much more important to my father than I was."

Kelsey's salmon was gone and she was almost done with her potatoes. "Then what happened?"

Theresa shrugged again. “I put myself through college, even though he offered to pay for it. I wanted nothing from him. I worked my ass off for four long years, got my degree, was hired by the same company I did my internship with, and I moved to New Jersey.”

“So you didn’t have to see Hannah get what was yours, up close and personal.”

“Exactly,” Theresa said, pointing her fork at Kelsey. “And I stayed away for a really long time. And I was—I am—very good at what I do. I’m very successful.”

“I’m sure you are. And now you’re back.”

Theresa nodded. “I am.”

“And that feels…?”

Theresa’s shoulders dropped and she looked like she was honestly contemplating her answer. “Good. Weird. Confusing. Right.”

“So many feelings.” Kelsey grinned.

“I’ve got a lot of ’em.” Theresa chuckled.

“You’re so complex,” Kelsey said, and finished her wine.

Theresa made a show of squinting at her. “Is that sarcasm?”

“A little bit. But mostly the truth. I like that about you.” Kelsey nodded as she held Theresa’s gaze. “I like a lot of things about you.”

“Yeah?” Theresa said in response, but her voice was quiet. Husky.

“Ladies? Dessert?” Mark’s voice might as well have been an air horn the way it cut through the delicate deliciousness of the sexual tension.

Theresa's eyes never let go of Kelsey's as she said, "No, I think we're good. Just the check, please."

"You got it." And Mark was off.

"I figured we'd have dessert at my place," Theresa informed Kelsey softly and with an underlying familiarity that had Kelsey's thighs clenching, her stomach tightening, and caused her to swallow audibly.

"Perfect."

Theresa paid the bill after snatching it out of Mark's hand before Kelsey had a chance to. "You get the next one," she said as a solution, and of course, the first thing Kelsey felt was joy at the idea of another dinner with her.

They didn't speak again until they were in the parking lot and Theresa asked where Kelsey was parked. They walked to her car, and before Kelsey had time to even form a coherent sentence about following Theresa to her place, she felt Theresa's hands on her shoulders turning her and pushing her back against the car while Theresa moved in close. So very close.

They stood that way for a long moment, bodies touching from knees to breasts, Theresa's warmth pressed against Kelsey's, her eyes searching Kelsey's for...something. Reciprocation? Permission? Kelsey had no idea. All she did know was that Theresa's mouth was way too close to not kiss her. So she did.

Were there fireworks going off nearby?

The question flashed absently through Kelsey's mind before all thought became laser-focused on Theresa's kiss. Heated but tentative. Tender but demanding. It was all those things, and Kelsey was reasonably sure she could stand there for an hour or two just making out with Theresa. She tasted like wine and beauty and desire. Her hands were holding Kelsey's face, both gently and possessively.

Air became a necessity for both of them, so Kelsey finally broke the kiss, but kept her forehead pressed to Theresa's. Ragged breathing was the only sound for several beats before Kelsey murmured, "Yikes."

"I have wanted to do that since I first caught you looking at me that day in Starbucks."

Theresa's voice was a whisper, her eyes were closed, and she swallowed audibly. When she opened her eyes again, they were dark. Heavy with arousal and need and want. She let out a small sound—a combined groan and whimper—and kissed Kelsey again. And this kiss was different. Primal. Raw. She pushed her tongue possessively into Kelsey's mouth and Kelsey let her, reveled in the feeling of Theresa wanting her as badly as she wanted Theresa. Kelsey pushed back, used her own tongue as a weapon as the delicious battle for control waged on in the darkened parking lot of Rinaldo's Italian Ristorante.

Another whimpered groan sounded and Kelsey was suddenly cold before she could even open her eyes. When she did, Theresa was still there, but both arms were straightened, her hands braced against the car on either side of Kelsey's shoulders, literally keeping her arms' length from Kelsey.

"We have to stop," Theresa whispered, chest heaving. "Or I will undress you right here in this parking lot."

"Presumptuous," Kelsey teased quietly, not recognizing the huskiness of her own voice.

"Oh, you'd let me," Theresa assured her with a nod and a quick raising and lowering of her eyebrows.

"I know."

Their gazes held then for a long, sensual moment. Finally, Theresa whispered, "Follow me home? I'm five minutes from here."

"Thank God. I might spontaneously combust if it's any longer."

Theresa gave one more groan and jogged off to her car. Kelsey was thankful she hadn't kissed her again because she wasn't sure they'd be able to stop. God, what the hell was it? What was this power? This raw, animal sexuality that Theresa exuded? Kelsey had never wanted somebody so badly in her life and she didn't even stop to think about that. She was going to have sex with Theresa. Tonight. After one date.

"Who am I?" she asked the empty darkness of the car, as both slight shame and giddiness rolled through her at once. She didn't do this. She didn't have random sex with just anybody who came along.

But Theresa wasn't just anybody. She'd known that from the second she'd laid eyes on her, felt it roll through her like a wave of heated desire. That very first time, Kelsey had known something about her was different.

She'd felt it.

She just hadn't understood what it was.

Despite the humidity of the evening, rolling down her window helped cool down her fired up bloodstream, and the rest of the ride allowed her to regain her equilibrium, steady her breathing, calm her racing heart. Theresa wasn't kidding about her place being five minutes away, and in no time, she was pulling into the driveway of a rather nice house. White siding, lush, well-kept lawn, pink Impatiens along both sides of the walk leading from the driveway to the front door.

"This is beautiful," Kelsey said as her eyes scanned the whole picture.

"Thanks," Theresa said, coming around her car and holding out a hand. "Come on."

Kelsey shouldered her bag and took Theresa's hand, the soft warmth of it making her feel oddly comforted and safe—two things that caught her by surprise. Theresa led her to the door, slid her key into the lock, and opened her house to Kelsey.

"Welcome to my humble abode," she said, waving an arm like a model on *The Price is Right.*

The first thing Kelsey noticed, of course, was the smell. It was lovely, and she inhaled quietly, taking it in. Cinnamon. Honey. Fresh-cut grass. And Theresa. Its aroma was all those things, and Kelsey felt instantly welcome. The living room was more modern than any other style, with a black leather couch and matching chair, sleek glass coffee table, and subtle flat-screen TV. The large area rug was a thick pile in a neutral color, and it encompassed the seating area but left the rest of the room to the hardwood.

"Wine?" Theresa asked, and her voice startled Kelsey for a moment.

She nodded.

"It's a gorgeous night for a swim. What do you think?"

"You have a pool?" Kelsey followed Theresa into the kitchen where she could look out the back window at the small, kidney-shaped pool, its light giving off a soft glow. "Oohhhh," Kelsey murmured.

"Like it?" Theresa was suddenly close enough to set all Kelsey's nerve endings tingling.

"It's beautiful."

"It's a big part of why I bought the house. Not that we get much swimming weather here, but..." She shrugged as she returned to the counter and opened a bottle of wine. "I've always wanted my own pool."

"Me, too." Kelsey smiled at her.

Theresa poured two glasses, then gestured to a hallway with her chin. "There's a powder room right there where you can change. There are beach towels in the linen closet next to the toilet. I'm going to run up and put my suit on. I'll meet you out back?"

"Sounds great." Kelsey waited for Theresa to disappear up the stairs before she took a huge slug of wine. "A little liquid courage," she muttered, then took her bag into the powder room, which was small and cute and sparsely decorated.

Now came the big decision.

She set down her bag and looked up at her reflection in the mirror. "What's it gonna be, Peterson? Play it safe with the one-piece? Or go crazy with the two?"

She pulled each one out. The one-piece was nice. A very acceptable navy blue with white pinstripes and a racer back. It looked just fine on her and she never worried she might accidentally fall out of it.

The two-piece... Well, hell, she should just call it what it was. A bikini. It was a bikini. She'd actually bought herself a black bikini last summer. She'd lost some weight, felt like she was almost over Janice, and wanted to do something to make herself feel good, confident. Sexy. Chris had gone shopping with her (something Chris *despised* doing) and after convincing Kelsey to let her see the bikini on, had gone utterly speechless.

Kelsey stood there in a panic. "Is it a good thing or a really, really bad thing that you're not saying any words?" Chris stayed quiet, just stared. "Chris! You're killing me. And also creeping me out a little bit."

Finally, Chris had blinked, looked up at Kelsey, and a big, tender smile broke out across her face. "Jesus, Kelserrific, you look...gorgeous. Amazing and gorgeous."

"Really?" Kelsey's voice was small, but hopeful. "You're not just saying that?"

"I am not just saying that. I promise"

"You'd tell me if I looked ridiculous?"

"Trust me. You look far, far from ridiculous. Whoever you wear that suit for will be one lucky woman."

Kelsey remembered that conversation now, smiled at the fact that the bikini had been in a drawer for well over a year, and the person she was about to wear it for was Theresa. She shed her clothes, folded them into a neat pile and left them on the vanity, then slipped the suit on. The bottoms were typically tiny, but hugged her curves, and the black was flattering. The top was a halter and tied behind her neck. Not ideal for swimming, but perfect for sunbathing. The center dipped lower than she was used to, and Kelsey had to gaze into the mirror, remind herself that showing a little bit of cleavage was okay, that it was allowed, that she wasn't the first woman in the world to do that. She was a little self-conscious, but did her best to shake it off.

As Theresa had instructed, she found beach towels in the linen closet and grabbed two, wrapping one around herself like a robe. Which was ridiculous, as it was still fairly humid out and she'd be sweating in a matter of seconds. Still...

She exited the powder room and saw no sign of Theresa yet, the wine glasses still on the counter. Kelsey grabbed them, opened the sliding glass door off the back of the house, and went out onto Theresa's back deck.

The powder room may have yet to be decorated, but Theresa had obviously focused on the backyard. The deck looked new, made from that synthetic wood that never needed to be stained or maintained and didn't give you slivers in your feet. A wrought iron high-top table and four chairs were tucked into the corner, and to Kelsey's left, a small hot tub bubbled away. Pots of flowers were scattered around the whole area, which was only slightly larger than the pool itself, but they lent little splashes of color that made the yard feel homey and welcoming. A six-foot privacy fence went all the way around, and Kelsey felt like she was tucked into a safe and private little resort.

A look back at the house showed her a light on in an upstairs window she assumed belonged to Theresa's bedroom, and she had a sudden flash of naked Theresa changing into her bathing suit. The flush that went through Kelsey's body then made keeping the towel on impossible, so she tossed it off and went to one end of the pool where she could see steps leading down into the water. She gently set the wine glasses down on the concrete and dipped a toe in. She'd never been the girl who just dives in all at once, and she wasn't about to start now. She had to step in carefully, gingerly, a little at a time. But the water was perfect:

not cold, but not so warm as to not be refreshing. Four steps down and she was in up to her stomach—her very bare, very exposed stomach. She took another couple of steps until she was on the floor of the pool, and then she lowered herself until the water was at her shoulders.

She was looking around at the yard when lights along the fence turned on, throwing a soft, gentle glow over the space. Then the lights in the pool dimmed a bit, making it so Kelsey couldn't see her feet as clearly anymore.

Mood lighting. She grinned at the thought and turned toward the house.

Theresa stood there in a short, white robe with a hood, belted around her waist, her feet bare. Her eyes landed on Kelsey and held, and they stayed that way for a long, erotic moment.

Finally, Theresa spoke as she approached the pool. "You beat me in."

"You took too long."

Theresa arched one eyebrow and tilted her head slightly to the side. "Well, then. I apologize." She reached for the belt, untied it, and dropped the robe to the concrete.

Kelsey's mouth fell open and she stood there, staring like some kind of pervert, but she didn't care. She couldn't pull her eyes away. Theresa's white bathing suit was one piece and barely there. It covered her breasts, but the neckline plunged low enough to show her belly button and Kelsey felt her mouth water at the thought of following the edge of the fabric with her fingers, with her tongue. One strap went from the left side of the suit around Theresa's back to the right side and that was about it. It fastened behind Theresa's neck and Kelsey suspected that with one simple flick, she could have it open and off. That made one corner of her mouth pull up mischievously.

"You should get in here," she said, that unfamiliar, husky tone returning. "Right now."

"Is the water fine?" Theresa asked teasingly as she walked to the end where the steps were.

"It'll be perfect once you're in it." Kelsey was *not* teasing. Judging by the suddenly serious look on Theresa's face, she got that.

Theresa waded into the pool, walked toward Kelsey as if she had all the time in the world—though the intensity in her eyes just then was sizzling. Sexy. Undeniably erotic—and Kelsey swallowed hard as their eye contact held.

"Why are you so far down in the water?" Theresa asked quietly. "I can't see you."

"Maybe that's the idea," Kelsey said, her bravado suddenly replaced with self-consciousness. She took a subtle step back. Then another as Theresa continued her slow approach. In four steps, Kelsey couldn't touch the bottom anymore and began to tread water, still backing up slowly, finding it surprisingly sensual to wonder if Theresa would follow her.

Theresa did, swimming and undeterred, and now a rather mischievous glint had appeared in her eyes. The pool wasn't big and Kelsey had backed up against the far wall before she expected to. "There's a ledge that runs all the way around," Theresa said, almost to Kelsey now. "You can stand on it instead of treading water."

Kelsey's feet found the ledge and she stood, still keeping the water at her shoulders by bending her knees, and leaned comfortably against a curve that was almost a corner.

Theresa stopped in front of her and braced a hand on the edge on either side of Kelsey's head. "Hi," she said softly.

"Hey," Kelsey replied, and her smile seemed to appear all on its own. Theresa was beautiful up close like this. Her skin—so much skin—looked creamy smooth even in the dim pool lights, the ends of her hair wet and hanging around her shoulders. Kelsey felt Theresa's feet looking for purchase on the ledge, felt them against the insides of her own feet. She continued to hold on to the edge of the pool, but her face was no more than a couple inches away from Kelsey's. When her gaze dropped from Kelsey's eyes to her mouth, Kelsey felt everything below her waist tighten in excited anticipation and in the next breath, Theresa's mouth claimed hers.

The kiss started slowly, again as if Theresa had all the time in the world. She began with a gentle melding of lips. It was warm and soft and blissful, and Kelsey felt light, like she was floating. Long moments went by like that until Theresa deepened the kiss. Little by little, she increased the pressure, used just the tip of her tongue to coax Kelsey along on the same path. But once Kelsey opened her mouth to the request, all bets were off. The kiss went from gentle to firmer to almost demanding. Tongues came into play as the two women battled for the upper hand. Which Theresa claimed easily by pushing her body into Kelsey's and using her feet and knees to push Kelsey's legs apart and up until Kelsey was pretty much straddling her thighs in the pool. Kelsey's legs wrapped around

Theresa's waist anchored Theresa so she was able to let go of the edge and use her hands for other, more delicious activities. Like digging her fingers into Kelsey's hair. Like cupping Kelsey's ass and pulling her more tightly against her own stomach. Like running the back of her finger over Kelsey's nipple through the fabric of her suit, causing it to poke forward as if looking for more contact.

The kiss never broke. Theresa's tongue was deep in Kelsey's mouth when both of her hands closed over Kelsey's breasts, kneaded them, scratched her thumbnails across the nipples. Kelsey finally had to wrench her mouth away so her moan would have somewhere to go.

"God, Theresa," she whispered as their gazes met. Kelsey had one hand around Theresa's shoulder for balance. She laid the other palm against Theresa's cheek, ran her thumb across Theresa's swollen bottom lip. "You're so beautiful," she said quietly.

Theresa grabbed Kelsey's hand and kissed the tip of that thumb. "Thank you. You should maybe check out a mirror once in a while because *you* are stunning. And this suit?" Kelsey followed Theresa's gaze down and realized the the underwater lights in the pool were at a much better angle in this spot; Theresa could see Kelsey's body very clearly and she seemed to appreciate the view. "Yeah, you're killing me with this suit." When she looked back up at Kelsey's face, her eyes had gone even darker and more hooded than they'd been ten seconds ago. "And I want it off," she said, her tone low and sexy, before crushing her mouth to Kelsey's.

Kelsey heard a small whimper, was puzzled for a split second before realizing it had come from her own throat. She'd never been this aroused, this utterly and undeniably turned on. She didn't understand what it was about Theresa Keene, but my God. Kelsey was beginning to understand how intense it all was, that the woman could look at her from across the room and soak Kelsey's underwear with only her eyes. How was that even possible? *When did I become so easy?* That train of thought faded away as she felt Theresa's hand behind her neck, tugging at the tie on her top. And just like that, she was naked from the waist up. Theresa's hands on her had felt like sensual magic through her bathing suit top, but now? The pleasure of her touch increased tenfold for Kelsey as all barriers between Theresa's fingers and her breasts were gone. Theresa was gentle...and then not. She kept kissing Kelsey even as her hands explored Kelsey's breasts, stroked them, cupped them, rolled the nipples between her thumbs and forefingers until Kelsey thought she might lose her mind from being too aroused.

Was that even a thing?

Time seemed to fade away then. Kelsey couldn't explain it, she only knew that everything dimmed except for Theresa's hands, Theresa's mouth, Theresa. Kelsey did her best to give as good as she got, and she ran her hands along the bare skin of Theresa's back. When her fingers came to the clasp of the strap that ran from one side of her suit to the other, Kelsey didn't even think about it. She slid her other hand up Theresa's back to behind her neck, flicked both clasps open, and Theresa's bathing suit fell away from her body like it had simply let go, held to her now only by her thighs. The surprised gasp she let out was so sexy, so hot, and it made Kelsey smile against Theresa's lips before closing her hands over both newly bared breasts.

God, she felt good. Her breasts were small, but that only meant they fit more perfectly into Kelsey's hands. Theresa's nipples pushed into Kelsey's palms, making themselves known and demanding attention, which Kelsey gave with her fingers. She wanted her mouth on them in a big way, but the water made that difficult. She was debating whether she could lift Theresa high enough to taste her nipples without drowning when all coherent thought was chased from her mind by fingers slowly and gently stroking between her legs, over the fabric of her bathing suit bottoms. Kelsey sucked air in through her teeth, dropped her head back...which Theresa took as an invitation to run her tongue along Kelsey's throat.

"Oh, my God," Kelsey whispered as Theresa kept a slow and steady rhythm.

"Nope, just me," Theresa whispered back. Kelsey lifted her head so she was face-to-face with Theresa, their eyes locked, Theresa watching her expression closely as she continued to play Kelsey's body like a beautiful, much-loved instrument. "You feel so good."

Maintaining eye contact during sex was not something Kelsey had ever been any good at, but so many things were different with Theresa, and that was one of them. Their eyes stayed locked. Even as Theresa grabbed Kelsey's bottoms with one hand and slid them down her legs and off, their gazes held. And when Theresa helped Kelsey adjust her position, wrapped her legs tightly around Theresa's waist, their gazes held...and stayed that way until Theresa's fingers finally, *finally* touched

Kelsey's heated and swollen center. Then their eyes closed as they rested their foreheads together, Theresa moving slowly through wetness that had nothing at all to do with the pool.

Kelsey felt like her entire body might simply combust, just burst into flame, pool water or no pool water. When she opened her eyes, Theresa was looking at her, into her, and Kelsey could feel waves of heat coursing through her body, guided by Theresa's fingers. Part of her wanted to shriek at Theresa to hurry, to put her out of her misery, to tip her over the edge. *Now. Please.* But another more powerful part thrilled at the slow and steady strokes, at how intently Theresa was focusing on taking her time, judging by the way her brow had furrowed slightly in concentration. When Theresa finally broke eye contact, it was because, once again, her gaze fell to Kelsey's lips, and Kelsey nearly cried out loud with joy when Theresa kissed her again, as if she'd been missing that mouth so badly (and she had).

How is it possible to feel this good?

It was the only thought in Kelsey's head, repeating again and again, more intensely as her own arousal ratcheted higher. She had one hand at the small of Theresa's back, holding on for dear life. Fingers of the other hand were dug deeply into the soft blondness of Theresa's hair, her palm against the back of Theresa's head, keeping their mouths melded. Theresa picked up the pace and her nipples brushed against Kelsey's below the surface of the water, causing Kelsey to make a sound deep in her throat. She was so close now, so close, and her hips moved on their own, following Theresa's rhythm, moving slightly left or right to help her find the exact right spot. And when Theresa pushed her tongue into Kelsey's mouth and her fingers into Kelsey's center at exactly the same time, that was it.

Kelsey tore her mouth from Theresa's and let out a small cry as every muscle in her body tightened into near-spasm. Theresa didn't stop; she kept up the rhythm and Kelsey could feel eyes on her face, knew Theresa was watching her intently, and she didn't care. Her body didn't care. The only thing on this planet right now was Kelsey's orgasm and the gorgeous woman causing it. She rode it out as colors exploded behind her eyes and her fingers gripped a handful of Theresa's hair. It seemed to go on forever, though Kelsey knew that wasn't reality. But her chest heaved and her body quivered and she never wanted to let go of Theresa. Ever.

And that was a very, very new feeling for her.

When the contractions inside her body finally began to wane, she gently reached down, closed her hand over Theresa's and whispered, "Okay. Stop. Stop. Stop." Theresa obeyed, but stayed inside, and Kelsey's breathing gradually returned to normal. When she finally opened her eyes and focused on the gorgeous face in front of her, Kelsey felt a lump in her throat. Swallowing it back down, she mentally admonished herself for getting sappy over a woman she barely knew. A woman she'd slept with on the first date. She should be annoyed with herself. She should be ashamed and she knew it. But one look at the tender smile on Theresa's face as they stayed in the same position, Kelsey's legs wrapped around Theresa's waist, Theresa's fingers still tucked snugly inside Kelsey, and the self-deprecation evaporated like a drop of rain on a hot sidewalk. Kelsey was able to simply bask in the glow of those beautiful blue eyes.

"That was..." Kelsey's voice trailed off and she shook her head.

"Horrible? A nightmare? The worst experience of your life?" Theresa's voice was low, coy.

"None of the above. It was...amazing. Mind-blowing. Possibly limb-melting since I can't seem to feel my legs right now."

"Oh, I feel them. They're there, don't you worry. In fact, I very much like them there."

Kelsey tightened her thighs, giving Theresa's waist a gentle squeeze. "There?"

"Right there, yes."

Kelsey smiled as she realized just how very much she liked Theresa so close to her. Her body, her face, her mouth. Everything was mere inches from Kelsey and she wished she could keep it that way. And now, she wanted nothing more than to touch Theresa's body, to feel *her* wetness, to make her feel as good as she'd made Kelsey feel. She grasped Theresa's hand, slowly pulled Theresa's fingers from her body—and almost whimpered with sadness at the loss.

"My turn," she said quietly and arched an eyebrow in expectation.

Theresa turned her hand so she caught Kelsey's. "Tell you what. Let's get out of the pool before we turn into prunes, have a little wine, dry off, and then we'll go inside and..." One corner of her mouth pulled up in a sexy half-grin.

"And...I get to touch you this time?"

Theresa nodded, then pushed herself away from the wall of the pool. Kelsey watched her swim and when she was able to touch the bottom, she pulled her suit the rest of the way off, tossed it up onto the concrete, and climbed the steps to get out. Completely naked. Kelsey's breath caught in her throat as she got the full view. From the back.

"I might not survive this night," Kelsey muttered to herself as she watched Theresa exit the pool, find a towel, and wrap it around herself. She turned to look at Kelsey and crooked a finger at her.

"Your turn," she said.

Kelsey felt a surge of arousal and knew she could easily be ratcheted up again. And probably would be. She unfastened the clasp holding her top around her rib cage, then tossed the top up onto the concrete as Theresa had done. Then she swam to the shallow end as it occurred to her that this was the first time she'd ever skinny dipped. Trying to ignore the feel of Theresa's eyes on her (impossible), Kelsey climbed out of the pool, found the other towel, and wrapped herself in it, relieved to be covered again, but wishing Theresa wasn't.

Theresa stepped close, wine glasses in hand, and Kelsey took in her scent. Chlorine, sex, and her usual nutmeg/cinnamon/honey blend that was so incredibly appealing. Kelsey took one glass. "That was..." She shook her head, at a loss for words, and sipped.

"I completely agree," Theresa said, smiling and not stepping back, for which Kelsey was grateful. She reached out her hand, stroked it along Theresa's bare arm. Yup. Creamy smooth. Theresa caught that hand and tugged Kelsey to the two lounge chairs parked side by side. "Come over here with me."

They each took a chair and stretched out, wine glasses in hand. It was peaceful and surprisingly quiet.

"I can't believe how many stars you can see tonight," Theresa commented softly.

Kelsey looked up as well, saw a canvas of a thousand little pinpricks of light in the midnight blue sky. "It's beautiful."

They were silent for a long moment before Theresa said, "I need you to know something, Kelsey."

Kelsey wasn't sure if she should be wary or nervous or calm. Theresa's tone was gentle, but with an edge of seriousness. "Okay. Tell me." Kelsey braced herself.

Theresa swallowed audibly, then took a sip of her wine, swallowed again. "This is...this is new for me. It's not something I do on a regular basis."

Kelsey pressed her lips together for a moment before turning to look at Theresa and asking, "This, meaning...laying out back at night and stargazing?"

The small grin made Kelsey feel a touch lighter. "No," Theresa said. "This, meaning..." She cleared her throat. "Having sex with somebody after, like, a date and a half. It's not normal behavior for me." She turned her gaze to Kelsey, her expression a mix of worry and shame.

Kelsey felt her own smile grow. "Well, thank *God*."

"What does that mean?"

"It means, thank God it's not normal behavior for you, because it's not normal behavior for me either."

"Thank God," Theresa said. A beat of silence passed, then they both burst out laughing.

"I was so worried what you might think of me."

"Which is silly, because why would I think poorly of you when I'm doing the same thing?"

"I didn't say it was logical," Kelsey said, still chuckling.

Their laughter died down. "I need you to know that...this feels different to me." Theresa sat up suddenly, raised one hand, palm out, in a placating gesture. "I'm not trying to freak you out or get too heavy or deep. It's just that..." She shrugged as if she'd run out of thought. "I wanted you to know."

Something in Theresa's voice, in her eyes, warmed Kelsey from the inside. "It feels different to me, too," she said quietly.

"Yeah?"

With a nod, Kelsey said, "If it didn't, I never would've agreed to meet with you because...Hannah." She grimaced.

"Yeah, I had the same concern. And came to the same conclusion: that it was worth it to see where this went." Theresa held out her hand. Kelsey took it, and they gazed up at the stars, fingers entwined until they'd each finished their wine.

"You know where I think this should go?" Kelsey asked.

"Up to my bedroom?"

"Exactly."

Theresa's bedroom seemed to be another place where she'd spent time and energy on the décor. The walls were a slate blue, deep and rich, but not too dark. Two dressers stood on opposite walls, one with a mirror, a makeup tray, and two framed photos Kelsey couldn't make out in the dim light. The comforter on the king-size bed was ivory with what looked like fifty pillows perched against the headboard, all in varying shades and patterns of blue. The bed itself was a four-poster, large and elegant and exactly what Kelsey would've chosen for Theresa.

"I like pillows," Theresa said when she saw where Kelsey was looking.

"I noticed."

Theresa came up behind her then, wrapped her arms around her from the back, and hugged her tightly. Her face near Kelsey's ear, she said, "I'm so glad you're here."

Her voice, her proximity, her body heat. All of it combined to make Kelsey literally weak in the knees, and she reached out to balance herself with a hand on one of the bed's posts. As expected, her arousal cranked up several notches, and Kelsey turned in Theresa's arms. They were almost exactly the same height, their noses almost touching. Kelsey grasped Theresa's towel with both hands, right at the top where one end tucked into the rest, and tugged it open. She held a corner in each hand, kept Theresa close with it as she let her eyes slowly rove over this spectacularly beautiful body before her. She hadn't had a good view in the pool, the water distorting what she could see, but now...she was struck speechless, so she simply continued to look. Bronzed skin (Kelsey was startled by how tan Theresa actually was, given that she'd initially thought her almost pale) that called to Kelsey to touch it, stroke it, kiss it. Small, but lovely breasts that made Kelsey's mouth water just from looking at them. Nicely rounded hips and legs that seemed to go on forever.

"You're going to give me a complex if you keep staring like that," Theresa said in amusement.

"Shut up. You're gorgeous and you know it." And with that, Kelsey dropped the towel to the floor, leaving Theresa standing naked before her. She grasped her face in her hands and kissed her. Not gently. There would be no gentle lead-up this time. Kelsey was too turned on. She had to have Theresa and she had to have her now.

A quick spin had Theresa's back to the bed and Kelsey only needed to take a couple of steps toward her to push her onto it. Theresa scooted backward until her head was near the pillows as Kelsey dropped her own towel and crawled after her.

The pool had been awesome, but it didn't compare even a little bit to actually being naked and on top of Theresa. Every nerve ending in Kelsey's body was on high alert, sizzling and hot. She shoved pillows out of her way as she made room for their bodies and brought her mouth down on Theresa's, pressed her tongue in immediately and was met with a moan and the feeling of Theresa's fingers digging into her back.

It had never been like this for Kelsey. Never in her life. There'd never been this urgency. This desire. This *need* to touch another person so badly she was afraid she'd go insane if she didn't. It scared her—the intensity, the unfamiliarity—and at the same time, it felt so completely perfect.

The clichéd sound of it was not lost on Kelsey, but they really did fit flawlessly together. There was no awkwardness. Not a stitch of uncertainty. They moved together, in syncopated rhythm, stroking and squeezing and pushing and rocking. Kelsey made her way down Theresa's torso using her tongue and her lips, kissing every millimeter of skin she possibly could. Theresa alternated between ragged breathing and contented sighs, and

Kelsey paid close attention to what move of hers caused each sound. When she passed Theresa's belly button, she raised herself up on her knees, wanting to get the full view before she continued on her journey. Theresa had one hand over her eyes, the other gripping the corner of a pillow tightly, and her chest was heaving.

"Theresa," Kelsey said softly as she placed a hand on each of Theresa's knees and slowly pushed her legs apart. When Theresa removed her hand and looked at Kelsey's face, Kelsey said simply, "You're beautiful." Theresa gave her a warm smile and Kelsey bent down to her center.

Kelsey's plan was to take her time, to work Theresa up slowly before sending her over the edge. As she made herself comfortable and used her thumbs to spread around Theresa's wetness—God, she was so wet—Kelsey realized keeping to her plan was going to be hard. Because the view from her spot looking up Theresa's naked and flushed body to her beautiful face, did nothing to keep her in check. And the musky scent of her was a bigger turn-on than Kelsey even expected. She touched her tongue to Theresa's hot, swollen flesh, and the tang, the salty sweetness of her was more that Kelsey could take. She dove in more firmly, stroking and tasting and loving the feel of Theresa writhing in pleasure that Kelsey was causing. The sounds she made were enough to push Kelsey shockingly close to her own orgasm. Soft moans, occasional whimpers, quiet whispers of, "Kelsey...oh, Kelsey..." were almost her undoing. But Kelsey forced herself to concentrate and reached up to fondle a nipple, which caused a gasp. Kelsey smiled against Theresa's flesh and the second she slid her fingers inside, Theresa's moans got louder. Kelsey felt Theresa's hand in her hair as she whispered, "Oh, God, yes. Right there." And then her hips lifted off the bed as she let out a long, strangled whimper.

Kelsey watched from her position, keeping her mouth pressed tightly to Theresa's center, not wanting to break contact, but wanting to watch the orgasm tear through her. Her back arched, the muscles in her neck stood out, everything was tensed, and it was beautiful...so, so beautiful. The most sensually erotic thing Kelsey had ever witnessed, right there, right beneath her, under her hands and her mouth. Kelsey stayed where she was for what seemed like hours, but was probably only a minute or two, until Theresa's body began to relax, until her back came down in contact with the bed, until her fingers in Kelsey's hair gave a gentle tug, instructing her it was okay to let go.

Kelsey gently took her mouth away, but placed a tender kiss on the spot before leaving it altogether. As she slid her fingers out, Theresa's leg twitched and she chuckled. Kelsey rubbed a hand up and down Theresa's thigh, loving the warm softness of it.

"Come up here," Theresa commanded, and Kelsey pushed herself up on all fours. She placed a kiss on Theresa's stomach, then stretched out next to her. Theresa immediately turned on her side, tucked her head under Kelsey's chin, threw a leg over Kelsey's, and draped her arm across Kelsey's stomach.

Nothing had ever felt more perfect in Kelsey's entire life, and she felt her eyes well up a bit, hoped Theresa didn't see.

"That was...you're amazing. I mean, that was...God."

"You know, I almost made fun of your lame descriptors, but the fact that you're kind of speechless is a pretty awesome compliment, so I'm going to take that."

"Please do," Theresa said, cuddling closer. "You deserve it."

Kelsey could feel herself blush, and she squeezed Theresa to her, wanted her closer than possible. "Wasn't hard," she said and placed a kiss on Theresa's forehead. There was a lot she wanted to say then, a lot she almost did say. But the fact that they still barely knew each other stuck in her head and kept her from mentioning anything that might send Theresa screaming into the street. Instead, she simply held Theresa tightly and snuggled in closer to her body.

They lay like that for long moments and Kelsey was just starting to doze when Theresa asked softly, "Do you want some water?"

Kelsey nodded, kept her eyes closed as she felt Theresa leave the bed, and she let out a quiet groan, disappointed at the loss. She heard soft footsteps as Theresa padded out of the room, and she took the opportunity to shift her position and get under the covers. A thought occurred to her then: would Theresa want her to go home now? Kelsey had no idea. Maybe she would, right? They'd only been together this once. Despite what they'd talked about earlier, they weren't exclusive. They didn't really owe each other anything. Maybe Theresa didn't sleep well with somebody else in her bed. Maybe she didn't enjoy sleepovers in general. Maybe they were too personal, too involved.

Pressing a hand firmly to her forehead did nothing to stop the whirlwind of these thoughts, and Theresa came back in at just that moment. A water glass was in each hand as she approached Kelsey's side of the bed in all her naked glory.

"You should never wear clothes," Kelsey said as Theresa set a glass down on the nightstand.

"I'd be cold for much of the year." Theresa went around to her side of the bed. "Oh, good. You got under the covers. I was starting to get chilly."

"It's August." Kelsey lifted the covers so Theresa could slide in.

"See? If I'm chilly in August with no clothes, how would I survive, say, December?"

"Good point." Kelsey held an arm out and Theresa settled right back into her spot on Kelsey's shoulder. "So..." Kelsey swallowed.

Theresa's head shifted on Kelsey's shoulder and Kelsey could feel her gaze. "So...?"

"Is it okay if I stay?" Kelsey's voice sounded small, and she hated that.

"Absolutely," Theresa replied, as if that was the silliest question she'd heard in weeks. Then her tone went more serious. "I mean, I'd like you to. But if you're uncomfortable and would rather leave, I get it."

"I am so far from uncomfortable right now."

"Oh, good. Me, too. You should stay."

"I think I'll stay."

Theresa lifted herself up on an elbow so she could look down on Kelsey's face. She bent forward and pressed her lips to Kelsey's in what Kelsey assumed was meant to be a simple and chaste kiss goodnight. But the feel of those soft lips, the taste of that mouth, they were more than Kelsey could bear and she shoved sleep aside with a surprisingly easy swipe.

And they were off again.

Sleep wasn't allowed back in the room until well after two in the morning.

CHAPTER TEN

THE BEEPING IN KELSEY'S head was unfamiliar, and she tried to analyze what it was without opening her eyes. She was way too comfortable. Snuggled into great softness, something very warm and smooth pressed all along the back of her body.

Which was naked.

That got her attention and she opened her eyes just as the warmth behind her shifted slightly and then groaned.

Theresa.

It all came flooding back and Kelsey's smile seemed to spread across her face all on its own. Theresa moved and the beeping stopped. Then she returned right back to the exact spot she'd been in, spooned up behind Kelsey. Her arm wrapped around Kelsey's torso as Theresa whispered in her ear, "We've got ten more minutes and then I have to get up." She pressed a kiss to Kelsey's temple, then settled back down against her back.

Yeah, I could get used to waking up like this every morning.

The thought tiptoed through Kelsey's head as she drifted off once again.

Ninety minutes later, they were both up, showered and dressed. Kelsey wore her clothes from the night before, but knew she had time to go home and change before opening the shop at ten. Theresa, on the other hand, had to go right into work. Kelsey had mentioned just going home and showering there, but

Theresa had pouted—*actually pouted!*—and said she wasn't ready for Kelsey to leave yet.

Yeah, this was going to be a problem if their relationship continued, because Kelsey was reasonably sure she'd give Theresa anything she wanted in the face of that pout.

Kelsey waited in the kitchen for the coffee to finish brewing and grinned when she heard the click of heels coming down the hardwood stairs. Theresa entered the room and Kelsey did her best to school her features so she wasn't staring, slack-jawed, like a teenager at a strip club for the first time. Which was really hard, as Theresa's beige dress pants, black sleeveless top, and black heels made her look fierce, entrepreneurial, and just sexy enough to warrant a second glance if you passed her in an office hallway.

She set down her briefcase and a pile that consisted of a few files and a blue binder logo'd with what looked like a house outlining a heart on the spine. "Hey," she said to Kelsey as she reached for the cabinet door near Kelsey's head. A slight lean and she was able to press her lips to Kelsey's. "Sleep well?" She pulled two travel mugs down and set them on the counter.

"Like a baby. You?"

"I slept great. I was worried you wouldn't be used to sleeping with an albatross hanging all over you." She gave a sheepish grin as she pulled the coffee pot off its pedestal and filled each travel mug.

"I actually enjoyed that very much. Who knew?"

Theresa's smile seemed very satisfied. "How do you take your coffee? I mean, if it's not a Frappuccino."

"Lots of cream and lots of sugar. I like it not to taste like coffee at all."

Shaking her head, Theresa said, "Why does that not surprise me?" She proceeded to add cream and sugar, checking with Kelsey to see when was enough. Then she screwed the lid on and handed it over.

"Thank you," Kelsey said, touched beyond words. She took a sip and it was perfect. Because of course it was. Mug still to her lips, she asked quietly, "Can I see you again?"

Theresa just looked at her for a long moment before replying. "You can." She sipped her own coffee, her eyes never leaving Kelsey's, and something in that look made Kelsey's stomach tighten.

At seven in the morning? Seriously, body? I am in so much trouble already with this girl...

"Good. When?" Kelsey asked.

Theresa set her mug down and pulled out her phone, scrolled through what Kelsey assumed was her calendar. "I've got late meetings today and tomorrow. This project is huge and it's taking up a lot of my time." She made a face that said she wasn't happy about it, and that made Kelsey feel warm inside. "Friday?"

"I can do Friday."

"Great. I'd like to cook you dinner. Would that be okay?" Theresa actually looked slightly hesitant, as if she was worried Kelsey would be all, "Oh, no, I'd rather you didn't. That's just silly."

"I'd love that. What can I bring? And what are you cooking? And will you be wearing an apron? And nothing else?" Kelsey waggled her eyebrows lasciviously, which made Theresa chuckle.

"There will be an apron, but sadly, there will also be clothes."

"Damn it."

"I have a few ideas for dinner. I need to think about it and then I'll text you Thursday to find out what you like and don't like."

"I like you." The words were floating out in the air before Kelsey even realized they'd formed in her brain. She felt her face flush, her ears got hot, and she took a sip from her mug to try to mask the embarrassment.

"I like you, too," Theresa said. Softly. Tenderly. The relief washed through Kelsey like a flood.

Their kiss goodbye was long and sensuous and amazing, a delicious display of push-pull, and Kelsey toyed with the idea of dragging Theresa back through the door, into the living room, onto the couch. Theresa pulled away first, before Kelsey could make any moves. She didn't step out of Kelsey's arms, but she pulled her mouth away, her hands still on Kelsey's face, holding her, cradling her.

"You are an amazing kisser," she said, kissed Kelsey once more—quickly—and stepped back a couple steps. "And if we don't stop now, I'm going to be *very* late for work."

"Understood. Sorry."

"Oh, no. No apologies from you. I think my boss should apologize to me for making me leave all of this"—she gestured with one hand up and down Kelsey's body—"gorgeousness."

Kelsey was pretty sure she blushed all the way home.

Common Scents was busy for a Wednesday. Which was good, because it made the day go by a bit faster. Kelsey wanted Wednesday and Thursday and Friday afternoon to fly by, super quickly, so she could be with Theresa again. Like, immediately. In fact, she entertained the idea of just popping in on her tonight, just driving to her house after the store was closed and surprising her. Luckily, she was intelligent enough to understand how that could maybe be viewed as semi-stalkerish behavior, and she wasn't willing to risk it.

What continued to amaze and bewilder her was how shockingly compatible she and Theresa seemed to be. *At least physically.* She had to add that little caveat because reality liked to pop its ugly face into Kelsey's storybook fantasies and remind her how little time she'd actually spent with Theresa, how little they really knew about each other.

"So far," Kelsey said aloud to her empty office. That would change. You always started a relationship not knowing the other person that well, right? Wasn't that the nature of a new pairing? It had only been one date. Was she expected to be able to write a biography on Theresa now? Because that was lame.

And you couldn't do it. The little voice again. That stupid little voice.

Kelsey spent the remainder of the day and into the evening taking care of paperwork, responding to e-mails, running the register while Jeanine took her break, and helping four different women choose the right scents for them. Honey Almond, Sugared Martini, The Jasmine in my Mind, and Autumn Hike, respectively. Jeremy had asked for the night off, so Kelsey hung out and closed. She tallied up the totals, smiled at the results of the day. Then she locked the front door, turned the lights to the "night" setting, gathered up her things and the garbage bag from under the counter, and headed out the back door.

As she walked toward the Dumpster the entire building used, she saw Jacob Kim heading in her direction. Jacob owned the dry cleaners next door to her shop.

"Hey, Jake. You're working late tonight."

Jacob opened the top of the Dumpster, tossed in his garbage, then held it for Kelsey. "No, just going through some papers. I assume you've been visited by the Wicked Rent Raiser of Westland?"

Kelsey grimaced. "I have. Can't say I enjoyed her company all that much."

"Yeah, no kidding." He paused, looked up at the sky for a beat before saying. "I don't think I can stay if she raises the rent by a lot."

Kelsey nodded. "I know. I'm in the same boat. I don't know where else I'd go. This was the best rental I could find for a business. I chose it purposely for that reason."

"My father is livid." Jacob had inherited the dry cleaners from his parents five years prior, and it had taken another three before his father had fully retired and let Jake run things on his own. "He says Mrs. Jenkins would never have done this."

"I know." She wanted to add that Mrs. Jenkins was beyond elderly and selling the building to her child wasn't really something all that surprising, just dumb luck and bad timing for them. But she didn't, because honestly, it was nice to have somebody else to commiserate with. Kelsey's anger, worry, sadness...Jake got it, because he had them as well.

"I keep waiting for the other shoe to drop," Jake said. "'Cause it's going to."

Kelsey nodded her agreement. "It is. Part of me likes that we've gone so long without contact. I can trick myself into believing she changed her mind and will keep everything as is. The other, logical part of me wants her to just get it over with so I can figure out my next steps and if I even have any."

"I totally get that. Same thing goes on in here." Jacob tapped a finger against his temple, then blew out a breath of what was most likely frustration. "Ah, well. It's business."

"It is."

"It sucks and I hate it, but it's business." He made a face that basically said, "What can you do?" Then they said their goodbyes and went their separate ways.

Kelsey loved the length of the days in the summer. It was after nine, but dusk was just beginning to shift the sky toward night. She loved closing the shop and still having almost daylight left to get her home, and she drove with a smile on her face, despite the conversation with Jacob Kim.

Whatever happens, happens. There's not a lot I can do about it.

The thought wasn't terribly comforting, but it was realistic and realism always had a way of making Kelsey feel like she was on solid footing again. She really, really didn't want to lose her shop, but it was a very distinct possibility, and if it was going to happen, she'd deal with it. She planned to do some research soon on other possible locations. She turned up the volume on the radio and hummed along as she headed home.

Once settled into her apartment for the night, Kelsey realized she hadn't had much to eat that day. Her stomach made its dissatisfaction clear by causing sudden uncomfortable roiling, letting Kelsey know just how empty it actually was. She was just about to scramble a couple eggs when her phone dinged with an incoming FaceTime call from Chris.

"I'm propping you up on the counter so I can cook," she informed her cousin by way of hello. "Hi there."

"Hey, you. Whatcha makin'?" The background of Chris's shot wasn't her office as usual.

"Scrambled eggs. Are you actually home?"

"It's ten thirty here, K-Pete. Even I don't work that late."

"Damn. I constantly forget the time change."

"Constantly." Chris chuckled, took a sip from a bottle of water. "What are your plans for the weekend? Specifically, Sunday."

"Why? What's happening on Sunday?" Kelsey used a fork to beat the eggs in a small glass bowl. She glanced at the phone's screen before opening the fridge for milk.

"It's very possible that your favorite cousin might need you to pick her up from the airport." Kelsey squealed in delight. Literally squealed, which made Chris laugh. "Wow, you sure know how to channel your inner three-year-old."

"Are you really coming?"

"If I wasn't already on my iPhone, I'd show you my confirmation e-mail from the airline."

"I can't wait to see you!"

"You're sure it's okay?" Chris ran a hand through her short hair, wrinkled her nose. "It's really last minute, and I'm sorry about that."

"Don't be sorry. Of course it's okay. I'm so happy you're coming to visit. How long can you stay?" Kelsey moved a pat of butter around the hot frying pan until it melted completely, then poured the beaten eggs and milk in. Surprised to find she actually had bread left, she popped two slices into the toaster.

"At least until Tuesday. Possibly longer."

Kelsey pursed her lips into a pout. "Two days isn't very long."

"I know. But I said possibly longer. We'll see."

Kelsey squinted at the screen as she scrambled her eggs. "You're hiding something," she said, and saw Chris's cheeks tint pink.

"I'm not hiding anything. I'm just...sitting on it for a bit." Chris bit down on her bottom lip.

"You're seriously not going to tell me? But you tell me everything! I'm going to have to rethink this entire relationship now. Thanks a lot."

Chris's chuckle came over the phone's speaker loud and clear. "I'm going to tell you, Kelsify, just not yet."

"Fine. Then I won't tell you *my* news." She stuck her tongue out at the tiny Chris on the screen.

"Yes, you will. You're bursting with it. I can see it on your face. You can't *not* tell me."

Kelsey made a sound of frustration because Chris was absolutely right. Kelsey was dying to tell her about Theresa. "I hate you sometimes. You know that, right?"

"I do. It's okay. Now tell me what's going on?"

Kelsey scraped her eggs onto a plate, buttered her toast, and set everything on the counter near the phone so she could talk to Chris and eat at the same time. She took a bite, chewed slowly.

"Aw, come *on*!" Chris glared at her, which Kelsey found endearingly amusing.

"I didn't sleep here last night." Boom. She left it right there and watched Chris's face.

"Get out."

"Totally serious. I slept at Theresa's."

"Wait. What? Who the hell is Theresa?" Chris's eyebrows shot way up into her hairline as her eyes widened in shock.

"Theresa is Lisa."

"Lisa." Chris squinted, then said, "The Starbucks chick?"

"That's the one." Kelsey wasn't sure why she hadn't mentioned her actually meeting "Lisa" at Hannah's. It had all happened so fast, cliché as it sounded. So she began at the beginning and told Chris all of it. Everything. Reiterating the first meeting in Starbucks, then on to the online dates to the spectacularly unexpected meeting at Hannah's house. And her relationship to Hannah, of course, as well as Hannah's less than favorable reaction.

"Are you making this up?" Chris's expression was dubious. "'Cause this is like a damn romantic comedy, and it's also the first time you're mentioning that the dream woman is an actual woman you've actually spoken to. Are you bullshitting me?"

"I promise you I'm not. Do you want to hear the rest? Or would you rather just whine and complain?"

Chris glared at her through the phone. "The rest, please."

"All right then." Kelsey went on with the story. The talk on the front porch at Hannah's house. Dinner at Rinaldi's. The pool.

"She has her own pool?" Chris said, obviously impressed.

"She does. And we had sex in it."

"What?" Chris asked, loudly. "Now I really think you're bullshitting me. My favorite cousin won't even skinny dip, let alone have actual sex in a pool."

"I know, right?" Kelsey's voice had the same level of incredulity that Chris's did. "I wouldn't believe me either." She put the last bite of eggs into her mouth and chewed. "But it's true. And holy shit, Chris, it was *so good*." She closed her eyes as she stressed the last two words.

Chris seemed to take time to absorb the story, all the details Kelsey had given her. "Huh," she said finally.

"What does that mean?"

"It means I believe you because...that dreamy look on your face tells me this girl is real. And that she's got a hold on you."

"She does." Kelsey dropped her chin into a palm as she leaned on the counter. "Which is very, very unlike me."

"It is and that's the only thing that's got me worried for you. You don't fall easily. You're a tough nut to crack. And this girl seems to have cracked you on the first try."

"I know."

There was a moment of quiet as the two of them simply looked at each other through the small screens of their iPhones.

"Will I get to meet her?" Chris finally asked.

"I'd really like that," Kelsey said, and she meant it. "She's cooking me dinner on Friday night. I don't know what the plans are, if any, on Saturday. I have the shop, as always. And then you come on Sunday. Maybe we can all have dinner on Monday or something?"

"I'd be up for that. I'll follow your lead. I just want to spend time with you and I want to meet this person who's swept my little cousin right off her feet. Face-to-face."

Kelsey felt a warm surge of love for Chris then, for her protectiveness and desire to keep her safe. She wasn't sure how Theresa would feel about meeting family members already. It was so early in all of this. "I'll talk to her on Friday. See how she feels about it."

"And how are things with Hannah?" Chris asked. "You having a fling with her sister can't be sitting well with her."

"Yeah, I'm sure it's not." Kelsey picked up her plate and turned her back to the phone so she could set them in the sink. "I haven't talked to her."

"Recently?" Chris asked. "Or since?"

"Since." Kelsey grimaced as she waited for the scolding. Which came immediately.

"You haven't even called her? Come on, Kels. You're better than that. She's been really great to you. You owe her at least an *attempt* at reconciliation."

"I know, I know. You're right." And she was. Kelsey was well aware that she should be making the effort, not waiting around for Hannah to eventually call or text. Because she probably wouldn't. Kelsey had chosen her sister over her. And even though that was a gross overgeneralization that left out a lot of important detail, that's how Hannah would be looking at it.

And Kelsey knew that. "I'll try to get in touch with her tomorrow."

"That's all I'm asking. The trying part."

They chatted for a few more minutes, but Kelsey hit the wall all of a sudden and after her third yawn, Chris smiled.

"You know, it's an hour later for me. I'm the one who should be yawning."

"I'm sorry, Chris," Kelsey said, a hand over her mouth. "I didn't get a lot of sleep last night." She arched one eyebrow to punctuate the comment.

"Sure, rub it in," Chris said, but her eyes sparkled. "Good for you, favorite cousin. I'm happy for you."

"Yeah?"

"Absolutely. It's been forever since you got laid. You needed it. Your nose has been scrunching up weird and you were getting cranky."

"Hey!" Kelsey pointed at the screen and made a threatening face that only made Chris laugh.

"Get some sleep. I'll text you the details of my flight tomorrow."

"I can't wait to see you."

They signed off. Kelsey rinsed her dishes and put them in the dishwasher, the whole time looking at the recent events in her life through Chris's eyes. It was no wonder she was worried. Concerned. Acting like a mama bear. Kelsey knew she'd be acting the same way if their roles were reversed. In fact, if Chris called and told her she'd met a woman she was insanely attracted to, went to one dinner with her, then slept with her that night, on their very first date, Kelsey would have an earful to give her. As it was, Chris had gone pretty easy on her.

She finished cleaning the kitchen, then headed to the bathroom where she brushed her teeth, washed her face, did everything she usually did before bed. Her mind was filled, of course, with Theresa. Visions of Theresa. Laughing. Flirting. Naked. Coming. Kelsey swallowed hard at the last one, wondering if they could do it again on Friday.

"No," she said to her reflection. "I need to get to know her a bit more first. That's the game plan. Talk. Then sex. Maybe. I mean, probably. Hopefully. Please can there be sex?" She stared at herself for an uncomfortably long time, studied her own face, her skin, her lips. She wondered what Theresa saw when she looked at her.

Once under the covers, Kelsey turned off the bedside lamp and stared at the ceiling. She was tired and just wanted to sleep, but Chris's words about Hannah kept running through her mind on a loop.

You haven't even called her? Come on, Kels. You're better than that. She's been really great to you. You owe her at least an attempt *at reconciliation.*

Guilt sat on her chest like an overweight cat. Chris was right, and Kelsey felt shame seep into her consciousness. What kind of friend was she? She knew how Hannah felt about her. She knew that her choosing to see Theresa would be hard on Hannah. Then a thought struck: did Hannah even know? And how was she to go about finding out? She couldn't just ask Hannah outright. *"By the way, you know I slept with your sister the other night, right? Amazing!"* Could she even ask Theresa without it being weird? *"So, how does your sister feel about us fucking in your pool?"*

Kelsey groaned as she felt sleep sliding further out of her grasp.

CHAPTER ELEVEN

THE SHOP WAS QUIET on Thursday morning, which was not helping Kelsey keep her mind off certain things. She preferred it busy. She could focus on customers and displays and then she wouldn't have to think about distracting things like the upcoming rent increase or how Hannah hadn't answered the text she sent more than two hours ago.

There were many possible reasons for the radio silence that did not mean "she hates me." Hannah was at work and busy (even though Kelsey knew she always had her phone in her pocket). Hannah was in a meeting. Hannah was off today for some other reason.

"Yeah, she hates me," Kelsey said to the empty office. She watched the security monitors for a moment before picking up her phone and typing out a second text.

Look, I know you're mad at me and I'm sorry about that. Let me make it up to you. Meet me for coffee? Or drinks? Dinner? Something? Please.

Then she added several emojis, including a tearful one, a grimacing one, one that just looked sad, and she threw on one that was a puppy, just because it was cute and made Kelsey smile. Maybe it would do the same thing for Hannah.

September had snuck up on her, but the weather was gorgeous, still in the seventies and with no sign yet of leaves changing colors or crunching underfoot. Kelsey decided to take a walk before eating her lunch, get some fresh air, absorb a little vitamin D from the sun and try to clear her head a bit, maybe wander around the park across the street. She told Jeanine she'd be back in half an hour, tops, and headed out the front door.

The building Common Scents was in was essentially a strip mall, though the surroundings were lush and very residential looking and it kept the strip from looking like, well, a strip mall. In addition to Jacob Kim's dry cleaners, there was a tax prep office that was like a ghost town this time of year, a nail salon with the super strong, not at all pleasant odor of acrylics wafting out the door any time somebody came or went, a tiny gift shop that Kelsey had never noticed a single customer patronizing, and the office of a CPA. The window said the CPA's name was Pat Blucas, but Kelsey had no idea if that was a man or a woman, as she'd never seen anybody in or out any time she'd been able to see the place. Weird.

All of these businesses must have gotten a visit from Betsy Siegler recently, and she absently wondered if any of them were as panicked as she was. They'd all been there when Kelsey had moved in, and from what she'd ascertained, most of them had been there for five years or longer. Betsy Siegler was going to shake up a lot of people. Kelsey suspected she'd enjoy every minute of it.

The phone in the back pocket of her jeans dinged, indicating a text. She hoped it was Hannah, but when she pulled the phone out, she saw it was better than that.

Theresa.

How do you feel about chicken French?

Kelsey smiled, loving the way her entire body flushed with warmth at the thought of spending time with Theresa.

I have no idea what chicken French is, but it sounds yummy, she typed back.

Do you like chicken? Butter? Lemon juice? White wine?

Kelsey stopped and typed again. *Yes. Yes. Yes. Absolutely.*

She walked for a moment or two, then came, *Fantastic. That's what's on the menu for tomorrow night. Do you like dessert?*

Kelsey gave a snort. *Are there people who don't? Like, actual people?*

I hope not. That would just be sad, Theresa replied.

Agreed. Kelsey paused to check traffic before crossing the street, then typed, *What can I bring?*

Theresa's response made Kelsey's smile widen and her cheeks heat up. *Bring your smiling face, your amazing mouth, and that hot body of yours. That's all I'll need.*

I'll see what I can do. Kelsey made a note to get a bottle of wine, as her mother had taught her never to show up to somebody else's house empty-handed. *Time?*

As they settled on when dinner would be, another text came through. Hannah.

"Okay, that's some bizarre timing," Kelsey said out loud to no one. When she finished her conversation with Theresa, who had to get back to work, thank God, she opened Hannah's text.

Sure, we can meet for drinks.

Okay, that was good. A little...sparse in the words department, but Kelsey decided she'd take it. As she started typing a response, another text came through.

And I'm not mad at you.

That was even better. Kelsey blew out a sigh of relief that surprised her and felt a little bit of the weight on her shoulders lift just a smidge.

They set up a time to meet after Hannah got out of work. Jeremy would be working at the shop tonight, so as long as they weren't suddenly inundated with customers (which wouldn't be a bad thing), Kelsey could leave without issue. The afternoon went by more quickly than expected. Not because of an influx of customers (there wasn't one), but Kelsey suspected it was because she had a tiny bit less guilt hanging over her head. She'd been going over things to say to Hannah, but hadn't settled on anything solid yet. They were set to meet in less than an hour, and Kelsey suddenly had a thought.

I'm having drinks with Hannah. You're okay with that, right? She sent the text to Theresa, before she reread it and realized it sounded very much like she was asking permission. Which she wasn't, but she thought Theresa should know they were meeting, that it would feel strange for her not to. When a response didn't come right away, Kelsey set her phone down and did her best to busy herself with e-mails. Nearly twenty minutes went by before her phone dinged.

Of course I am. Just know that she won't have nice things to say about me.

Kelsey bit at the inside of her cheek as she read. While Theresa's prediction wasn't a surprise, it still made her sad. Kelsey had no siblings, but she had Chris, who was as close to being a sister as one could get without the actual blood relation. She couldn't imagine saying anything bad about her to another person, even if she was hesitant about that person seeing Chris.

Here, Hannah and Theresa were actual sisters—well, half, but still—and they seemed to hate each other.

Noted, Kelsey responded, unsure of what else she could possibly say.

You can text me later if you want. I'll be here until late.

Kelsey nodded, sent a quick, *Will do*, and slid her phone into her bag. It was time to meet Hannah and she was both nervous and happy. She'd missed Hannah over the past week, and it was a realization that had surprised her. She spoke to or texted Hannah every day and going nearly a week with no contact at all felt...wrong. Unbalanced. Weird. So while she was nervous to talk to Hannah about Theresa, part of her felt like her world was being righted again after having tilted slightly off-kilter.

She hoped that part of her was correct.

Point Blank ran several Happy Hour specials on weeknights, so it was pretty busy for a Thursday evening. The smells of stale beer, fried food, and men wearing too much cologne made for an odd mix. Kelsey scanned the patrons, found Hannah sitting at the end of the bar, the only empty stool to her left. She had a draft beer in front of her and was watching the TV overhead that was tuned to a soccer game. Kelsey took a deep breath, tipped her head from side to side to crack her neck.

"Gear up," she whispered to herself, then headed Hannah's way. She was nearly there before Hannah saw her, and the smile that broke across Hannah's face was additional relief for Kelsey. Hannah looked happy to see her.

"Hey," Hannah said as she got off her stool and wrapped Kelsey in a hug.

Kelsey hung on, let Hannah let go first, then took the stool next to her. "Hi there. I've missed you."

Hannah gave a half-shrug. "I know. I've missed you, too."

Kelsey ordered a rum and Coke from the bartender and it arrived quickly. Then she turned to Hannah and asked, "How's work?" Kelsey started off with that question intentionally. It was good neutral ground and a subject that never failed to get Hannah talking. And talk she did. She went on about her week, about a couple of irritating patients, about the kid who threw up on Hannah's shoes on Tuesday, about one of the other women who worked with her and her complete computer ignorance. Kelsey grinned as Hannah went on, feeling again like maybe things were back to normal.

"And how are you?" Hannah asked, signaling the bartender for another beer. "Business good?"

"It's okay. I'm running a sale and it's brought in some extra cash."

"Heard any more from the landlady's evil daughter?"

Kelsey sighed. She hated the reminder, but knew that pretending the situation didn't exist wasn't helping. "Yeah. She's buying the building from her mother."

"Which means, I assume, she can raise the rent all she wants because your lease will no longer be valid."

"Exactly."

"What did your dad say about it?" Hannah sipped her beer, eyes focused on the soccer match as she asked the question.

"Yeah, I haven't told him yet." Kelsey hid her face in her drink.

As expected, that got Hannah's attention. "Kels, you need to tell him. He might have some good advice for you."

"Or more likely, he'll say he told me so and ask if he should have Mom get my old room ready for me." Okay, that was a giant exaggeration, but she didn't care at the moment.

Hannah saw right through her. "Yeah, I'm sure that's what would happen." She bumped her with a shoulder, trying to cheer her up.

It worked. Kelsey could feel a small smile creeping up on her. "I've missed you, goober."

Hannah's smile was tense. "I know. I had to...think about some things."

"Me and your sister?" Kelsey asked, her voice small.

"Half-sister. Yeah." Hannah's gaze was back on the soccer game. She sipped her beer and didn't look at Kelsey when she asked, "So...are you two together now?"

The stiffness of her body, the fact that she couldn't look at Kelsey, the way she scratched at the side of her neck, it all told Kelsey what an uncomfortable topic this was. Kelsey inhaled quietly, a deep, slow breath, then let it out just as slowly. "I wouldn't say that. We've had a date and spent some time together. We're having dinner tomorrow night."

Hannah rolled her lips in and bit down on them until they were barely visible. Several moments passed before she said, "I see."

"I'm sorry, Hannah. I'm sorry if it's weird for you. I don't mean it to be." Kelsey thought her own words sounded lame, but she didn't know what else she should say.

Hannah pulled her focus from the TV and stared into her beer as if looking for words in it. Finally, she turned to regard Kelsey. "I just want you to be happy, Kels. If it's Theresa and not me that does that for you, I need to step aside. I don't want to because, as you've probably figured out, she's not my favorite person on the planet, but this isn't about me or her. It's about you." Kelsey saw Hannah's throat move as she swallowed. "You're my friend. I love you and want you to be happy. That's all." Her eyes welled up and her expression immediately shifted to embarrassment.

Kelsey reached for her hand, closed her own over it. "Thank you for saying that. And I love you, too. This week with no contact from you has been...just wrong."

Hannah laughed, swiped a hand across her nose. "I know, right?"

They stayed that way for several moments, smiling sadly and holding hands. Finally, Kelsey signaled to the bartender for a refill. "So," she said once it had arrived. "Why do you guys dislike each other so much?"

Kelsey wasn't at all sure if it was a very complicated question or a deceptively simple one. Plus, she had Theresa's side, and she was curious to get Hannah's. She sat quietly and watched several emotions slide across Hannah's face. Uncertainty. Sadness. Hurt. Confusion.

"You know..." Hannah took a big sip of her beer, stared at it for a bit. "I'm not really sure, to be honest. I mean, I have issues with her. She has issues with me. We just don't have a ton in common and..." Her voice trailed off and she shrugged. "I don't know."

Kelsey wanted to push. She wanted to prod. She'd gotten more from Theresa, but not much more. Instead, she sipped her drink and stayed quiet.

"Even if I did get along with her," Hannah said, "I still wouldn't be thrilled to have you dating her."

Kelsey gave a slow nod. A slew of responses zipped through her head. *I don't even know if we're dating* and *it's not really any of your business* and *I'm really sorry this hurts you* and *I would probably marry her tomorrow*. Instead, she said simply, "I know." And she did. She did know. She hadn't planned this—whatever it was—with Theresa. And she'd never told Hannah she thought of her as anything other than a friend. So while she did understand where Hannah was coming from, she also found herself slightly irritated by the way Hannah was making her feel guilty, and she did her best not to let that surface.

"Listen," Kelsey said, forcing some cheer into her voice and hoping it didn't *sound* forced. "My cousin Chris is coming to visit for a few days. I'd really like you to meet her. She knows all about you 'cause I talk about you so much."

That last line did the trick, judging by the way Hannah's face lit up. "Oh, yeah?"

"Yup. She gets here Sunday. She's not staying terribly long, but I'm hoping we can all get together while she's here."

"I'd love that." Hannah grinned and picked up her beer, and it was as if the whole previous conversation had never happened.

Kelsey found that both cute and annoying. "Hey, we have a playoff game on Tuesday. You should bring her to that."

Kelsey liked the idea of having Chris meet some of the softball team. "She may only be here until Tuesday, but I'm going to try to convince her to stay at least a day longer."

"Yeah, work on that."

"I'll keep you posted."

They spent some time just talking about mundane things, and Hannah was her old, smiling self. Kelsey was super glad to have patched things up, but much as she was enjoying Hannah's company, she just wanted to go home and talk to Theresa.

A text from Jeremy kept her from doing that, however. He had a few customers more than he could handle, so Kelsey bid Hannah goodbye, promising to keep her updated on Chris's visit, and instead of going home to flirt mercilessly over the phone with the woman she couldn't stop thinking about, she headed back to work.

It was nearly ten by the time she made it back to her apartment. While she would never, ever curse an onslaught of customers, she wanted to curse this one a tiny bit simply because she was so exhausted.

Once home, she took a long, hot shower to get her body to relax. The nights were no longer hot and humid, but they weren't exactly chilly, so a hot shower might sound weird to some people. But Kelsey had learned long ago that when she was worked up or too wired to sleep, a hot shower helped soften her muscles, let her veg a little bit mentally, and overall, just made her feel better. By the time she got out and had slathered herself with the new Gingerbread Autumn Spice lotion Stephanie Bradley had sent, she felt a million times better.

A million and one after she glanced at her phone and saw the text from Theresa.

Missed you tonight...

Kelsey's entire body felt mushy. In that good way. Theresa had sent a couple texts earlier telling Kelsey she was still at the office, but had been thinking about her. Kelsey had texted back a short note telling Theresa she was slammed at the shop, but was thinking about her, too. And that was all either of them had been able to do until this latest text from Theresa, which had come while Kelsey was in the shower.

Missed you back. Which seemed like an odd thing to say given they'd only spent a short amount of time together. Was it possible to miss somebody you didn't really see that much?

The shower had done the trick. Kelsey was beat. She climbed between the sheets with the phone and turned off the lights, texted in the dark.

You home? she asked.

Just, came the reply. *You?*

All curled up in bed. Kelsey burrowed down into her pillows, thankful for the gentle night air that let a gorgeous breeze come through her open windows. Coming from someplace that got as warm as North Carolina, she wasn't used to open windows. More often than not, places were closed up and the air conditioning was running, at least in her parents' house. This open window thing was sort of new to her. She liked it. A lot.

Well, that paints a lovely picture.

Kelsey smiled at the words on her screen. *Yeah? It'd be lovelier if you were here with me.*

A beat went by before the reply came. *Lovelier, maybe. But less sleep would be had.*

Kelsey chuckled to herself, wondering how it was possible for a woman to make Kelsey blush while she lay in bed in the dark all by herself. She placed a hand against her heated cheek. *Very true*, she texted back.

Listen, I would love nothing more than to chat with you all night, but I am wiped out from my fourteen-hour day. Kelsey could hear Theresa's voice in her head, could actually hear the regret in the apology when it arrived. *I'm sorry...*

Kelsey shook her head as she typed. *No need to be sorry. I get it. I feel like I got run over by a truck tonight. As long as I get to see you tomorrow, I'm good.*

A few seconds more went by this time before a reply, and Kelsey could picture Theresa in her bed, dozing a bit. *You do. Can't wait.*

Me neither. Sleep tight.

An emoji with a line of z's was all that came next. Kelsey ran a fingertip over them as her eyelids became heavy. She gave it another minute to make sure no more was coming, and the image in her head of Theresa asleep made her feel gooey and warm and happy. She plugged in her phone, set it on the nightstand, and rolled onto her side, breathing in deeply and then letting it out slowly.

For once, sleep claimed her easily.

CHAPTER TWELVE

"OH, MY GOD, IT smells amazing in here." Kelsey lifted her head and sniffed, like a dog getting a whiff of a hamburger. Only this was not hamburger. It was chicken. And wine. And Theresa. And the combination was strangely intoxicating.

"Why, thank you," Theresa said with a little bow. "Hopefully, it will taste as good as it smells and you'll enjoy it." She was relaxed, which was nice to see given how busy her week had been. Her cheeks had a lovely pink blush, her blue eyes were bright as she met Kelsey's gaze. She'd had time to change into jeans before Kelsey arrived and they looked worn, soft, and perfect for her. A royal blue tank was covered by a black apron. Her feet were bare, red polished toes waving at Kelsey from under the cuffs of the jeans.

"This is for you," Kelsey said, handing over the bottle of Cabernet. "I think white probably goes better with chicken, but this is a really good one."

"It's perfect. There's white *in* the chicken, so we'll drink the red." Theresa took the bottle and gave Kelsey a quick peck on the lips. She pulled back before Kelsey could even register it, which was probably a good thing, and stepped aside, waving Kelsey in with a flourish. "It's good to see you. Follow me."

Kelsey closed the door behind her and followed Theresa from the foyer past the living room to the kitchen in the back of the house. She hadn't had a lot of time to take it in during her last visit, so she scanned slowly this time. White cabinets and a black and gray granite countertop in a large U-shape anchored the room. The floor was a light hardwood, the fixtures on the cabinets and sink a deep, brushed ebony. All the accents in the room were black: utensil holder, towels, canisters, and the appliances were stainless steel. It was an average size house, but Theresa had filled the kitchen with top-of-the-line stuff.

"What can I do to help?" Kelsey asked as Theresa returned to the salad she'd been apparently making.

Theresa opened a drawer in front of her, pulled out a corkscrew, and handed it to her. "You can open the wine. I'm ready for a glass. It's been a week."

"I hear that," Kelsey said, and did as she was told. Theresa pointed to her left and up before Kelsey could even ask, so she opened that cupboard and found a beautiful set of lead crystal wine glasses. She filled two, then sidled up next to Theresa and leaned a hip against the counter. "Cheers," she said, handing over a glass.

Theresa took hers, touched her glass to Kelsey's, and sipped. "Oh, that's yummy."

"I know." Kelsey watched as Theresa chopped celery. "I was wondering if you'd be able to get out at a decent time tonight."

Theresa glanced at her. "I wondered the same about you."

"Jeremy's great in the evenings. Unless he gets totally buried like he did last night, I can usually stay in the office or even leave. He calls if he needs me."

"He had to call last night?" Theresa picked up her cutting board and scraped the diced celery into the salad bowl.

"Yeah, he got slammed around seven."

"And where were you? With Hannah?"

It wasn't at all a trap or a test—there was nothing suspicious or sinister in Theresa's tone or in her face when she glanced at her—but Kelsey felt both anyway. "Yeah, at that bar her softball team goes to," she said, after a pause.

"Ah." Theresa nodded. "Point Blank."

"Right."

"I like it there."

"Me, too."

There was a pause in conversation, no sound but Theresa's knife against the plastic cutting board. Finally, Theresa spoke. "Did you guys...talk?"

Kelsey wanted to be completely honest with Theresa. Always. It was imperative if this was going to go anywhere. At the same time, it made her feel the tiniest bit uncomfortable. "We did. Didn't really get into anything in depth, but...it was fine."

Theresa made a sort of soft grunt of agreement, but didn't say any more. A part of Kelsey really wanted to dive in, to pry open that vault and make her talk. Better yet, she'd like to make Hannah and Theresa sit down together, each with a cocktail, and just talk it out. But the other thing she really wanted was a peaceful, enjoyable, maybe a little bit sexy evening with Theresa and throwing her sister—sorry, *half-sister*—into the mix was probably not the smartest of moves to make that happen.

"Tell me about your day," she said instead as Theresa finished up the salad, wiped her hands on her apron, and picked up her wine.

"It wasn't bad." Theresa took a sip of her wine, then reached across the two feet that separated them to wrap a lock of Kelsey's hair around her finger. "Given how busy the week was, today was pretty bearable."

"What's made the week so hard?"

"My boss is a fan of throwing several things at his employees at once, which means once I start on a project, no matter how big it may be, I know in the back of my mind that another one is probably coming shortly."

Kelsey cocked her head. "I would take that to mean you're good at your job and your boss knows it."

"Oh, I am and he does." Theresa tugged the lock of hair playfully, then let it go. "He just doesn't always think about workloads and such. Since I'm not married and don't have kids, he assumes I have nothing in life but my job. Which isn't far from the truth."

"Until now," Kelsey said softly, then wondered how the hell *that* had escaped her lips.

But Theresa was undeterred, amused even, given the arch of her eyebrow. "Until now."

Their gazes held for a beat before Kelsey broke it and asked, "How did this happen?"

Theresa evidently didn't need explanation. "I've wondered the same thing." She set down her wine and kissed Kelsey a second time. This was more than a peck, though. Not demandingly sexual, but tender and definitely intimate. Then she turned to another part of the counter near the stove where she had a battering station all set up. "Come talk to me while I cook the chicken."

Kelsey was happy to oblige. In fact, there wasn't much she'd rather do. "You caught my eye immediately in that Starbucks," she said as she watched Theresa turn on the burner and place a pat of butter into a frying pan.

"Oh, I know."

Kelsey slapped playfully at her arm. "Shut up."

"I totally busted you looking." Theresa dredged a chicken breast in flour, then in an egg wash and repeated the process with a second one.

Kelsey covered her eyes with a hand. "I know. So embarrassing!"

"I thought it was cute. And kinda sexy." Both chicken breasts went into the frying pan, sizzling as they made contact with the heat.

"You did?"

"Absolutely," Theresa said with a nod.

"Well, that's a relief." Kelsey sipped her wine and watched Theresa's beautiful hands as she worked. "Where'd you learn to cook?"

"My mom's a chef," Theresa said. "Didn't I tell you that?"

"Nope. That is something I'd remember. Plus, last time we were together, we were a little...busy, if you recall."

"I recall." The heated expression Theresa shot her way made Kelsey's knees go weak for a moment.

"What restaurant is she at?"

"None." Theresa flipped the chicken so the golden brown side was facing up. "She's a personal chef."

"Like, she goes to people's houses and cooks for them?"

"Exactly like that, yes." Theresa watched the chicken as she spoke. "She learned this dish when she was working for a guy from upstate New York when he requested it. It's really popular there, but if you go a little ways west or south, people have never heard of it." She pushed the chicken a bit with a fork, picked an end up to check the bottom. "I used to love shadowing her in the kitchen and she taught me how to cook from a pretty young age. I made my first Bolognese sauce when I was eight."

"I'm impressed." And Kelsey was.

"Don't be," Theresa said, leaning close and lowering her voice to a whisper. "It's super easy to make."

"Maybe you could teach me sometime."

Theresa smiled at her. "I'd be happy to." She removed the chicken from the pan and put both pieces in a small baking dish. Then into the frying pan went more butter, some lemon juice, chicken stock, and a little bit of white wine from an open bottle Theresa pulled from the refrigerator. "You're supposed to use sherry for this, but I like white wine better. Gives it a nice tang to go with the lemon juice."

"It smells like heaven," Kelsey said, inhaling deeply. "I mean, you had me at butter, so..."

Theresa chuckled as she finished up the sauce and poured it over the chicken. Then she covered the dish with foil and put it in the oven. "I'm just gonna let it warm through in here. About fifteen minutes and we'll be ready to eat."

Dishes were brought down from a cupboard and Kelsey helped set the table. "Are you and your mom close?" she asked.

Theresa nodded. "Very. You?"

Kelsey bobbed her head from side to side. "Fairly close. She had a hard time with me moving here."

"Understandable. You have siblings?" At Kelsey's head shake, Theresa said, "Yeah, that's why she had a hard time. Her only baby moving, what? Four states away? Five? That's got to be rough on a mom."

Kelsey gave a quiet sigh. "I know."

"What about your dad?" Theresa raised her eyebrows at Kelsey's snort.

"My dad can be kind of a prick."

A laugh burst from Theresa's mouth. "Seriously, Kelsey, don't sugarcoat it or anything."

Kelsey joined in the laughter. "That was probably a little harsh. He's not that bad. I'm just in kind of a..." She searched the ceiling for the right word. "Sensitive place with him right now."

"How so?" Theresa went back to the oven to remove the chicken.

"Without going into long, drawn-out, incredibly boring detail, I'll just say that he's a businessman. Has been for decades. He likes to remind me of that and to point out any business decisions I make that he would not have." Kelsey carried the wine bottle and their glasses to the table while Theresa plated the chicken.

"Ah, I see. And how did he feel about you moving here and opening your own business?"

"Let's just say, he wasn't as supportive as I'd have liked."

Theresa turned to regard her, a small frown on her face. "I'm sorry, Kelsey."

"Thanks." Kelsey refilled their wine glasses. "It's not that big a deal, but I've got some changes coming at work and I'm really hoping he doesn't have an opportunity to say he told me so." Theresa approached the table with plates. "Anyway. What about you and your dad? I mean, you went to his barbecue, so I'm assuming you get along at least a little bit?"

Theresa gave a slow nod that seemed somewhat uncertain. She went back to grab the salad and returned to set it in the middle of the table. "We do now. It took a long time. But I really like Liz."

"That's a plus," Kelsey said, remembering how nice Hannah's mother was.

"It took me a while, but I finally realized that my issues with my father aren't her fault, you know?" Theresa took off her apron, waved a hand for Kelsey to sit, then she did the same.

"I do."

They dug in and the burst of tangy deliciousness that hit Kelsey's tongue caused her to hum in delight. "Oh, my God," she said. "That's fantastic."

"You like it?" The smile on Theresa's face was sweet and slightly relieved, as if she'd been worried.

"I love it. I want to take a bath in this sauce."

"I'd pay good money to see that."

Kelsey gave her what she hoped was an expression considered "smoldering," though she wasn't sure how successful she was. A glance out the window reminded her of her last visit to Theresa's house. "How long do you keep the pool open?"

Theresa craned her neck around so she could see the wall behind her where a calendar hung. "The pool guys come in two weeks to close it."

"Not a very long season."

"Sadly, no. Not around here. But I'll take what I can get. I swam in high school, so always promised myself I'd have my own pool one day." She chewed a forkful of salad before asking in a low voice, "Wanna go for an after-dinner swim?"

"I don't know," Kelsey replied. "After I finish making a giant pig of myself, it's possible I'll just sink to the bottom. Ask me again in twenty minutes."

They finished dinner in less than that and cleaned up together like they'd been working as a team for years. Kelsey cleared the table. Theresa rinsed the dishes, and, together, they loaded the dishwasher. It was shocking, companionable, and utterly perfect how well they worked together, and Kelsey didn't want to dwell on that. Except that maybe she did want to. The same questions kept returning to her brain: How is this possible? How can I be so comfortable with a woman I barely know and have spent less than thirty-six hours with in total? Should I be concerned, or should I run with it?

She had no answers. To any of them. Ignoring them didn't make them go away, sadly, but she did so anyway. All she knew was that when she was with Theresa, she didn't want to be anywhere else. She wanted time to stand still so she could get to know this woman without other obligations interrupting the process. Kelsey watched Theresa finish up in the kitchen, watched her wipe down the counter and stove, drape the towel over the handle to the oven, watched her turn to look at Kelsey with a look on her face that could only be described as a little bit hungry, but not for food.

"Feel like watching some TV?" Theresa asked as she reached out to play with Kelsey's hair.

Kelsey nodded, absurdly happy just being here. They took their wine and went into the living room. The black leather couch was shockingly comfortable, and seemed to almost hug Kelsey as she sank into it. Three remotes lined up neatly and a hardcover by Lisa Scottoline occupied the surface of the glass coffee table. A large flat-screen television sat on another dark table in the corner, and Theresa picked up two of the remotes and hit some buttons. The picture sparked to life.

"Any requests?" Theresa flopped down on the couch and sank in next to Kelsey as she hit a button and popped the guide on.

They settled on an episode of *Sugar Showdown* and laughed and made fun of the contestants when they failed miserably at a challenge. Which was kind of mean, but still fun because nobody knew except the two of them. After the first show and into the second, Kelsey burrowed in against Theresa, snuggling in close like it was something they'd done every day for years. It certainly felt like it was. Theresa's arm was around her shoulders, and she squeezed, pressed a soft kiss to Kelsey's forehead.

"This is nice," Kelsey said quietly, keeping her eyes on the guy making little crowns out of sugar glass, which Kelsey never knew was a thing.

"It is," Theresa agreed. "Very nice."

The timing felt right, so Kelsey turned her head so she could see Theresa's face. "Hey, my cousin is coming to visit for a few days. How do you feel about meeting her?" Kelsey scrunched her nose. "Would that be weird?"

Theresa furrowed her brow. "Why would it be weird?"

Kelsey shrugged. "I don't know. I mean, it'd be meeting family. I wondered if it was too soon."

"You mean because we've had exactly two dates?" Theresa's half-grin kept the mood light.

"Because of that, yeah."

"I can tell you, in all honestly, I'd love to meet your cousin."

"Yeah?" Kelsey shifted a bit so she got a better view of Theresa's expression, which was open and smiling.

"Mm-hmm."

"I think you'll really like her. She's business-y like you."

"You're business-y," Theresa pointed out.

"No, I'm retail-y. Not the same. You and Chris are, like, corporation-y."

"I'm a fan of this new vocabulary you've created."

"Good. Most people are just jealous because they're not as definition-y as me."

Theresa threw her head back and laughed, which was an amazing sound, like a soundtrack to the picture of her long, elegant throat right in Kelsey's eye line. Kelsey couldn't help it; she leaned forward slightly and pressed her lips to that gorgeous column of flesh.

Theresa's laughter faded quickly and she brought her gaze to Kelsey's, and just like before, all sound seemed to fade away for Kelsey. There was no television babble, no traffic noise of tires against pavement, no random dogs barking in the neighborhood.

There was nothing but Kelsey and Theresa, their quiet breathing and the steady beating of their hearts.

Kelsey moved first, lifting a hand to Theresa's face, pushing her fingers into Theresa's hair and pulling her head closer. She kissed her tentatively at first. Lightly. Gently. A simple pressing of lips to lips as she kept her eyes open, studied Theresa's face. When she pulled back slightly, enough to focus, Theresa's eyes had gone dark, her lips were parted. The tip of her tongue darted out to wet them, causing Kelsey to swallow hard as a surge of desire tore through her with unexpected force.

She pulled Theresa to her again and this time, there was nothing tentative about it. It was a hungry kiss. Demanding. Kelsey shifted her position so she pushed Theresa to her back on the couch and settled her hips between Theresa's jeans-clad legs. A thought ran absently through Kelsey's mind then, a thought that said this was her spot. Her place. Where she belonged and where she was supposed to be. Right here, tucked snugly against Theresa's body with Theresa's arms holding her tightly. It was warm and comfortable and sexy and perfect, and Kelsey would be completely satisfied to spend her remaining days right here, just like this.

After two dates. What is happening to me?

Before she could shove the thought away, it was driven out of her head by Theresa, by Theresa's tongue in her mouth, by Theresa's hand sliding up the back of Kelsey's shirt, and Kelsey let herself melt into this woman, let everything go, chose to live in the moment and not sweat the small stuff...or at least save it to sweat over later. The warm palm on the small of her back, the soft-but-assertive mouth on hers, it was bliss. It was heaven.

Kelsey redoubled her efforts, determined not to let Theresa wrestle the upper hand from her. There was tandem giggling as Theresa suddenly made an effort to roll the two of them so she could be on top, but Kelsey held firm, didn't let it happen.

"Nope," she said, her voice husky as she slipped a hand under the front of Theresa's shirt. "My show."

"Your show? Well, aren't you the bossy..." Theresa's voice trailed off, followed by a soft intake of breath as Kelsey found a nipple and toyed with it through her bra.

"You were saying?" Kelsey asked playfully, her hand still moving.

Theresa's eyes drifted closed and she whispered, "Nothing. I was saying nothing."

"That's what I thought."

There were no more words after that. Kisses pressed ever deeper, Theresa's legs wrapped around Kelsey's waist, hands were everywhere—in hair, under shirts, along bare skin—and when Theresa's orgasm ripped through her simply from Kelsey's hand moving against her center through her jeans, surprising them both, Kelsey grinned like the Cheshire cat, absurdly pleased with herself and at the same time utterly, undeniably happy. Her brain chose that moment to poke at her, to suggest some analysis, but Kelsey managed to shut it down, to just revel in the beautiful woman beneath her who was breathing raggedly, one arm tossed over her eyes.

"Oh, my God," Theresa whispered, still catching her breath.

"That was pretty awesome." Kelsey kissed Theresa's elbow, since she couldn't get to her nose.

"Awesome? Oh, no. Better than awesome. Way better than awesome." Theresa swallowed and cleared her throat. "For God's sake, all my clothes are still on."

Kelsey's satisfied grin widened. "I know."

Theresa moved her arm, and her eyes caught Kelsey's. Held them softly. She reached up to stroke her fingertips across Kelsey's cheek. The touch was gentle. Sweet. Kelsey got the feeling Theresa wanted to say something—honestly, so did Kelsey—but neither of them spoke. They simply looked at each other as something...tender passed between them. Long moments went by as they lay there.

"I say we go upstairs," Theresa said, her voice barely above a whisper. "And we take them all off. Mine and yours. You in?"

Kelsey nodded. "I think that's a very good plan. I'm in." She kissed Theresa once more, then carefully extricated herself from the tangle of limbs they'd created. Once standing, she held out her hand. Theresa took it, and Kelsey pulled her to her feet. When the television was off and the front door was locked, they headed upstairs.

Sleep came much, much, *much* later.

CHAPTER THIRTEEN

"I'M SO HAPPY YOU'RE here," Kelsey said as she raised her beer glass and touched it to Chris's. "I don't like going months without seeing you. Feels weird, you know?"

"I totally get it." Chris gave a nod and took a sip of her beer. She looked like her usual self: short, sandy hair; bright brown eyes; an aura of cheer, kindness, and fun. But there was something else Kelsey noticed. Chris looked tired. Not just a little tired, but *really* tired. Like, beaten down tired. Like, not getting enough sleep and not eating well and working too many long hours. That kind of tired. Her skin had a slight gray pallor to it. She was way too thin. The dark circles under her eyes were visible to Kelsey, even through the makeup Chris had obviously used to cover them (and Chris rarely wore makeup). And she seemed...the tiniest bit sad.

"Hey," Kelsey said and waited until Chris looked at her before continuing. "Are you okay?"

Chris nodded, made a face that said, "why would you think otherwise?" and said, "Sure. Fine."

Kelsey propped her chin in her hand and studied her cousin. "Yeah, I don't believe you."

Chris dropped her head in defeat, her chin at her chest, obviously aware that she couldn't pull one over on her favorite cousin so she shouldn't even try. She blew out a breath and when she looked up at Kelsey, her eyes seemed clearer. "I have an ulterior motive for coming to see you."

"Okay," Kelsey said, drawing out the word. "Tell me."

"I have a job interview."

Kelsey's eyebrows shot up. "What? Here? Why? When? With who? Doing what? Are you moving here?" The questions came out quick and staccato, like gunfire.

Chris laughed and held up a hand traffic cop style. "Easy there. It's like I'm having lunch with the Riddler."

"Sorry." Kelsey joined in the laughter. "You just took me by surprise."

"I know. I apologize."

"Well? Fill me in!"

Before Chris could begin her story, they were interrupted by a voice from behind Kelsey. "I see they'll let anybody in here. So much for avoiding the riff-raff."

Kelsey turned to look and smiled at the sight of Hannah. "Hey, you."

"Sorry I'm late. Got stuck helping my mom with her computer." Hannah's eyes stopped on Chris and lingered for a beat before she stuck out a hand. "You must be Chris."

"I am." Chris did a half-stand, the best she could do given the booth they were in and Kelsey noticed her do the same linger in return. "And you're Hannah, right? It's nice to meet you. My cousin has told me all kinds of stories about you." Chris winked at her and Hannah chuckled.

"Please keep in mind that your cousin lies. Like, a lot. It's a huge problem."

"Has been since we were kids," Chris deadpanned.

"Hey," Kelsey said in protest. When the other two started laughing, Kelsey couldn't help but join them. "Yeah, you two are hilarious."

Hannah slid into the booth next to Kelsey. "Are you guys having lunch?"

"We are," Chris told her, eyes sparkling. "We just wanted to start with a beer to celebrate since we haven't seen each other in a while."

"Can I join?"

"Of course." Chris flagged down the waitress and Hannah ordered a beer, which arrived a few moments later. They clinked glasses.

"Okay, so back to this interview," Kelsey said.

"Job interview?" Hannah asked for clarification. "So...you're looking to move here? 'Cause that'd be cool."

"You two." Chris shook her head good-naturedly; Kelsey could tell by her gentle expression. "I'm just feeling some things out, weighing my options."

"She works like crazy right now," Kelsey said to Hannah. "Too many hours. Way too many. In a great city that she never has time to explore."

"Boston, right?" At Chris's slight look of surprise, Hannah added, "Kelsey's mentioned it before."

"For a minute there, I thought you might be stalking me." Chris punctuated that with a flirty little grin and Kelsey was struck with the sudden realization of what was happening here. She decided to add a little fuel to the newly kindled fire.

"Well, you follow her on Instagram, so maybe you're the stalker." Kelsey covered her smile with her beer glass, ignored the subtle, startled look Chris shot her.

"You do?" Hannah tilted her head.

"I, um, follow Kelsey and she follows you, so..." Instead of looking chagrined, Chris held eye contact with Hannah and smiled.

"Well, that's pretty cool." Hannah took a gulp of her beer. "Where's the interview?"

And just like that, Kelsey watched the beginning of...something. They didn't exclude her. Of course they didn't. But Hannah talked directly to Chris. Chris responded, then would glance at Kelsey, who would give her a smile. They ordered lunch, it arrived, and things continued. Hannah asked all the same questions Kelsey would have, so she didn't feel she was missing out on any information. Instead, she took it all in—both the information on Chris's interview and the crazy-obvious chemistry between her cousin and her friend. It was amusing and fun to watch. Kelsey was a little bit envious, but then she thought about Theresa and decided she had nothing at all to be envious about. Nothing. At. All.

When they'd finished eating and argued over the check (Chris won and paid for the whole thing), Hannah said, "So how long are you staying?"

Chris moved her head from one side to the other. "I haven't decided yet. I can't be away for too long. My interview is tomorrow. I was thinking of flying back on Tuesday."

"You should stay until Wednesday."

"I should? And why is that?" They moved down the aisle toward the door, Chris and Hannah side by side, Kelsey behind them.

"Because my softball team has a playoff game Tuesday night. You could come watch, go out with us, then fly home on Wednesday morning."

Chris turned to look at Hannah as they pushed through the doors and out into the sunlit Sunday afternoon. Kelsey watched her cousin's profile and knew she was actually considering it. She tried to smother her grin, not wanting to be too obvious about what she was witnessing...or that she was witnessing it.

"You know what?" Chris asked as they stopped next to Kelsey's car in the lot. "I think I'm going to take you up on that." With a glance at Kelsey, she asked, "Are you going to the game?"

"Well, I'm kind of important in the cheerleading department."

"She totally is," Hannah agreed. "Been to every game."

"All right then. I'll see you Tuesday." Chris held out a hand to Hannah, who looked at it, chuckled as she shook her head, and instead, wrapped her arms around Chris's neck.

"I'm a hugger."

"She is," Kelsey agreed, then watched as Chris hugged back. With both arms.

Well, isn't this interesting?

They said their goodbyes to Hannah, who was parked two rows away, and got into Kelsey's car. She keyed the ignition and put the A/C on full blast...which only served to blow hot air on them.

"That was fun to watch," Kelsey said as they waited for the air to cool.

"What was?"

Kelsey arched an eyebrow in a silent, *Really?*

Chris had the good sense to look sheepish. "She's cuter in person than in her Instagram photos. And just so you know, I follow her on Instagram so I can see what *you're* up to."

"Mm-hmm." Kelsey simply grinned as she backed out of the parking spot and headed toward her apartment.

"Seems like we've got a lot in common, too." Chris was watching out the window as they drove. She could've been talking to herself, given the soft, almost dreamy quality of her voice.

"Seems like it."

Chris turned to her. "Hey, you don't mind if I tag along to the game, do you? I didn't even ask." She grimaced, which only made Kelsey love her more.

"I don't mind at all. Besides, you're probably going to need somebody to wipe all that drool off your face while you watch Hannah play."

Monday was pretty dead at the shop, which did not make Kelsey happy. An order from Earthly arrived thanks to Stephanie Bradley, so Kelsey busied herself stocking the shelves and posting the banners Stephanie had included that announced the new products were cruelty-free. Kelsey took one of each scent of lotion and marked it as a tester, then rubbed some of the

Pumpkin Nutmeg Latte one into her hands. It smelled so delicious, she wanted to lick it, which made her giggle softly when Jeanine threw her a look.

"It smells like pumpkin bread," she explained. "And I'm hungry."

"Me, too," Jeanine said.

"Split a sub?"

"Yes!"

"I'm on it." Kelsey headed to her office where she grabbed her money and then scooted off to Marco's.

The deli was also a bit slow on this Monday. Well, slow meaning it wasn't packed wall-to-wall with customers, which was its usual situation. Two orders were in front of hers, so Kelsey wandered the very small shop and then gazed out the window while she waited. The day was gray, overcast, perfect for a Monday. At least the temperature was nice. Her phone buzzed in her back pocket, interrupting her musings on the weather, and she pulled it out immediately, expecting a text from Chris telling her how the interview went.

Even better, she thought as she saw the text was from Theresa.

Hey, sexy. How's your day?

Theresa had been swamped with a big project at work, so Kelsey hadn't heard much from her at all since leaving her house very reluctantly—on both their parts, judging by the intensity of their goodbye kiss—on Saturday morning. Theresa had gone into the office and had worked there all weekend.

Slow, she typed. *But better now.* She added a smiling emoji to punctuate the statement. *Yours? Still buried?*

Ugh. Yes. I might be late to dinner. I have a couple of property visits to do and then a meeting to report my findings to my boss. Could be quick. Could take forever.

Kelsey pressed her lips together. She really wanted Chris to meet Theresa, to sit and have dinner with the person who'd been taking up so very much of Kelsey's head lately. She wanted to see them interact. She wanted them to laugh and joke together and become friends.

She wanted Chris's approval.

That was the crux of it. What her cousin thought was very important to Kelsey. It always had been. And Kelsey was 99.9 percent sure that Chris and Theresa would get along great. But she wanted to see it happen. She wanted to be able to tell the story later, years down the line, about how Chris and Theresa first met.

And then she literally shook herself. What the hell was she thinking? Years down the line? Seriously?

Her phone buzzed in her hand, pulling her back to the present.

Are you mad? Theresa had texted. With a frown.

Kelsey had let too much time pass between texts. *No! Not at all. Sorry. Waiting on lunch. It's not a problem. Just get to the restaurant when you can. We'll be there at 7.*

The guy behind the counter called Kelsey's name and she moved forward to grab her sub

If I'm not there by 7:15, start without me.

Kelsey blew out a disappointed breath, even though she knew it wasn't Theresa's fault. She had a job to do. Kelsey, being the boss in a retail operation, certainly understood that. "It'll be fine," she said aloud as she left Marco's and got in her car. She sent an okay off to Theresa and went back to work.

The rest of the afternoon stayed fairly quiet, so Kelsey was able to remain holed up in her office. She'd sent an e-mail earlier to Stephanie Bradley to let her know the order had arrived and how much Kelsey loved all the new scents. A response had been waiting in her inbox upon her return from Marco's, so they went back and forth a couple of times, then opened an instant message conversation so they could chat more in real time. They talked about their experiences—both bad and good—with other cruelty-free companies. Stephanie seemed impressed by Kelsey's knowledge of the industry, and Kelsey told her that it was important to her, that she only wished "cruelty-free" didn't also tend to be synonymous with "more expensive."

If Jeanine hadn't dropped a large bottle onto the floor—not shattering it, but making a hell of a noise—Kelsey wouldn't have snapped her head up to look at the security monitors. If she hadn't done that, she'd have missed a familiar figure wandering slowly through her store. A big smile spread itself across Kelsey's face as she watched Theresa pick up a lotion, sniff it, set it back on the shelf. Then she stood still and looked around the shop, turning in a slow circle. Next, she walked slowly toward the back, her eyes on the wall to her right.

Kelsey was thrilled she'd found her shop, almost giddy about it. She sent a quick note to Stephanie that she had to run, then headed out front.

"Hey," she said with genuine enthusiasm and a big grin. "You found it."

Theresa turned her way and for a split second, looked surprised to see her. No, not surprised. Shocked. "Hey," she said and reached out to hug Kelsey. "This is your shop, huh?"

"It is. Welcome to Common Scents. My baby." Kelsey looked around proudly. "You find some free time this afternoon after all?"

Theresa nodded. "Just a tiny bit, though. I was in the neighborhood and thought I'd give myself five minutes to get a little air, pop in and say hi."

"I'm so glad you did." Kelsey held her arm out toward the back. "You wanna come back to my office for a couple minutes?"

"Oh, no. I can't." Theresa shook her head quickly. "I wish I could, but..." She glanced at her watch. "Gah. Yeah. I have to get back."

"You sure?" Kelsey tried to hide her disappointment. *It's her job. It's her job. It's her job.*

"I am. I'm sorry." Those gorgeous blue eyes met Kelsey's. "I'm really sorry."

Kelsey waved it off. "Eh. No biggie. You've got to work. I get it." She leaned forward and kissed Theresa on the cheek. "Okay. Go." She playfully waved her away. "I will hopefully see you tonight."

Theresa nodded, took one last look around, then scooted out the front door. With a quick wave back at Kelsey, she was gone.

"Was that...?" Jeanine was next to Kelsey now, her gaze lingering on the door.

"It was." Kelsey felt herself blush the tiniest bit.

"Wow. She's beautiful."

"I know, right?"

Jeanine gave her upper arm a squeeze, then went back to the counter where the one other customer in the store had set down a few items. Kelsey sighed happily and headed back to her office.

Before she could even sit down, her phone buzzed with a call. Kelsey saw Chris's name on the screen and her heart rate picked up.

"And? How'd it go?" she asked when she hit the Answer button.

"I think really well." Chris's voice was just a bit hesitant, as if she didn't want to jinx herself. But there was also an air of confidence. "I'm definitely qualified. I think I have more experience than they were expecting."

"How many people?"

"I interviewed with one first. She must've been the screener and I passed because then she took me into a room with three others. A couple of senior account executives and a VP. I was with them for over an hour."

"Wow!" Kelsey let out a little squeal of happiness. "That's awesome. Meeting with the big wigs has to be a good sign."

"I think so, too."

"What happens now?" Kelsey flopped down into her chair.

"I should hear in the next couple of days."

"Man, that's fast."

"I know. Makes me a little nervous."

"But you covered all your bases, right?" Kelsey asked, trying to allay that tone of slight unease. "You told them you need to give two weeks' notice? You told them how much vacation you'd like and you named your price?"

"I did."

"Good. And they still sat with you for over an hour. I think you're in good shape."

"I think you're right." Kelsey could almost see Chris nodding. "I am so looking forward to going out tonight."

"Me, too," Kelsey said with a glance at her watch. "A couple more hours."

"See you when you get home."

They signed off and Kelsey rocked happily in her chair. Despite the slow business, it had been a good day so far. Chris's interview went terrifically. Theresa had popped into the shop unannounced to surprise her. And they were all going to a nice restaurant for dinner tonight.

Things were looking up.

CHAPTER FOURTEEN

"HOW DO I LOOK?"

Kelsey stood in the doorway of her small bathroom, smoothed her hands over her hips and wet her lips. She was nervous. She wasn't entirely sure why. She always got butterflies when she knew she was going to see Theresa, so that wasn't new. But this was different. She wanted Theresa to be wowed by her. And she wanted Chris to be wowed by Theresa.

Chris finished brushing her teeth, then made a show of looking closely at Kelsey, at the casual black dress, the low-heeled shoes (she was not graceful in heels...at all), the bounce she'd put in her hair with the curling iron. "That's quite a neckline," Chris finally said, and Kelsey wasn't sure if it was a positive comment or a negative one.

"What are you, my dad?" Kelsey asked with a small chuckle. She glanced down, saw the cleavage, didn't look again.

"You look great," Chris responded, her grin finally letting Kelsey off the hook.

"Thank you."

"And me?" Chris turned away from the sink, waved a hand from her own chin down her torso. She hadn't brought anything dressy aside from her interview suit—and dresses weren't really her thing anyway. She wore a nicely pressed pair of khaki pants and a sharp button-down camp shirt in an emerald green. Brown loafers were on her feet and her hair was swooped to the side in a rakish wave.

"Aww, you want to impress the woman I'm seeing?"

"The woman you're...oh, um..." Chris suddenly looked embarrassed. She rubbed her chin with one hand and wrinkled her nose as she said, "Shit, I forgot to tell you."

"Tell me what?"

"I invited Hannah to join us."

Kelsey gaped at her in disbelief for a beat. Two beats. "You did what?"

"I didn't think you'd mind." Chris made the I'm-sorry-but-I-know-you-love-me-and-will-forgive-me face that had gotten her out of every dumb thing she'd ever done with regard to Kelsey their whole lives.

"Hannah and Theresa don't get along, Chris. I told you that." Kelsey was feeling slightly exasperated, knowing there was no way to uninvite Hannah now without looking like a jerk, and knowing she didn't want to warn Theresa for fear she'd back out. She threw up her hands, then let them slap down to her sides. "What are you doing to me?"

"I know, I know. I'm so sorry."

"All right, here's what you're going to do." Kelsey toyed with the ring on her forefinger, spun it around as she thought. "Theresa is probably going to be late, which means you'll have some time to spend with Hannah before she gets there. But," she said sternly and held up a finger. "If things start to get awkward, you will take Hannah to the bar. Or somewhere else. Away from Theresa and me. You'll excuse yourself altogether if you have to and just leave. Understood?"

Chris sighed. “Yes. Fine. Understood.” She shook her head as Kelsey fussed with her own hair. “Why don’t they get along again?”

“It’s complicated.”

“I’m sure it is.” Chris shrugged. “I’ll ask Hannah. She’ll tell me.”

Kelsey raised her eyebrows. “You two been doing a lot of chatting? You only met her yesterday.”

“She may have texted me to ask about my interview. I may have texted her back after I talked to you.” Chris turned back to the mirror, kept her eyes on her reflection as she smoothed her hair. “She may have called me after that.”

“Wow. You guys BFFs now?” Kelsey heard the subtle tone of snark in her own voice and had to consciously not wince at it.

Chris snagged Kelsey’s gaze with her own, held it. “I’m sorry, are you possibly insinuating that I’m moving too fast? Because if I recall correctly, somebody in this room had sex on the very first date recently.”

This time, Kelsey did wince. “Ouch.”

Chris merely gave a half-shrug.

“I know,” Kelsey said, reaching out a hand in apology. “You’re right. I’m sorry. Ignore me.”

“Never.” Chris grabbed the offered hand. “But seriously, is my being friends with Hannah a problem?”

“Absolutely not,” Kelsey assured her. Was it? Why would it be? Kelsey knew the answer, but also knew how horrible it made her look, so she chose to ignore it. “Let’s get moving or we’re going to be late.”

Cline wasn't what Kelsey would call a "fancy" restaurant, but it was definitely a bit more on the upscale side of what she was used to. She avoided the valet parking, found her own spot in a lot across the street, and strolled arm-in-arm with Chris to the front door.

"Cline? Kind of a weird name for a restaurant, don't you think?" Chris asked quietly as they entered.

"I think it's the owner's name."

"First or last?"

"I have no idea." Kelsey smiled at the hostess. "Hi. Reservations for Peterson. I made them for three, but we have four now. Is that okay?"

"That's fine." The hostess was pretty in a very nonspecific way. Smooth skin. Sleek, dark hair. Black clothing, heavily lined eyes, and she seemed nearly devoid of any and all personality. "This way." She turned on a very high heel and began walking away from them.

"I guess the others will just have to find us," Kelsey whispered as she gave Chris a playful shove in the direction of the android.

The dining room was warm and inviting, with round tables covered in burgundy cloths, dim lighting emanating from small pendulum lights, and heavy wooden chairs. Aromas of steak, garlic, and melted butter wafted through the air, and Kelsey's mouth watered as she sniffed. She wondered if Theresa would ever recommend a place that disappointed instead of wowing her.

The robot hostess handed them their menus, told them their waitress would be right with them, and left without another word.

"Can you see the front?" Kelsey asked as she adjusted her chair so it was closer to Chris.

Chris craned her neck. "A little." She pulled out her phone. "I'll tell Hannah where we're sitting. You tell Theresa."

With a nod, Kelsey obliged.

Ten minutes later, Hannah arrived. Kelsey was so used to seeing her in either softball clothes or some kind of scrub shirt with cartoons on it for work, that she nearly did a double take at her now. Black slacks, low-heeled black shoes, a white button-down shirt. Her hair was shiny and swooped to the side in a style Kelsey'd never seen on her. She looked great, and Kelsey felt bad that the fact surprised her. Hannah's green eyes sparkled and—did they widen a bit when they landed on Chris? Kelsey was pretty sure they did. And also that her smile grew.

"Hey," she said, and looked from Chris to Kelsey, then back at Chris, who stood up and hugged her. Kelsey followed suit.

"I'm so glad you came," Chris said.

"Me, too," Hannah replied with a grin, then glanced at Kelsey. "I hope you don't mind. I know Theresa is coming."

Kelsey took a moment to just blink at her. The fact that Hannah knew Theresa was coming and still chose to tag along spoke volumes about how much she wanted to see Chris. Volumes. "Full disclosure, I haven't told her you'd be here. Somebody forgot to tell me until about half an hour ago." She shot Chris a look. Her cousin had the good sense to blush.

"Yeah, that one's on me," Chris said. "Any sisterly drama that occurs is totally my fault."

"We're big girls," Hannah said, closing her hand over Chris's. "It's not like we're going to throw drinks in each other's faces, okay?"

Chris chuckled and nodded. "Bummer. That might've been fun to watch."

The waitress stopped by at that moment, asked about the remainder of their party, and took drink orders. Kelsey glanced at her phone, saw that it was 7:20, and blew out a disappointed breath. "Theresa said if she wasn't here by seven fifteen to start without her, so we can get ready to order if you want."

Hannah gave a small snort—though not small enough that Kelsey and Chris missed it. The waitress returned with their drinks: wine for Hannah and Kelsey, a dirty martini for Chris. Kelsey asked for a couple more minutes so they could look at their menus. She hoped Theresa would show up by the time they were ready to order.

"So, what's the deal with you two?" Chris asked as soon as the waitress was out of earshot.

Hannah glanced at Kelsey, who shrugged. "Go ahead. I'm curious as well."

Hannah took a sip of her wine, set the glass down, turned it slowly in her fingers. It was as if she was evaluating each word she wanted to say, trying to predict which ones to use and which to discard. "There's a big age difference, first of all," she said finally. "She's thirty-seven. I'm twenty-five."

"Twelve years," Chris said, nodding. "Not a huge gap, but a pretty good-sized one."

"And we didn't grow up in the same house. She lived with her mom and I lived with my mom and our dad."

"So she's a child of divorce and you're not." Kelsey pointed out this fact, feeling herself bracing to defend Theresa, even though she wasn't sure she'd need to.

"Yes. That's true. And she was...unhappy about that." Again, choosing her words carefully.

Which didn't matter to Kelsey. "Of course she was. Why wouldn't she be? Her dad left her mom for yours." Hannah sucked in her bottom lip and waited. Kelsey could feel Chris's eyes on her.

"I'm only saying that to shed some light on my next comment," Hannah explained. "Which was that Theresa pretty much stayed away. From all of us. She had no desire to be around any of us when I was growing up. Which is really hard on a kid, you know? Here I had this amazing big sister that wanted nothing at all to do with me. My dad was always talking about her, telling us how terrific and smart and funny she was. And as we grew, he'd report on her successes. Graduating from high school as the salutatorian—she missed valedictorian by two hundredths of a point. Graduating from college magna cum laude. Getting hired by a national real estate developer. Every time she helped broker a big commercial deal, my dad walked around the house gushing." Hannah finally stopped to take a breath. Then a sip of her wine.

Kelsey made no comment, even when she wanted to. She'd heard Theresa's side. It was only fair that Hannah get to tell hers uninterrupted. And frankly, some of this information was new. Theresa had never said she'd stayed completely away. She'd made it sound like she wasn't welcome. And she'd never even hinted at her father's pride in her. Maybe she didn't know?

Hannah took a deep breath and continued. "It started to feel like I'd never measure up. Anything I did, Theresa had done way before me. And better. So many times I wanted to scream at my dad, *Why do you care how successful she is? Why do you care about her life? She obviously doesn't care about yours. I'm right here. Focus on me, the daughter who gives a shit about you.* But I never had the balls. He always looked so happy when he was singing her praises. And he always seemed so crushed when she missed a Father's Day or his birthday or a Christmas. BTW, she missed most of those. She doesn't really have time for other people."

Bitterness had crept into Hannah's tone, so when the waitress came by at that moment, it was perfect, as Kelsey felt like they all needed a second to take a breath. She saw a look pass between Chris and Hannah, and Kelsey was almost envious. Theresa wasn't here, Kelsey was beginning to think she wasn't going to make it at all, and that made her sad. Which made no sense because Theresa had warned her she might get stuck at work. With a soft sigh, Kelsey ordered chicken Florentine, then handed her closed menu to the waitress. Theresa's empty chair felt loud somehow.

"So," Kelsey prompted. "She started coming around eventually. I mean, she was at the barbecue and she knew her way around the house, around the kitchen cupboards. When did that happen?"

Hannah pursed her lips. "That started when she moved back here. So, not long."

"Did something...prompt that?" Chris asked, speaking her first words in quite a while.

"I'm not sure." Hannah propped an elbow on the table and rested her chin in her hand. "I guess maybe she decided it was time. Maybe she called my dad. I don't know. All I do know is that she started coming around. Not for lengthy visits, mind you. She doesn't come for dinner or anything. But she's been showing up for parties my parents throw, gatherings and stuff. I think it's easier for her if there are people besides the immediate family so she can slip out without anybody noticing." Hannah finished off her wine. "She likes my mom and my mom likes her."

"Yeah, I got that impression from the barbecue." Kelsey remembered Liz, her friendly smile, her openness.

"But you guys can't seem to get past any of it, huh?" Chris asked, her eyes on Hannah, her expression a little bit sad.

Hannah blew out a heavy breath. "It's hard for me, because I feel like she took so much of my dad's attention from me. I have a tough time pushing through that to get to the other side."

"You know what?" Kelsey asked, holding up a finger. "Theresa feels the same way about you."

Hannah furrowed her brow. "What do you mean?"

"She feels like *you* took your dad's attention from *her*. That you got her life."

There was silence for a long moment as Hannah seemed to take that in. Long enough for their dinners to arrive. Kelsey basked in the wonderful smells of their entrees. Her chicken wafted up a buttery, savory aroma. Chris's filet stuffed with Gorgonzola gave off a grilled, melty cheese aroma that had Kelsey's mouth watering. Hannah's wild mushroom ravioli was covered in a warm, basil-laden red sauce that was almost too gorgeous to eat. Almost.

The waitress asked if they needed anything else, and both Kelsey and Hannah ordered a second glass of wine, then looked at each other and laughed. That helped to break the slight umbrella of stress that seemed to be hanging over them.

"How about we talk about something fun and cheerful?" Chris suggested and she sliced into her steak and moaned at the perfect light pink color in the middle.

"I think that's a great idea," Kelsey said with a nod. A surreptitious glance at her phone told her it was eight o'clock and the chances of Theresa showing up at all now were slim to none. She tried not to let her disappointment show and pasted on a smile when Hannah spoke.

"Tell me about your interview," she said, pointing a fork at Chris.

For the next half hour, Chris talked about the people she'd met with, the position itself, and listed pros and cons. Hannah was surprisingly attentive, offering up unexpected insight, and Kelsey found herself looking at her friend in a different light. Doing her best to put Theresa in a box on a shelf for now, Kelsey focused on her cousin and her friend, laughed with them, offered support and suggestions, and overall had a really, really nice time.

Chris looked down at her plate and an expression of alarm appeared on her face. "Holy crap, did I eat that whole filet?"

Hannah chuckled. "You did. And I don't think Kelsey or I even got a *taste*."

"I know I didn't," Kelsey teased.

Chris's head snapped up. "Oh, my God, I'm so sorry. I'm usually so good about that."

"Must've been awesome." Hannah shrugged and set down her fork, a ravioli and a half still lounging on her plate. "Mine was."

"It was," Chris agreed. "Kels? You didn't eat much."

"Sure I did. And it was delicious. I just got full." Kelsey had eaten half her chicken breast and most of her potato, but the truth was that her stomach felt a little off and food didn't seem to be sitting well. "Lunch for tomorrow," she said, injecting cheer into her voice as Chris eyed her leftovers with skepticism.

"Anybody up for dessert?" the waitress asked as she seemed to materialize out of thin air.

The three of them looked at each other, back and forth around the table, before agreeing they were done. Kelsey excused herself to the ladies' room while they waited for the check.

The bathrooms were just as elegant as the dining room of Cline, with small baskets on the counter containing feminine hygiene products, scented hand sanitizers, and linen towels instead of paper. The air freshener was tough to identify, but had a slight citrus edge to it that Kelsey liked a lot. She closed herself in a stall, blew out a huge breath, and felt herself relax for the first time since Hannah had arrived. It was as if Kelsey had been on stage all night, playing a role, smiling and nodding and laughing when that's not really at all how she felt. And while part of her was relieved that there had only been one Keene sister at the table, she'd have much preferred it had been Theresa. She glanced at her phone and saw no texts. The disappointment that fell on her was surprising in its weight.

I don't want to feel like this.

That was the big thing. The logical part of Kelsey's brain continually reminded her that she didn't know Theresa all that well. As was her usual path, she wanted to argue, point out that they were slowly getting to know each other, that she knew Theresa better now than she had last week and that was progress. But it was the fact that she felt so tied to her already, so drawn, so connected. She could understand becoming enamored of somebody in fairly short order, but...to have her feelings be so enmeshed in Theresa's behaviors—good or bad—was kind of disconcerting for Kelsey. She was an independent woman. She didn't need anybody. So the fact that so much of her overall mood seemed tied to Theresa wasn't sitting well with her.

Her reflection in the mirror as she washed her hands showed her shaking her head slightly, a bit of a grimace tugging at one corner of her mouth. *This has to stop.* She picked up a towel, dried her hands, and shook herself free of the melancholy mood that had overtaken her. *Enough. Theresa knows where I am. She knows how to find me.* With one determined nod, she pulled the door open and headed back to the table.

"All set?" Chris asked as she stood.

Kelsey pulled her wallet from her purse. "Gotta pay first."

"Taken care of." Chris waved her away.

Kelsey blinked at her. "What?"

"You're letting me stay with you. You're spending all kinds of time with me. The least I can do is buy you dinner."

Kelsey tilted her head to the side and smiled. "Thank you, favorite cousin of mine." She kissed Chris on the cheek.

"You're welcome."

They gathered their belongings and headed out the door. Once outside in the lovely warm night air, Hannah waved goodbye to Kelsey and headed to her own car, which seemed weird until Chris leaned close to Kelsey and said, "Listen, would you mind terribly if I spent a little time with Hannah? She said she'd bring me home later."

"Oh, of course," Kelsey said, hoping she didn't sound overly enthusiastic. Why would this bum her out? Chris and Hannah had hit it off and that was good for both of them. Kelsey knew them both well and wasn't at all surprised they liked each other.

Was she jealous?

Not liking that possibility *at all*, she forced even more cheer into her demeanor. "Absolutely! Go. Have fun." She smiled, hoped it seemed genuine to Chris, who knew her well enough to be able to see when she was faking something.

"Great. You're the best." Chris squeezed Kelsey's shoulder, then waggled her eyebrows as she added, "Don't wait up."

And she was off, darting across the parking lot to Hannah's car.

Kelsey waved as they pulled away, then sighed a bittersweet sigh as though the last of her children had just moved out of the house. She was happy for Chris. She was sad for herself.

Once home, she got a pint of Chunky Monkey ice cream out of the freezer, flopped down on her couch, and flicked on the TV. After several minutes of channel surfing, she settled on *House Hunters* so she could watch people who were much more ridiculous than she was.

Some time later, she opened her eyes and blinked in confusion at the man on her screen showing her some strange silicone tray with holes it it that, apparently, made flipping pancakes much easier. “Is using a spatula that hard?” she whispered, puzzled.

The clock told her it was nearly two in the morning.

She dragged herself up and trudged off to her bed, no sign of Chris and no text from Theresa. Kelsey was happy to close her eyes and shut the world out again.

CHAPTER FIFTEEN

THE CHAMPIONSHIP GAME HAD come down to the wire and three extra innings before Hannah's team scored a run and the win. It had drawn a big crowd and the majority of both teams and all spectators headed to Point Blank to celebrate. As usual, the bar smelled of stale beer, warm popcorn from the machine in the corner, and infield dirt that was spread all over team shirts, sneakers, and the plank wood floor.

"Next stop, world domination!" Hannah shouted at the bar, holding up her beer to the cheers of everybody around her. She'd played one the best games Kelsey had ever seen her play and guessed that was due, in no small part, to the fact that she was trying to show off a little bit for Chris, who'd decided to stay until Wednesday after all—which came as no surprise when she'd arrived back at Kelsey's apartment long after Kelsey had fallen asleep the night before.

This morning hadn't started off well. Kelsey opened her eyes and immediately checked her phone to find...nothing. No text from Theresa. No missed calls. Nothing at all. She'd immediately typed one herself and sent it.

Everything okay? Haven't heard from you since yesterday. I'm a little worried.

That went unanswered. Kelsey had sent two more texts throughout the day, but in addition to her worry, a bit of doubt and a sliver of anger began to seep in to keep that worry company. "Is it so hard to send a quick text?" Kelsey had said to her empty office as she stared at her phone in mid-afternoon. "What would it take? Ten seconds? Say you're fine, just busy? Is that so hard?"

No response came. None. Kelsey headed to the game at six fifteen and at that point, had heard nothing. She felt annoyed, hurt, and more than a little bit ticked off.

"Well, that's an interesting development." Ree said now, her voice close to Kelsey's ear, and Kelsey found herself relieved to finally be in the presence of somebody who wasn't affecting her emotions in any way at all. She followed Ree's gaze to where Hannah stood next to Chris, talking to a couple other players. Suddenly, they all laughed and Hannah tossed her arm over Chris's shoulders.

"It is. I'm trying to keep a close eye on things."

"Why?" Ree's question sounded innocent enough, devoid of accusation. "Do you not trust one of them?"

Kelsey shrugged and sipped from the beer bottle in her hand. "I'm just protective of my cousin. I always have been. She's the same way with me."

"You know Hannah pretty well. I'm sure they're fine. They seem to really like each other."

Kelsey gave a nod, but said nothing, just watched the pair.

"Is there something else going on, Kels?"

Goddamn it, Ree was so freaking observant. Kelsey turned flashing eyes on her. "How is it that you know me so well and we hardly spend any time together?"

Ree chuckled, tipped her beer bottle in Kelsey's direction. "You, my dear, are not hard to read. Not by any stretch of the imagination."

Kelsey groaned and hung her head. This was not news. With a great, put-upon sigh, she lifted her head again, looked at Ree, and spilled. "I'm kind of annoyed at Theresa, who seems to have disappeared off the face of the earth, and I'm jealous of Chris and Hannah, probably because I'm kind of annoyed at Theresa."

Ree raised her eyebrows, seemingly impressed, and gave her head a tilt. "I see. Well, at least you know exactly what's going on in your own head."

Kelsey snorted. "Took me a while to get there." She waved a dismissive hand. "It's fine. Really. I don't know if anything will happen with Chris and Hannah, but they're having fun and enjoying each other's company, and that makes me happy."

"That's the spirit." Ree touched her bottle to Kelsey's. "And you deserve your own happiness as well, my friend. Just keep that in mind, okay?"

"I know." And she did. She hadn't really worried about it much until Theresa came along. With her gorgeous eyes and her quick wit and her rockin' body. And now Kelsey couldn't get her out of her head. Even now, after she'd vowed to just back off, to leave it alone. It was possible Theresa had lost interest, didn't want to see Kelsey anymore. While it would be nice to know, they'd only spent a handful of times together. They were not exclusive. Just because they'd had sex (amazing, mind-blowing, off-the-charts-hot sex) didn't mean they were now beholden to each other. Kelsey had to accept that this might just be Theresa's way of bowing out (as she forced herself not to dwell on

Theresa's whole "this feels different" speech). She hated it, but *had* to admit that it was a possibility.

Time to shake it off, she thought, and the Taylor Swift song immediately flooded her brain, making her groan softly. *Terrific.*

Kelsey could not put into words the depth of her hatred for Chicago's O'Hare airport. It was crowded, hard to navigate, and something was almost always delayed.

"Next time, fly into Midway. It's still crazy busy, but much easier to deal with." She turned to follow the signs for departing flights.

"I know. I made the reservations really fast and wasn't thinking," Chris told her.

"When will you be back?" Kelsey was surprised to feel herself getting a little emotional, which was kind of new in this situation. There was something in her, though, that didn't want Chris to leave. Chris felt like home to Kelsey, and right now, given everything she'd been dealing with, she was missing home in a big way.

Chris turned and gave her a tender smile. "Hopefully very soon. I should hear about the job sometime next week. If things go my way, it starts in a month, so..."

"You'd have a ton of things to get done." Kelsey stopped behind a taxi and waited.

"Exactly."

"I'm trying not to get excited about the idea of you living close to me again."

"Me, too."

"And what about Hannah?" Kelsey had been wanting to ask all morning, but felt a little weird prying, given how testy she'd been initially.

"What about her?"

"How did you guys leave it?"

Chris pursed her lips, took a moment before speaking. "We're playing it by ear. I mean, we like each other a lot and we're pretty...compatible."

Kelsey grinned as she saw Chris's face flush pink. "Yeah, not another word about me sleeping with Theresa on our first date," she scolded playfully.

"We just talked!" Chris said, eyes wide in shock. "I swear. There may have been some making out, but that's all." Kelsey wasn't sure she believed her and Chris knew it. "I swear. Anyway, we want to take some time to get to know each other, so...a little bit of long distance will be good, I think."

"I've been trying to picture you guys as a couple," Kelsey said honestly. "I wasn't sure at first, but seeing you together last night at the bar...you both looked really happy." She reached over and squeezed Chris's knee.

"I like her, that's for sure. I can tell you, though, that I have no desire to date somebody who still lives with her parents. Call me superficial."

Kelsey grinned. "I know. She's working on that."

"She is. We talked about it."

"You did?" Kelsey wasn't sure why she was surprised.

"There was no way I was going to do anything more than making out with her parents in the house." Chris said it as though Kelsey's question was the most ridiculous in all of mankind, which made Kelsey laugh. As they pulled up to the drop-off area, Chris became more serious. "Listen, K-Pete, I'm really sorry I didn't get to meet Theresa."

"Yeah, so am I." Kelsey had told Chris the whole story, how not only had Theresa not come to dinner, but that Kelsey hadn't heard from her since.

"You should drive right over to her house, ask her flat out what's going on."

Kelsey sighed sadly. "Yeah, I'm not going to do that."

"I know. I'm just venting for you." Chris unclipped her seat belt and pushed herself out of the car. Kelsey popped the trunk and followed her.

Behind the car, Chris shouldered her bag, then held out her arms and pulled Kelsey into a a warm, firm hug. Kelsey squeezed back, and for one tender moment, everything was okay in her world. No Theresa. No threat to her business. Just her cousin's love.

"Text me when you land," Kelsey said softly.

"I will. Call me if you need anything, even if it's just to talk."

"I will."

Kelsey stepped back and Chris squeezed her shoulders. "You're worth more than a silent blow-off, Kelsey. Remember that." She gave her a lopsided smile, then turned and headed into the airport.

"Bye," Kelsey said softly, and watched until an annoyed beep sounded behind her. She jumped, startled, and waved at the person behind the wheel waiting for her spot. "Sorry."

Jeanine had opened Common Scents that morning, so things were running smoothly and a customer or two were meandering around the shop when Kelsey arrived.

"Chris get off okay?" Jeanine asked, using an X-ACTO knife to slice open a box.

"She did. Everything okay here?"

"Yes, ma'am." Jeanine handed over a stack of envelopes. "UPS and the mailman were already here."

Kelsey took the stack with her to the office, dropped it on the desk, and got herself situated for the day. She stuck a pod in the tiny Keurig her mother had given her as an "office-warming" gift, booted up her computer, and glanced at the security monitors. The same two women were perusing shelves. The front door pinged, letting her and Jeanine know that another person had entered the store.

When her coffee was done, she tossed in two packets of sweetener and a bunch of powdered creamer. She preferred actual milk or cream, but hadn't yet purchased herself a tiny dorm-sized fridge for her office. She meant to, she just hadn't gotten to it yet. *And now I may not need to.* Coffee sufficiently sweetened, creamed, and tasting as little like coffee as she could manage, Kelsey flopped into her chair and got to work.

The next time she happened to look at the time, it was almost five o'clock in the evening and Jeremy was walking through the front doors, as she could see on the monitor. It must not have been a terribly busy day if Kelsey hadn't been alerted by the door buzzer very often. She gave a sigh as Jeremy came in, said hello, and dropped his stuff onto a chair. Then he went back out and relieved Jeanine. Kelsey watched them chat, then Jeanine left with a wave to the camera, which made Kelsey smile. With another sigh, she turned to the stack of mail on her desk.

Most of her business correspondence tended to come via e-mail, but she had to admit that she enjoyed getting regular snail mail. There was something satisfying about tearing open an envelope, unfolding a sheet of paper. Maybe she was just old fashioned, but she enjoyed going through the mail. She put three invoices in a pile—one from Stephanie Bradley's company, one electric bill, and one from a supplier of bath salts she'd given a shot to. Seven promotional ads from different vendors trying to get her business made up another stack. She'd take those home and look at them tonight.

A rap on her doorframe sounded and pulled her focus from the mail. Jeremy stood there waiting for her to look up. "Jake from the dry cleaners next door is here to see you?" His phrasing the announcement as a question mirrored what Kelsey was thinking. What was he doing here? He never stopped by at random.

"Oh. Okay. Sure, send him back." Kelsey waited only a beat before Jake blew into the office like a windstorm.

"Did you get the letter?" he asked, tossing a sheet of paper onto Kelsey's desk. His voice was surprisingly calm and measured considering the urgency of his body language. Kelsey picked up the letter, which was from a Carter Mayfield Real Estate Development, its house-shaped logo under the name. She scanned the body, somehow surprised and unsurprised by what it said. Basically, Betsy Siegler had already sold the entire building, which the developer was going to level (the letter said "restructure," but Kelsey wasn't stupid and neither was Jake) and replace with condominiums. The letter was to inform the current tenants that they had, as detailed in their individual leases, sixty days to vacate the premises.

"Two months?" Kelsey, again, was surprised and unsurprised at the same time.

"Two months," Jake confirmed, holding up two fingers and shaking his head in what seemed to be a combination of disgust and sadness. Then he folded his arms and leaned against the wall, his neatly pressed khakis and light blue oxford giving him the air of complete calm despite the subject matter. "My store has been here for almost forty years. I've already been researching because I had a feeling this was coming, but there's nothing in this area that even comes close to the rent I'm paying now. Mrs. Jenkins both helped and hurt us."

"She did." Kelsey blew out a long, slow breath as she handed the letter back to Jake. "I imagine everybody in the strip got this letter." She pushed through the remainder of her mail and found the now-familiar blue logo on the corner of the bottom envelope.

"I don't know what I'm going to do," Jake said. "My clientele is all here in Westland. I could relocate to another suburb, but there's no guarantee I could build the business back up, you know? People don't want to go out of their way to pick up their dry cleaning. They want it to be between work and home. Most of my customers live nearby."

Kelsey nodded as she spun the ring on her forefinger. She had no advice to offer. Jake was obviously looking for commiseration and she could certainly give him that, but beyond it? She had nothing. She had her own livelihood to worry about. Even though she'd known from the moment Betsy Siegler had set foot into Common Scents that losing her shop was a possible outcome, now that it was very nearly a reality, she wasn't ready.

They sat there in miserable silence, Kelsey and Jake, for a good three or four minutes before he pushed himself off the wall. "Well," he said and then shrugged.

"Yeah."

"This blows."

"It does." Kelsey nodded.

Their faces made twin expressions of, *Well, what can we do? This is our lot in life right now. And it sucks.* Then Jake took his leave. Kelsey watched the monitors as he made his way through the store and out the front door. Then she fell back in her chair and whispered, "Shit."

Time limit. She needed a time limit.

Kelsey's mother had taught her the time limit trick. When something was bothering her or upset her or made her seethe with anger, she said to give it a time limit. "Pick an amount of time," she'd told college-age Kelsey when she'd gotten a C on an economics test she was sure she'd aced. "Say, half an hour. It can be anything you want, though. Whatever you think would work. Ten minutes. Three hours. A whole day. But stick to that limit." Kelsey could still hear her mother's voice over the phone, just as clear as if it was happening right now. "So today, you're going to allow yourself to be angry about this test for half an hour. You can cry. You can scream. You can punch things. Whatever you need to do to embrace the emotion. And after that half hour is up, you're done being angry. You put it away and get on with your life."

It had sounded so corny. So simplistic. Imagine Kelsey's surprise when it had actually worked. She'd shed some tears. She'd screamed into a pillow. She'd envisioned doing terrible things to her professor. And when her timer had gone off marking the end of thirty minutes, she'd told herself she was done. And she was.

"Okay," she said aloud now. "That's what we're doing today." She sat up and pulled her chair closer to the desk so she could reach her keyboard. "First, we're going to find and watch a boatload of cute kitten videos on YouTube. And then we're going to wallow for an hour. And that will be that." Not for the first time, she wished she had a plant or a goldfish or something that she could conceivably be talking to should somebody walk in, rather than the air.

After another glance at the monitors to make sure Jeanine was doing okay alone, Kelsey clicked her way to YouTube and several adorable animal videos. There was one of cats eating ice cream and then getting brain freezes that made her laugh out loud. She was just calming herself down when the phone rang and she was pleased to hear Stephanie Bradley on the other end.

"Oh, good, I caught you. I thought I might be too late in the day." Stephanie's voice was businesslike, but with a nice gloss of friendliness over the top. "Just checking in to see how your customers like our products."

"So far, so good. I actually took some home to try myself and I love it."

They spent several moments chatting about the different scents, the lotions versus the creams, and some of the new holiday products coming up.

"I'd like to come in and show you a few," Stephanie said. "Not next week, 'cause I'm booked up, but what about the week after? That's pushing us almost into October, so I don't want to wait much longer than that."

For a split second, Kelsey considered telling her exactly what was happening, that in all likelihood, Common Scents might not be there for the holidays. But something held her back. Pride? Shame? Both? She wasn't sure. All she could manage to do was set up an appointment to meet with her a week from Monday.

She hung up the phone and immediately felt exhausted from the forced cheerfulness. Maybe now was the time for that hour of anger wallowing. She looked at the monitors, saw Jeremy dusting the shelf displaying the bath bombs, and nobody else in the store at the moment. A wave of melancholy washed over her then, and she felt surprisingly disappointed to be sad rather than angry. Rubbing both hands over her face, she took a deep breath and blew it out loudly. Before her brain had a chance to whisk her off into more wallowing, her cell rang. She glanced at the screen. Her mother.

"Hey, Mom," she said, not bothering to inject any false cheer into her tone. Her mother would see right through that.

"Hi, sweetie. How are you? I felt the need to check."

It was silly and adorable at the same time, the way her mother checked in on her as if she were still a ten-year-old. Kelsey could roll her eyes and act all insulted by it, but the truth was, it warmed her heart. They spoke for a few minutes about things back home. A neighborhood block party. The book her mother was reading for book club. A new wine she'd discovered in the discount barrel at the Harris Teeter grocery store. As

Kelsey listened and her muscles began to relax a bit, letting go some of the stress tension, she accepted that it was as good a time as any to get things out in the open.

"Hey, Mom, is Dad there?" At her mother's positive reply, Kelsey asked for him and soon the low timbre of his voice was tickling her eardrum.

"Kelsey." He didn't have pet names for her. She was never "sweetie" or "honey" or "darling." She was "Kelsey."

"Hey, Dad."

"How's business?" Right to the chase.

Kelsey blew out a breath. "I'm having an issue." She told him the whole story, beginning with Betsy Siegler's first visit and ending with the letter Jake had shown her, the one she had her own version of, sitting on her desk unopened.

Her father gave a grunt, then said, "That's too bad. I'm sorry you're dealing with that."

"I was wondering if you had any suggestions." She told him about the research she'd done for a new location, that Jake was having the same problem finding something even close to the same range. "If you can think of anything I'm not doing…"

"I told you that rent was almost too good to be true," he said, and Kelsey could picture him shaking his head slowly.

"I know."

"You should've chosen a location that cost a little more. That might have ensured something like this didn't happen."

"Yeah, well, sadly, I'm not psychic, so I don't think I'd have had any way of knowing something this would happen." Kelsey could feel her ire growing.

"I would think your solution is probably to close the shop and find another job. You gave it a shot. You failed. Not much else to be done if you can't find comparable rent." He was so blunt, so matter-of-fact, that Kelsey had to take a moment to sit there with her mouth open. He was a super successful businessman and had been for nearly forty years. Yet he offered no suggestions. He offered no money to help her (and she'd be damned if she was going to ask him for any). *You blew it. Find another job.* Those were his helpful daddy-daughter words of wisdom.

The fact that he was right, despite his lack of compassion about it, made her want to cry.

"Okay, well, I guess I'll have to do that," Kelsey said, this time definitely forcing cheer into her voice. There was no way she wanted him to see that he was crushing her right now. She needed to get off the phone. "Thanks for the advice, Dad." Before he could respond, she hit End and tossed the phone onto her desk with more force than necessary.

But she was so goddamn mad right now. Hurt and heartbroken and angry. She propped her elbows on the desk, dropped her head into her hands, and let the tears come quietly.

They didn't last long, though, as a thought poked at her right then. Hard, like an ice pick prodding at her temple. She furrowed her brow as she tried to figure out what her brain had latched onto. After a moment, she looked down at her desk, at the mail strewn about in piles, some open, some not. And that blue logo caught her eye.

"Noooooooo......" she said, in quiet disbelief, as she picked up the envelope and ran her finger over the Carter Mayfield Real Estate Developers logo. The house outlining a heart.

She'd seen that logo before.

On a binder.

At Theresa's house.

Facts began to click into place like pieces of a jigsaw puzzle finally coming together, and Kelsey could do nothing but stare at the envelope for a very long time.

When she finally blinked herself out of her trance, she moved her fingers to her keyboard and did a Google search on Carter Mayfield. She clicked on the website that appeared and a photo of a distinguished-looking older gentleman filled her screen, along with background on how he went from a little-known real estate agent in Chicago in the seventies to the CEO of one of the largest and most successful real estate developers in the entire Midwest. She checked the menu bar at the top, saw the option of "Staff," and clicked.

A vertical row of small photos popped up, looking very much like school pictures, each person dressed in a nice outfit and smiling widely for the camera.

All except for one.

She wore a classy bright blue top in what was probably silk. Her blond hair was wavy, its gentle curves of gold falling down around her shoulders. Her smile was subtle, like she knew something that nobody else did. And her eyes sparkled with both intelligence and mischief. Had Kelsey not already known Theresa Keene—intimately—she'd certainly want to. There was a pull, like a powerful magnet drawing paperclips across the surface of a desk, giving them no choice but to submit.

Almost instantly, the wonder over that draw was squashed by a sudden, blinding anger so intense Kelsey actually growled. She clicked out of the "Staff" page and closed the site all together. Palms on her desk, she pushed herself to a standing position, as if she wouldn't be able to rise otherwise, as if the white-hot anger had crippled her.

It sure felt like it had.

With a sudden determination that almost frightened her, Kelsey snatched up the letter and her purse and stomped out of her office. She could feel Jeremy's eyes on her as she marched up the aisle to the front door, calling, "I'll be back in an hour, tops," over her shoulder.

Forming coherent thoughts as she drove proved to be difficult, and for that, Kelsey was thankful. She didn't want to go over and over it all in her head. She wanted to face Theresa, to look in her eyes, to understand somehow even though that seemed impossible at the moment.

Traffic was heavy and she cursed it more than once, banging on the steering wheel and shouting expletives she rarely used. All the while, mixed in with her anger, was an enormous pain and sadness that she couldn't bring herself to think about. No, the anger was easier. She'd stick with that.

She made it to Theresa's house in one piece—and she'd left the others on the road intact as well, shockingly. When she pulled up out front, she was surprised to see Theresa's car in the driveway, then surprised at her surprise, since it had never occurred to her what she'd do if nobody'd been home. Stomp on some flowers? Jump up and down in the lawn and flail her arms? As it was, she had no plan, hadn't really thought it through.

Before she could second-guess herself, she pushed out of her car and marched with great determination across the front lawn and up to the door, the crumpled letter in her fist. She poked the doorbell and then knocked on the door anyway. Hard. When nobody had answered in three seconds, she banged some more.

Finally, the door flung open, startling Kelsey nearly as much as Kelsey's presence on her front stoop seemed to have startled Theresa. Her beautiful blue eyes were wide and as Kelsey watched, her face drained of all color until it was chalky white.

"Kelsey," she said quietly, and just that one word made it clear to Kelsey that Theresa had not expected this, had not expected her to show up on the doorstep of her house.

"Did you know?" Kelsey shoved the letter at Theresa, who took it without looking right away. She merely looked at Kelsey, searched her face for...what? Kelsey wasn't sure.

"Come in," Theresa said softly and stepped aside.

"Did. You. Know." Kelsey didn't move.

"Kelsey, please. Come inside."

Kelsey felt her nostrils flare at the directive, but Theresa's voice wasn't angry. Or bossy. It was pleading. "Fine." Kelsey stepped into the foyer, determined not to go any farther into the house and determined not to look at Theresa at all. Not to notice how cute she was in her casual clothes or how soft her hair looked or the sadness in her eyes. No. She kept her eyes on the letter in Theresa's hand and several beats went by before she said again, through gritted teeth, "Did you know?"

Theresa finally smoothed out the letter, gave it a glance, but it was obvious she already knew what it said. "Not right away, no." Her eyes stayed on the letter. Her voice was quiet. "Not until Monday morning."

Kelsey stared hard at her. She wasn't going to make this easy for Theresa. No way. She was too angry. Too hurt. Way too hurt.

Theresa cleared her throat, apparently realizing Kelsey wasn't going to speak. "And even then, I didn't know it was your store until I actually went in."

"When you were sizing it up, yes?"

Theresa met Kelsey's eyes then, but couldn't hold them, gazed somewhere over Kelsey's left shoulder. "I was checking out the layout, the structure of the entire building." She said it quickly, as if it embarrassed her. "I went into all the businesses."

"And you didn't think maybe it was a good idea to tell me then?" Kelsey's eyebrows raised up, her eyes widened.

Theresa inhaled, then swallowed audibly. "I was still trying to absorb it myself. I didn't know what to say." She grimaced, as if realizing how lame that sounded.

"Really. You didn't know what to say." Kelsey nodded slowly, let her eyes roam around the space but didn't actually see any of it. "How about, 'Hey, Kelsey? I think we need to talk about something?' How hard would that have been? How about, 'I need to talk to you before dinner tonight?' Although you blew that off, so that probably wouldn't have worked."

"I'm sorry I didn't call. I just..." Theresa let her voice trail off.

"Didn't know what to say?" Kelsey supplied with great snark.

"Right." Theresa looked down at her hands.

Silence reigned for several long moments as Kelsey felt herself slowly running out of steam, that sadness threatening to usurp the anger. Finally, she took a deep breath in and let it out. "You know what's hard?" she asked quietly. "The fact that I thought we had something, you and I. I mean, I know it's only been a short time and we would've had a lot of getting to know each other to do, but..." She swallowed, felt her eyes well up and wrinkled her lip in a snarl over the fact. "I thought maybe we had something."

"I think we do, too." Theresa's use of the present tense wasn't lost on Kelsey, who forced herself to scoff.

"Yeah, well, you certainly took care of that, didn't you?"

Theresa seemed to gain a little energy then, to stand up a little bit straighter, but her voice stayed quiet. "Kelsey, what did you want me to do? Huh? I was just as blindsided as you were on Monday. Should I have just blurted it out right there in the store in front of your employees and customers? 'Gee, sorry, but this building's been sold and you're going to have to vacate. Have a nice day.'" Kelsey had no immediate response and Theresa let the point sit for a moment before continuing. "I realize I should have contacted you by now—"

"Ya think?" Kelsey muttered, still angry, though the miserable look on Theresa's face was making it difficult for her to stay that way. She gave her head a subtle shake and said, "I've got to get back."

Theresa's hand closed on her upper arm, stopping Kelsey from taking another step. "Please, Kelsey," she whispered. "I'm sorry."

Kelsey looked at the hand on her arm, got a brief flash of that same hand on her naked skin, causing goose bumps and heat and arousal and want and...she squeezed her eyes shut, pushed the memories from her brain. "Yeah. So am I." She gently pulled her arm free.

Walking across the yard to her car, Kelsey tried to ignore the tears that had gone beyond welling and had spilled over to run hotly down her cheeks.

CHAPTER SIXTEEN

"MY FEET ARE KILLING ME."

Chris dropped into the passenger seat of Kelsey's car and immediately took off her shoe so she could rub her foot.

"Dude. Seriously. You're stinking up my car." Kelsey keyed the ignition and pulled out of the parking lot of the twelfth apartment they'd looked at since nine that morning.

"My feet don't stink," Chris said with mock indignation.

Kelsey snorted. "I've known you your whole life. I know exactly what your feet smell like."

Chris laughed. "And you love me, so you don't mind."

Kelsey allowed a small grin, and they drove the next few moments in silence.

"You doing okay, little cousin?" Chris's voice was quietly serious this time. Kelsey could feel the weight of her concerned gaze.

"Yeah. I'm fine." Kelsey turned to her, flashed her a quick smile, and moved her focus back to the road.

"You've been really quiet and..." Chris looked out the window.

"And what?"

"And you don't seem happy. Not like the last time I was here. You hardly smile at all. You just seem...sad."

"Yeah, well, my store is closing in less than a month, so I think I'm allowed a little sadness." Kelsey tried not to sound snippy, but was pretty sure she failed. Which wasn't fair. She wasn't mad at Chris.

"I know. I know. I just...I think it's more than that."

Kelsey furrowed her brow, played clueless. "Why would you think that?"

Chris tilted her head and gave Kelsey a look. "Known you your whole life, remember?"

Kelsey sighed. "I'm fine. I promise." But she couldn't look at Chris and she was certain her voice lacked the conviction she'd attempted to put into it. Because the truth was, she wasn't fine. Not by a long shot. She was losing her store. While she hadn't completely given up the search for a new location, she'd had no luck so far finding someplace she could afford. Leaving Westland wasn't something she wanted to do, though, which meant she probably needed to start looking for a job...something that proved difficult when all her energy was poured into making as much money as possible in the store's last few weeks.

And then there was Theresa.

Theresa, who hadn't stopped texting since their confrontation at her house two weeks ago. She'd called. Dozens of times. She left messages of apology. She sent texts of apology. She e-mailed apologies. Every day. Every day some sort of contact arrived. And Kelsey hadn't responded to a single one, which felt like righteous indignation at first. But now? Now, the anger was pretty much gone, and she was just so sad. It overwhelmed her, and she just didn't have the energy to deal with her own emotions. Theresa deserved more from her—two weeks was a long time to keep knocking at a door that nobody ever opened—but Kelsey couldn't manage to suck it up. She knew she *should*, but...

What if she stops?

It was a question Kelsey asked herself often. It was *the* question. Because Theresa was bound to give up at some point. And Kelsey honestly didn't know if she'd be relieved or crushed when that happened.

Chris, thankfully, left it alone and they drove in silence for a little while before Kelsey slickly (she hoped) changed the subject to something cheerful.

"I can't believe you're moving here." This time, her smile was genuine, as it was going to be such a relief to have some family nearby. Kelsey hadn't expected to miss hers as much as she did. Even her father.

"I can't either," Chris said. "But I'm really excited. I think this is going to be great. I already know more people here than I do in Boston, and I've been there for a while."

"Well, hopefully this new company won't work you a million hours a week and you'll actually have time for a social life."

"A what? I'm not familiar with that term."

Kelsey chuckled. "Speaking of that unfamiliar term, how's Hannah with all of this?"

"All of what? My moving here?"

"Your moving here and taking it slowly with her, yes. I was surprised you didn't have her come with us to look at apartments."

Chris pressed her lips together in a straight line and seemed to ponder things for a bit before answering. "She's doing okay, I think. I mean...I really like her, you know?" Chris's eyes were soft as she glanced in Kelsey's direction. "I want to give it a chance and not just jump in headfirst."

"I think that's smart," Kelsey said, and it was true. She hadn't spoken to Hannah much since Chris left, and things with Theresa had fallen apart. They'd texted here and there. They'd grabbed a drink or two. But for every text of Kelsey's Hannah answered, three others went un-responded to. So Kelsey attended the first softball game of the fall league, but hadn't been to the second or third. Things with Hannah weren't quite the same and Kelsey was sad about that, knew that it was her doing, inadvertent or not.

"That being said," Chris told her, "we've been invited to dinner at her house tonight."

"At Hannah's?" Kelsey couldn't hide her surprise.

"Yep."

"Both of us?"

"Mm-hmm."

"Wait." Kelsey glanced at Chris. "She invited both of us or she invited you and you invited me?"

Chris's eyebrows rose as her expression conveyed innocence. "She invited both of us." She held up a hand. "Scout's honor. Her mom is cooking and told Hannah to have us over."

Kelsey thought back to Hannah's mom, how nice she was at the barbecue, how friendly and inviting. "Okay. I'm up for it."

"Good." Chris finally put her shoe back on as Kelsey pulled into the parking lot of a large apartment complex. "Last one?"

"Last one," Kelsey said with a nod, then pulled her door open.

The second Kelsey had entered Hannah's house, she felt at home, because that's exactly what it smelled like: home. A warm, savory dinner was cooking. Some kind of candle or incense with a hint of cinnamon was burning. And despite it being early fall and still mild-ish weather, Kelsey felt as if it was winter and she'd walked directly into a warm, cozy hug after being out in the cold.

By the time Kelsey had finished her last bite of meatloaf an hour later and had barely three bites of mashed potatoes left on her plate, she was ridiculously glad she'd come. Such a classic, home-cooked meal filled her heart and made her feel less homesick than she'd been in a while. And Liz Keene was so charmingly sweet that Kelsey was pretty sure she'd developed a little crush on Hannah's mom.

"There's more, girls" Liz said, looking from Kelsey to Chris to Hannah and back as she refilled Kelsey's wine glass with a delicious red blend.

"If I eat one more bite, I will explode all over your lovely kitchen," Chris answered. "I haven't been this full since I moved out of my mother's house. Thank you so much."

"Same here," Kelsey said. "That was delicious. I haven't had meatloaf as good as my mom's, like...ever." With a grin, she added, "Let's keep that between us, shall we?"

Liz's laugh was soft and feminine, a musical tinkle of sorts. "It'll be our little secret." She finished refilling glasses, then sat back down. "I'm sorry Hannah's father couldn't join us. He's in the city for a business dinner."

Kelsey was sorry, too. The idea of getting to know the man responsible for half of Theresa's genes appealed to her.

"Chris, have you found a place yet?" Liz's question pulled Kelsey back to the table.

"We've narrowed it down to three," Chris nodded, then sipped her wine.

"How many did you look at?" Hannah asked.

"Nine hundred and thirty," Kelsey said, garnering laughter around the table. "Sure felt like it."

"It did," Chris agreed.

"Did you ask Theresa for help?" Liz's voice was innocent, but something in her eyes—a twinkling, a sparkle of mischief, something—told Kelsey that was an illusion.

"Why would they ask Theresa for help?" Hannah asked, eyes on her plate as she scooped up some potatoes.

Liz looked at her with that subtle sternness a mother has the ability to convey using only her eyes. "Because she's in real estate and she's your sister and she's friends with Kelsey." There was just enough of a pause before the word "friends" to let Kelsey know Liz knew full well they were—or had been—more than that.

"Mom, please." Hannah rolled her eyes. "You know she's tearing down Kelsey's building. That she's got to close her store because of it. I don't think Theresa's high on her list right now." She turned to Kelsey, obviously looking for solidarity. "Right, Kels?"

Kelsey blinked at her, the proverbial deer caught in the headlights. She glanced at Liz, who chewed her dinner and waited for Kelsey to answer, her expression impossible to read.

"I..." She thought of all the texts, calls, e-mails that she'd left unanswered, and suddenly felt deeply ashamed.

"Theresa was just doing her job," Liz said simply, then picked up her wine glass. "It's not like she chose the building or put it up for sale or decided to tear it down. Kelsey knows that. Right?" Her eyes were less gentle now as they clicked to Kelsey's and stayed there. Her demeanor wasn't mean. It wasn't angry. It was...firm? That was the only word Kelsey could think of as a description, but she knew without a shadow of a doubt that Liz knew exactly what was going on. Kelsey felt a sadness well up inside at the fact that she hadn't realized Theresa and her stepmom were close enough to talk about such personal things.

Kelsey cleared her throat. "Right," she answered, but it still sounded like she'd swallowed a frog.

Liz nodded as if Kelsey had answered a quiz question correctly. "She felt terrible about it. So terrible that she gave up the account altogether. You guys know that, right?"

Forks that had been moving stopped. Any sounds of utensils against dishes ceased. Kelsey stared at the one small bite of mashed potatoes on her plate and couldn't tear her eyes away, even as she felt Chris's on her. A few seconds went by, then a few more, and when Kelsey finally looked up, Liz was continuing to eat her dinner as if she hadn't just dropped a live grenade in the middle of the table.

Hannah also looked a bit like Kelsey felt at the moment—shocked, embarrassed, selfish—and she wondered if her own expression mirrored Hannah's.

Kelsey swallowed audibly before saying, "No. No, I didn't know that."

"No? Huh." Liz continued to eat, sipped her wine, her face friendly and open.

"Me neither," Hannah said quietly as she set her fork down.

"Well," Liz said, dabbed the corner of her mouth with a napkin and shrugged. "It's not like she'd announce something like that. She's pretty private about some things. But she felt terrible and went right in to her boss's office to tell him so. Then she asked to be removed from the account altogether. She was the senior account executive, so her boss wasn't happy with her. It'll probably be a while before she gets a project that big again." Liz made a sympathetic face.

Kelsey thought back to the texts and e-mails and messages. They were all apologies. They all begged Kelsey to talk to her. Not one of them said she'd given up the account.

"Who's ready for dessert?" The sound of Liz pushing her chair back on the linoleum floor jerked Kelsey back to the present. Without waiting for a response, Liz took four small plates down from a cupboard and pulled what looked to be a chocolate cheesecake out of the refrigerator. In a few minutes, they each had a generous slice in front of them. Chris dug in. Hannah hesitated a moment before forking off a bite.

Kelsey simply stared at hers.

"This is delicious, Mrs. Keene," Chris said after a quick glance Kelsey's way. "Thank you so much for having us."

Liz chuckled. "Please. Mrs. Keene is my mother-in-law. Call me Liz. And I'm very happy you came. I always enjoy getting to know Hannah's friends."

Hannah snorted. "She used to pop into my room whenever I had friends over." She grinned at her mother "All. The. Time."

"I was just saying hello. Being friendly." Liz took a bite of her dessert, a twinkle in her green eyes that were so much like Hannah's.

"You were spying," Hannah said, pointing her fork.

"That, too."

Laughter went around the table and lightened the mood considerably, and for that, Kelsey was grateful. She had to figure out what to do about Theresa. If anything. There was so much to think about, so much to analyze, but...she just couldn't right now. Forcing herself to shake it all away, at least for the moment, she shoveled a large bite of cheesecake into her mouth and did her best to tune into the current conversation.

She wondered what Theresa was doing right now.

CHAPTER SEVENTEEN

THE RIDE HOME WAS quiet.

They'd stayed another hour after Liz Keene had pried open the Theresa situation and poked at Kelsey's handling of it all. There had been coffee and more cheesecake (for Chris and Hannah) and continued laughter and conversation. But all the while, Kelsey felt herself sitting slightly removed from it all, replaying her last words with Theresa, the barbs, the hurt and anger. From both sides.

"Was I too hard on her?" she asked from the driver's seat.

"God, finally," Chris said. "I've been waiting forever for you to say something."

Kelsey smiled tenderly and glanced at her cousin. "I'm surprised you didn't start interrogating me the second the car doors closed."

Uncharacteristically serious, Chris said, "No, I was waiting until you were ready to talk about it."

Kelsey waited for a couple of silent beats while they sat at a red light. "Do you think she planned that? Liz?"

Chris wet her lips, shrugged. "I don't know. Maybe. Did you know she was close with Theresa? Seems like they're pretty tight."

Kelsey shook her head. "I didn't. I mean, I knew they got along well, but it never occurred to me that they'd share personal stuff. I don't know why. Did you know?"

"Hannah's never said anything, but I get the impression she doesn't talk about her sister much."

"Half-sister," Kelsey corrected with an eyebrow arch.

"Right, right, right."

"Was I too hard on her? Theresa?" Kelsey was back to the question that had been bugging her since Liz first brought up her name at the dinner table. "That's kind of the impression I was getting from Liz."

"What do you think?"

Kelsey took a moment to ponder the question, then answered as honestly as she could. "I think I was angry."

"Righteously so," Chris agreed with a nod.

Kelsey waited for the anger to begin a new simmer, but it didn't. "I mean, it would've been nice to get a heads-up, you know?"

Chris didn't exactly nod. She sort of tipped her head one way then the other, like she wasn't sure.

"What? What does that mean?" Kelsey asked.

Chris inhaled slowly and seemed to measure her words. "I was just wondering how far in advance Theresa knew. Knew your store was part of this project." She looked at Kelsey. Kelsey could feel the weight of her gaze, but kept her eyes on the road. "You say a heads-up would've been nice, but...maybe she really didn't know ahead of time. That's what she told you, right?"

"That's what she told me." Kelsey's voice was soft, filled with a trepidation that scared her because...what if that really was the case? Then a memory hit and forced some of that trepidation back into a corner. "But she disappeared then. She didn't call me. She didn't text or answer my texts. She blew off dinner."

Chris nodded. "Yeah, that wasn't cool."

"It wasn't."

"Except she *did* tell you she may not be able to make it because of work. So not *exactly* a textbook definition blow-off."

A moment of silence passed.

Another.

Kelsey pulled into her parking lot and they went into her apartment. Once inside, Chris collapsed on the couch while Kelsey leafed through the mail without actually looking at it.

"You like this girl," Chris said, not a question, her voice sounding startlingly loud in the quiet of the apartment. "She's got a hold on you. Even after everything that's happened, you haven't let her go yet."

"I did like her. I liked her very much."

"You still do. I can see it on your face. I could see it during my last visit and I can see it now." Chris looked at her, and her eyes told Kelsey not to bother arguing. Instead, she gave a reluctant nod. "She apologized?"

"She did."

"By text?"

"And e-mail. And she left a couple messages."

Chris nodded slowly. "And you haven't responded." Her voice had grown firm and this wasn't a question.

"No."

Chris held her gaze for what felt like a long time before saying, "Man, you're hard, Kels."

Kelsey wasn't sure she'd heard right.

She blinked at her cousin in shock. "I'm sorry?"

"What else could she have done?" When Kelsey didn't respond, Chris went on, her voice moving from firm to quietly stony. "She told you she didn't know ahead of time it was your store. She's apologized up and down for...how long now?"

Kelsey swallowed. "Two weeks," she said, barely above a whisper.

"Two weeks. Two weeks with nothing from you, and still she keeps trying. That's a long damn time to eat shit, you know?"

Kelsey looked down at her feet as her eyes welled with tears.

Chris stared at her for a moment, then said, "You know, I like Hannah. I like her a lot. I'd like to wing it with her, see what happens. But I know for a fact that when I talk about her, my face doesn't look like yours does when you talk about Theresa. Even while you're furious at her, you still have that gentle tone, that soft look in your eyes, that tenderness for her. Most people don't have that with somebody. And most people wish they did. And you were well on your way, my friend, to something amazing, and you just..." Chris shook her head. "I love you, Kelsey, I do. But I'm sorry, you really screwed this one up." Silence sat in the middle of the room like some large boulder. Kelsey didn't know what to say. Chris didn't look at her. Instead, she pushed herself to her feet. "I'm gonna take a shower." She left the room without so much as a backward glance at Kelsey, who remained standing all alone in the living room. For the first time she could remember in life, her cousin was disgusted with her.

That reality sat like a lump of clay in the pit of her stomach.

You really screwed this one up.

The worst part, believe it or not, wasn't that she was hurt by what Chris had said.

It was that she was worried Chris was right.

There was very little conversation for the rest of the night. Chris opened the bathroom door after her shower and the scent of the Pumpkin Spice Cookie body wash Kelsey kept in the shower wafted out with the leftover steam. It was a lovely smell, all warm and autumn-like and inviting, but it did nothing to make Kelsey feel any better. She was too busy mentally beating the crap out of herself.

She headed into the bathroom to wash her face and brush her teeth. She toyed with the idea of soaking in a warm bath, but was worried that would give her too much time to think and it was pretty clear she didn't need any more of that. Besides, it was nearly eleven on Friday night and she had to be to the shop early tomorrow to help with the Going Out of Business Sale.

The thought broke her heart a little bit.

Of course, sleep eluded her. Long after she could hear Chris's soft snores coming from the couch, Kelsey lay wide awake, her brain spinning like an overloaded washing machine, unbalanced, knocking loudly, and in danger of flinging everything all over the place.

How had she ended up here? In less than six months, she'd gone from leaving everything familiar to becoming a successful small business owner to racking up some amazing new friends to meeting somebody who might actually matter...to all of it completely dissolving around her like a sandcastle in the rain.

How did I end up here?

Tears filled her eyes as Theresa's face filled her mind, doing nothing to alleviate the stress, worry, and self-flagellation she'd been drowning in for—she glanced at the clock that might as well have laughed at her as it reported it to be closing in on three o'clock—more than four hours now. For the first time, she let herself think about what it must have been like to send endless texts, messages, e-mails asking for forgiveness, only to be met with nothing but utter silence. How much that must have hurt.

Kelsey tried to put herself in Theresa's shoes.

She didn't like it there.

"I'm really going to miss this place," a nice-looking woman in yoga clothes said to Kelsey, as she placed a Bed of Pine Needles candle in her hand basket. "I mean, I know you weren't here that long, but I really love your stuff. I'm sad you're closing."

"Thank you," Kelsey said. "I appreciate that."

It had been that way all day, customers buying up the remaining stock while lamenting how much they were going to miss Common Scents. The other repeated comment was a question: are you opening somewhere else? That was the hard one to answer. Maybe down the line, she could try again. Kelsey knew that. But for the time being, it just wasn't in the cards. More than once, she quietly headed to her office in the back to pull herself together. The emotion was unexpected.

Also unexpected was the end of contact from Theresa.

It was almost as if she'd gotten wind of the conversation Kelsey and Chris had had the previous night and had decided that was it, she'd had enough. For the past two weeks, Kelsey had received at least one text a day from Theresa. Sometimes more, but always at least one. The begging and apologies had changed to simple "thinking of you" statements that came at the end of the day, usually between five and six, probably once Theresa was home from work. And Kelsey had grown to expect them. To rely on them. And she hadn't even realized it until yesterday. When they'd stopped.

She woke up that morning to still no new texts, which meant she didn't get one at all yesterday. It was now closing in on five in the afternoon and she had received nothing from Theresa yet. She was surprised how much that bothered her.

You really screwed this one up.

Chris was on a plane on her way back to Boston, but her critical voice was still lodged uncomfortably—and loudly—in Kelsey's head. Had been all day long.

"Thank God," Kelsey muttered when the intercom sounded and Jeremy, who'd come in early to help with the sale, told her she had a phone call. Anything to take her mind off this crap. "Hello?"

"Kelsey? It's Stephanie Bradley."

"Hey, Steph. How are you?" Kelsey was always happy to hear from the Earthly Products rep.

"Better than you, apparently. What's this I hear about you closing? I was just there a couple weeks ago."

God, she hated this. She hated having to tell the story because it felt like admitting her failure, even though it was no such thing. She gave Stephanie the abbreviated version.

"Well, that sucks," Stephanie said bluntly, and Kelsey burst out laughing because she really had summed it up perfectly.

"It totally does. And thank you for saying so."

"Listen..." There was a pause, as if Stephanie was gathering her thoughts before voicing them. "This might actually be perfect."

"What might?" Kelsey sat back in her chair.

"I got a promotion. That's one of the reasons I was calling. They're bumping me up to Manager of Midwest Sales."

"Stephanie! That's fantastic! Congratulations. You must be thrilled." Kelsey's grin was wide. Stephanie was good at her job and Kelsey had no doubts she'd continue to succeed. "You'll be managing other reps?"

"Exactly. There are twelve reps in the Midwest, and I'll be overseeing them and their sales."

"That sounds great."

"Which leaves my current position open..." She let her voice trail off and waited for Kelsey to catch up.

"Oh." Kelsey nodded as Stephanie's words sank in. Then she sat upright in her chair. "Oh!"

"There you are," Stephanie said with a laugh. "Honestly, I think you'd be great and you really seem to like our products and believe in what we're doing. That goes a long way in selling them."

"Your products are awesome," Kelsey said with conviction.

"I get to help hire my own replacement, so you'd already have an in. What do you say? Interested?"

This was falling right into her lap and that always made Kelsey nervous. Things that seemed too easy made her nervous. Still. She needed a job. She was good at sales (she'd done it before moving to Westland). She believed in the product. Also, she *really* needed a job.

"Definitely."

"Terrific! E-mail me your resume and I'll make sure it goes to the top of the pile."

Kelsey was clicking along on her computer as Stephanie spoke. "Done."

"Great. You know," Stephanie said, and her voice softened. "I'm really sorry your store is closing, Kels, but at the same time, I think this might be the perfect fit. I'll be in touch."

What just happened?

Kelsey sat there for a long moment, just staring at the phone. When she finally shifted her gaze to the security monitors, she stared there, too. Sat for a long while and just watched the inner workings of her little scent shop, her dream, the dream she'd made a reality. And even though it hadn't lasted, she was still proud of it, no matter what her father said. Maybe it was meant to be a short stopover, just a blip in her life. Maybe this was the path she was meant to take. Maybe working for Earthly Products, selling cruelty-free items to others like her, was what she was supposed to be doing next. She had no idea. But weirdly, it felt right.

Kelsey had no explanation for that.

Back in the store, she spent the next couple of hours with Jeremy, waiting on customers and offering scent advice to those who asked. She'd definitely miss this part if Stephanie hired her, interacting directly with the end user. Kelsey enjoyed it and was good at it.

When the last customer left and Kelsey's watch said 9:05, she locked the front door and sent Jeremy home. As she went through her nightly routine, counting up the cash drawers, adding up the sales, putting money in the little office safe to be taken to the bank tomorrow, she only had one thing on her mind, and it wasn't the possibility of a new job.

It was Theresa.

A glance at her phone told her this was the second day with no text from her and that made it pretty clear to Kelsey that Theresa was finished with her. That was fine, she supposed, except for one thing.

She wasn't finished with Theresa.

Traffic was fairly light, which wasn't really a surprise given that it was nearly ten at night. Kelsey blasted the radio, hoping to keep her own thoughts at bay, because the truth was, she had no idea what she was going to say when Theresa answered the door. *If* Theresa answered the door. For all Kelsey knew, she might not even be home. She might not even be in town. But calling ahead hadn't been an option. She wanted the element of surprise. For both of them.

Once she had turned onto Theresa's street, her radio felt obnoxiously loud, so she turned it off. The fall evening was beautiful, the temperature in the high fifties, the streetlights casting a warm, yellowish glow on the neighborhood, the moon high and full. Theresa's lights were on inside her house and her car was in the driveway.

Kelsey's heart rate went from a jog to a full-on sprint.

Ten minutes later, she was still sitting in her car, parked in front of Theresa's house, working on her nerve. It was only when a man walked by with his black lab and gazed at her as he did that Kelsey realized how suspicious she looked sitting in her car on the street in a neighborhood that wasn't hers at ten o'clock at night.

"Get moving, Kelsey, before somebody calls the cops on you," she muttered.

With a deep, and what she hoped was fortifying, breath, she pulled on the handle and opened the car door. Then she stood looking over the top of her car at the house, which suddenly loomed much larger than life and looked alarmingly daunting, like a haunted mansion in an old-timey horror movie.

Summoning every ounce of courage she could, she began her trek across the front lawn and up onto the front stoop of Theresa's house. Where she stood. Doing nothing. Again.

Kelsey hung her head and stared at her own feet for what seemed like long moments. She wasn't a woman who was often at a loss, but she felt that way right now. And it made sense because...she'd put herself here. She'd vilified Theresa—whether she'd intended to or not, that's exactly what she'd done. She'd acted like a spoiled child and she was annoyed with herself that it had taken Chris to point it out. For God's sake, she was thirty-one years old—old enough to know better than to behave like she had.

She was thinking about how disappointed her mother would be in her when the door was pulled open. It startled Kelsey so much that she gave a little yelp and took a step backward, nearly stumbling off the stoop, but catching herself at the last minute. When she'd righted herself, Kelsey looked up into beautiful blue eyes. Beautiful, but not sparkling. Not twinkling. Not soft. Hard. Hard eyes. Stony eyes. Eyes that very clearly stated their owner was not pleased with this intrusion.

"Theresa." Kelsey wet her lips, tried not to look away from that unimpressed gaze. "Hi."

Theresa said nothing, simply stood leaning against the edge of the front door, not opening it any farther, not making any room for Kelsey to come in.

"Um, listen," Kelsey said, then cleared her throat, hating how uncomfortable she was. "I wanted to talk to you."

Theresa arched an eyebrow and tilted her head to one side, but said nothing. She didn't need to; her expression made her thoughts clear. *Oh,* now *you want to talk?* She didn't move. She just waited for Kelsey to continue.

"So, um..." Kelsey took a deep breath, wishing more than anything that she'd rehearsed some sort of dazzling speech, something that would make Theresa swoop her up in a hug or smile at her or...God, *something*. Anything besides this silent staring. "Listen. I've been thinking and I owe you an apology."

Blue eyes stared.

Kelsey swallowed. *Okay, it's all or nothing here.* She really hoped it didn't end up being nothing. "In my defense, I had just been informed that I wasn't about to get a possibly-insurmountable rent increase, as I was expecting. That would have at least given me a chance. Instead, I was told I had sixty days to vacate my shop entirely. Close it down. After being open for roughly five months. I had looked for another location in the previous weeks and found nothing I thought I could afford, so I was dealing with the fact that I was going to lose my shop. And I had just spoken with my father about it, and he was his usual less than warm and fuzzy self, and that stung. And I'd been dealing with all of that for less than a couple hours before I confronted you." She looked at Theresa and was met with the same unemotional gaze. "I know you were just doing your job. I get that now. I should've gotten it sooner." Again, Theresa raised an eyebrow in expectation, as if waiting for Kelsey to say something specific. She gave it a shot. "And I should have responded to your texts and stuff." That was embarrassing, as she now understood how childish it had been to simply ignore any attempts at contact. "I'm really very sorry."

Kelsey was done now. She took a deep breath, blew it out, and waited. A long pause went by before Theresa finally spoke.

"Is that it?" Her voice was quiet, nearly devoid of any inflection at all.

Kelsey took a beat. "Um, yeah. I think so."

Theresa nodded subtly, then stood up straight and closed the door with a quiet click, leaving Kelsey standing alone on the stoop.

"Oh," she said out loud. "Okay then. I guess that's that." She gave it another moment before slowly turning away from the door and heading back to her car, feeling such a mix of things, she didn't know what to do with them all. Relieved that she'd apologized. Thrilled to have laid eyes on Theresa again. Uncomfortable that Theresa hadn't let her in, had left her standing on the stoop. Disappointed and sad that she had said exactly three words to Kelsey the whole time. And such shame, she didn't know what to do with it. So many feelings in such a jumble.

Back in her car, she leaned her forehead against the steering wheel. "Well, that was loads of fun," she muttered to nobody.

And then the tears came.

"Goddamn it," Kelsey whispered as she kept her head against the steering wheel and wept. She wasn't sure how long she was there, but when the tears subsided, she dug a tissue out of the glove compartment and wiped her nose, dabbed at the tracks of mascara on her cheeks.

It was done now. Not the conclusion Kelsey had hoped for, but she really had nobody to blame but herself. Regardless, it was done. She glanced once more at Theresa's house as she started her car and thought she saw a part in the mini-blinds in the front window close quickly, but she couldn't be sure. It was dark. Her eyes were swollen. And she was so very sad.

She put the car in gear and went home.

CHAPTER EIGHTEEN

OCTOBER 10 STARTED OFF and progressed like any other day at Common Scents. Well, with the exception of the very sparse stock. And the empty shelves. And the way the whole place looked like an unfinished painting with missing pieces and colors creating large holes of nothing on a canvas that was once so vibrant. And had smelled so good.

A few customers still mingled, walking around hoping to scoop up some as-last-minute-as-possible products, and some of them succeeded. Kelsey had been fairly chipper in the morning, but by mid-afternoon, her mood had tempered, become gray and sad, and though she did her best not to show it, it was almost impossible. She'd caught Jeanine looking at her from across the store more than once, her face etched with sympathy. Kelsey would give her a lame smile back, trying to reassure her that everything was fine. But Jeanine was a mom, and she knew better.

Deciding she needed a little air, Kelsey went out the front door and wandered down the sidewalk of their little strip mall. The CPA was gone, the windows dark, the inside empty. The tax prep place didn't look any different than it usually did when it wasn't tax season: quiet, dark, and uninhabited. The nail salon was still going strong, a sign in the window trumpeting their new address, opening in two weeks just three blocks away. Kelsey felt a pang of envy. Jake's window sported a very different sign:

Going Out of Business After 40 Years. Kelsey's envy quickly changed to sympathy. Yes, her store was closing, but at least she didn't have forty years of history behind it. At least it didn't have her family's blood running through it. Jake was heartbroken. Kelsey was sure of it.

And she knew where she was going next. That was also a good thing. Stephanie had offered her a job with Earthly Products the day after receiving her resume, so there'd be no scramble for rent, as Kelsey had been afraid of. She didn't want to ask her parents for money, even though she knew they'd help. She had the next two days to clean out the store, she'd have Sunday to chill, then she'd start working for Stephanie Monday. No breaks, which was probably good, as Kelsey didn't want to wallow. Which was the reason she'd turned down the offer from Hannah and Chris to take her out for drinks after she closed tonight. No, she needed to do this alone and then get herself ready for the next chapter in her life.

Things were moving quickly and that was good. But despite the bright future ahead, her heart still ached. She was still sad. Letting go of her store was harder than she'd expected.

She pulled out her phone and opened her texts, then typed one out.

Today is it. I close the doors for good at 6. I'm so sad I can barely breathe.

She hit Send before she could second-guess herself.

The irony wasn't lost on her. She wasn't sending texts to Theresa daily, but she was sending them regularly. Since that night on Theresa's doorstep, she'd sent maybe eight or ten. They'd all gone unanswered and Kelsey chalked it up to Karma wanting her to know how it felt to be completely disregarded and ignored.

It sucked. That's how it felt. She got it. Loud and clear.

She blew out a breath, tucked her phone into her back pocket, and walked to the end of the strip mall, then did an about-face and headed back. She was almost to her door when her phone beeped. She pulled it out and looked at the text.

I'm sorry. That's got to be hard. Hang in there.

"It is," Kelsey said out loud while staring at the screen, unable to believe Theresa had texted back. A million replies whipped through her brain like race cars shooting past the bleachers at Daytona.

I could use a hug.

I miss you.

I'm sorry I said it was your fault. I was so wrong.

I miss you.

Have dinner with me.

I miss you.

She thought about—and discarded—every one of those before typing simply, *It is. Doing my best.* She sent it, tucked the phone away, and went back inside, her ears hyper-tuned to the sound of a text beep. But another one didn't come.

At 5:31, she hugged Jeanine, thanked her for everything, and sent her home.

At 6:01, she locked the front door, went back into the darkened store behind the counter, and leaned forward. Her arms on the counter, she rested her chin on them and just took it all in—the empty shelves, the signs, the few remaining bottles, the cheery, lime green walls, the linoleum floor—all of it. She stayed that way for long moments before the tears began. They came quietly, almost gently, rolling softly down her cheeks.

October 10.

The day she let go of a dream.

By late October, things seemed to have settled into some semblance of normality and near-comfort, at least for some of the people in Kelsey's life. For that, she was thankful. Chris was making huge strides in her new job and Kelsey had never seen her cousin so happy. She had a cute little apartment about ten minutes from Kelsey's, and she and Hannah had been dating, slowly and steadily getting to know each other. Kelsey tried her best not to feel any envy or jealousy, but there were times when she wondered what she and Theresa would have been like if they'd given each other a chance, if Kelsey hadn't been so pig-headed.

She was still trying to let go of Theresa—but her efforts were half-hearted at best. She still texted her, and once in a while, she'd get a text back. But they were always short, fairly impersonal, and never led to an actual conversation. Kelsey still went to Starbucks here and there. She'd tell herself she needed caffeine, but in reality, she was hoping to run into the sexy blonde who caught her eye what seemed like forever ago. She'd recall how much fun it was to flirt with her, remember the feel of her hands on Kelsey's body, her mouth on Kelsey's mouth. And then her phone would ring or somebody would call her name, yanking her out of the pleasantness and back to reality.

Like now, she realized, as she picked up her phone to see the text that had just pinged through from Hannah.

My place tonight. Small gathering for Chris. Bring wine and your smiling face.

Kelsey blew out a breath. She wasn't really up for a party, though it was Friday night and "small gathering" sounded harmless. Ree would probably be there, and she hadn't seen her in a while. And even though Hannah was actively looking for an apartment now, she still lived at home. Which meant Liz would most likely be around. Kelsey hadn't seen her since the dinner last month and she was less excited about that. But the gathering was for Chris, presumably to welcome her and introduce her to the group.

"And probably recruit her for the softball team," Kelsey said quietly, joking.

"Recruit who?" Stephanie Bradley stuck her head around the green fabric of the cubicle wall and grinned at Kelsey.

"Nobody. Just talking to myself." Kelsey smiled at her new boss.

"I think geniuses do that, talk to themselves. Isn't that what they say? I do it, so..." Stephanie handed over a sheet of paper as Kelsey chuckled. "Here's a new store that opened up in Aurora. Give them a call?"

"Will do." Kelsey nodded and took the paper. As she scanned it, she felt Stephanie still standing there, and she glanced up, raising her eyebrows.

"You're doing great, Kelsey. I just wanted you to know. I know closing your store was hard, but...I'm glad you came on board." Stephanie gave Kelsey's shoulder a squeeze and went back to her own office.

Okay, that felt good, not gonna lie.

Kelsey had battled some mild and unexpected depression after closing Common Scents, and she worried she wouldn't be able to throw herself into this new job. But she'd done okay, apparently. And she liked it. The products were high-quality, they smelled amazing, and selling cruelty-free items was almost a no-brainer. She'd found herself sucked into doing research and learning all she could, and before she knew it, she felt better. Which seemed odd, as it had only been a couple of weeks. She was given a handful of existing customers and a list of possible customers for her to cold call. She surprised herself by jumping right into the cold calls first, and after her third day at her new job, she'd set up six appointments for herself. Maybe this was what she was meant to be doing after all.

An e-mail came later that day letting the sales reps know there were some new scents in the conference room for them to smell, try out, and give their opinions on. This was the second time since Kelsey had been there that she'd been invited to check out the new products, and it had quickly become a favorite aspect of her job. She was the only one in the room when she got there, and spotted the six bottles on the table. Three lotions and three body fragrance sprays. Kelsey picked up each one. The Lavender Vanilla was really nice. Nothing new or earth-shattering. Rather, a fairly common scent combination, but a winner nonetheless. Sandalwood Musk was also pleasant, if not a tiny bit masculine for Kelsey. The third one was called School's Out for the Summer. It held notes of coconut, sunshine, and what Kelsey was sure was a tiny hint of chlorine. She closed her eyes and inhaled slowly, took in as much as she could. It actually smelled a little bit like a swimming pool...

And just like that, Kelsey was transported back to that night, to Theresa's pool. The star-sprinkled sky above them, the underwater lighting illuminating just enough of Theresa's body, the warm softness of the water, the smooth nylon of that white swimsuit under Kelsey's fingertips, the heat from Theresa's body, her hands, her mouth...

Kelsey's breath shuddered slightly as she let it out. "God," she whispered.

"You like that one?" a voice from behind her said, scaring the crap out of her.

Kelsey turned, one hand pressed to her chest to see Dina, another sales rep, smiling at her.

"Did I startle you? I'm sorry. My mother always told me I move like a cat." Dina reached around Kelsey and picked up the bottle of the School's Out for the Summer body fragrance spray, gave it a sniff. "Not bad." She sniffed again. "Smells like summer vacation. Which I suppose is the point, huh?" She laughed and Kelsey joined her, albeit less enthusiastically, as she was a little miffed at being yanked from her reverie. With a sigh, she headed back to her desk, but for the next hour, couldn't get that lovely little flashback out of her head. She picked up her phone and stared at it for a long moment.

"Screw it," she finally muttered as she began typing.

Just smelled a new lotion that flashed me right back to your swimming pool...

Kelsey knew if she hesitated even an extra second, she wouldn't send it, so she hit Send before she could think about. Almost immediately, she made a little yelp of horror and dropped her phone onto her desk with a clatter, the panicked phrase "What have I done?" ripping through her brain like a hacksaw. She picked the phone back up, tossed it into a desk drawer, and slammed it shut. Eyes closed, she shook her head back and forth while wondering why Apple hadn't yet created a *Wait! I Take it Back!* button for retrieval of texts that should never have been sent.

It took a great deal of effort, but Kelsey threw herself into work, making calls and setting up appointments, and after about an hour, she'd completely forgotten about the text. Until she opened her drawer to grab a stapler and saw her phone sitting there. When she picked it up, the screen came to life and let her know there was a text waiting. Holding the phone in her hand for what felt like hours, Kelsey forced herself to just breathe. Finally, *finally*, she clicked the text open.

Sadly, the pool is closed now. ☹ But I've had the same flashback. More than once. Have you gotten any winter clothes yet? You're gonna need 'em...

Kelsey's eyebrows shot up into her hairline. Theresa's had the same flashback? Theresa thought about them in the pool? More than once? Kelsey wasn't sure what to do with this new information, and the tightening in her stomach that it caused was both delicious and a little alarming. She took a moment, reread the text again and again. And again. And once more.

There was a question in there. Theresa had asked if Kelsey had gotten any winter clothes. A question meant an answer was expected, right? Why wouldn't Kelsey's brain work? She rubbed her fingers against her forehead, willing her thoughts to clear. She set the phone down on her desk and stared at it. She toyed with the ring on her forefinger and stared some more.

A question needs an answer. Expects *an answer.*

Phone back in her hand, she typed.

I have not and I'm freezing!

This time, the response came in an instant, as if Theresa was waiting, phone in hand, much like Kelsey.

My offer to shop with you still stands.

"It does?" Kelsey didn't mean to say it out loud, but she was so surprised that it slipped out. Surprised and...a little giddy, if she was going to be honest. What was happening here?

Kelsey looked up from her phone and glanced around. Her cubicle walls were low enough that she could see over the top if she lifted her chin a smidge. Everybody was busy. She could see Stephanie in her office on the phone. The gentle hum of conversation traveled through the open area like a soft breeze, other reps on calls with their clients. Kelsey should be doing the same thing. *A little preoccupied here*, she thought as she wrinkled her nose.

This was a big step. Kelsey realized that as she reread the text. Theresa was putting herself out there; she was obviously much braver than Kelsey. Theresa had extended an invitation and had no way of knowing how Kelsey would respond. That was gutsy. And impressive. And sexy somehow.

I would like to take you up on that.

Again, Kelsey hit Send before she could second-guess herself.

Waiting for a response was the hardest part. If Theresa didn't answer right away, it could mean many things. It could mean she was only being polite and she didn't actually want to go shopping with Kelsey. It could mean she got called into a meeting. It could mean she had an appointment. It could mean she was on the phone. It could mean she was in the ladies' room. So many possibilities, most of which were *not* Theresa avoiding the conversation. But that didn't matter. Kelsey's mind was already sprinting down the hall toward the room marked The Worst Possible Option. She was saved, though, when her phone pinged.

Tomorrow?

One word. One question.

Yes! This time, there was no hesitation on Kelsey's part.

There's a place I know near my house. Pick me up at noon?

Was this a date? Was it an official date? Because...they probably should talk about some things, right? Kelsey shook the worries free. For now, she wanted to bask in the giddiness she used to feel when talking to Theresa.

I'll be there.

And then bask, she did. She sat back in her chair and grinned like she knew something nobody else did.

Was it tomorrow yet?

By nine o'clock that night, Kelsey was thankful she'd agreed to go to the party for Chris because she knew if she hadn't, she'd be sitting home, bouncing off the walls with nervous energy that would have flooded her system in anticipation of seeing Theresa tomorrow. This way, she was surrounded by friends, her attention was taken up by something other than tomorrow, and the time went by much faster than if she'd been at home alone.

Hannah had invited about a dozen people, including Chris and herself, most of whom made it. Liz had been flitting around the kitchen all evening, helping with drinks and hors d'oeuvres, and she'd been nothing but friendly and warm to Kelsey. So there was that.

There were about nine people gathered in Hannah's mother's dining room, six of them seated around the table playing poker. Kelsey was terrible at poker and Ree hated it, so they'd opted to sit this one out, relaxing on the loveseat in the attached living room where they could both watch the card game and chat with each other.

"How're you doing, kid?" Ree asked quietly as they watched each player fold or bet. "I know closing your shop must've sucked."

Kelsey scoffed. "Did it ever. I mean, I knew it would. I expected it to. But when the time came, it was harder than I'd prepared for. I stood behind the counter in the dark and just cried."

"Aw, you poor thing." Ree patted her leg, the warmth in her voice genuine and kind and yet another reminder of how much Kelsey liked her. "And how's the new job?"

"Oh, you mean the one that fell right into my lap?" Kelsey laughed.

"That one, yes."

"It's good. I like it a lot. It's a good company that makes a good product."

"Can't ask for much more than that." Ree sipped from her red Solo cup and they watched the poker action for a few moments. Chris seemed to be raking in the chips to teasing cries of the game being rigged.

"No, you really can't." Kelsey had brought a lovely Cabernet and sipped from her glass now, letting the smooth red coat her tongue before swallowing it. A burst of laughter shot up from the table and though Kelsey didn't know what had happened, the sound was contagious. Soon she and Ree were both chuckling along.

"And how's the rest of you?" Ree asked once the group had refocused on their cards.

"The rest of me?"

"Yeah. You know, the non-work parts." Ree's eye contact was just this side of intense, as if she was trying to telepathically clue Kelsey in on what she was really asking.

Kelsey simply raised an eyebrow.

"I heard about Theresa."

Kelsey sighed quietly. "Yeah, Hannah never misses an opportunity to slam her."

"Sounds like this time, it was warranted?" It was a question, and Ree seemed to honestly be looking for Kelsey's response.

"I thought so, initially, but..." Kelsey took a sip of wine, recalled how hard she'd been on Theresa. "I maybe jumped the gun a bit. Was harsher than I should've been."

"Interesting," Ree said, sipping from her Solo cup, her eyes never leaving Kelsey's, obviously waiting for more information.

"We're going shopping tomorrow."

Ree's brow furrowed. "You and Hannah?"

"Me and Theresa."

The shift of Ree's eyebrows from furrowed to springing up into her hairline was almost comical, and Kelsey smiled at the sight. "Seriously?"

"Seriously."

"I'm going to need details. Stat." Kelsey grinned as Ree snuggled herself more comfortably into the cushions of the love seat, shifted her body so she was fully facing Kelsey, and propped her chin in her hand. "Tell me."

So Kelsey did. In hushed tones, she told Ree everything. She wasn't sure if Ree knew about the two weeks of unanswered texts and other correspondence, but she was sure that Chris probably told Hannah. If Hannah knew, Kelsey had no doubt she'd passed it along, grabbing onto any chance to badmouth her half-sister. So she told Ree all of it, right up to yesterday's text session.

Ree listened quietly through the whole story, never interrupting, never interjecting her own opinion. She kept her eyes riveted to Kelsey's and simply nodded here and there. When Kelsey finished, Ree seemed to take a few moments to absorb it all before she finally spoke.

"Well." She took a healthy gulp from her cup, finishing her drink. "I have two things to say to you. One: I did not see that coming. And two: go, you."

"Really?" Kelsey was surprised. "I kind of got the impression most of Hannah's crew doesn't like Theresa."

"If it was up to Hannah, we wouldn't. Luckily, I have my own mind and can form my own opinions. I don't know Theresa well, but I've always thought she was nice. Also? Girl is *hot*." Ree gave a snort. "Like I have to tell you that."

Kelsey held up a hand, palm out. "I'm trying to go into this tomorrow with no expectations. None." She lowered her voice. "And I haven't told anybody but you, so..."

"My lips are sealed." Ree twisted an imaginary key in front of her lips, then tossed it over her shoulder.

"I have no idea what will happen and I don't want to jinx it." Trying to portray nonchalance, Kelsey gave a half-shrug. "We're just doing this as friends. I need winter stuff and she was born here, so she's going to be my guide."

Ree gave her a knowing look, but said nothing other than, "Mm-hmm."

"I mean it." And Kelsey did, despite being fully aware of what she *really* hoped would happen tomorrow...

CHAPTER NINETEEN

SATURDAY DAWNED GRAY AND cold, perfect weather to shop for cold-weather gear. Instead of being lulled into melancholy by the overcast skies, Kelsey was smiling, chipper, almost giddy. She needed to be careful of that, she kept reminding herself. She and Theresa had a lot of baggage now, which seemed almost ridiculous, given their short stint of almost-togetherness.

Choosing what to wear on this shopping excursion had proven an exercise in frustration because nothing seemed quite right. She didn't want to overdress, thereby giving the opinion that this was possibly a date and she was trying to be impressive. On the other hand, she didn't want to be *too* casual, as she—admittedly—wanted Theresa to find her attractive and to know she'd put in at least *some* effort.

She'd settled on tasteful simplicity by going with a dark pair of jeans, a cream V-neck sweater, and a lightweight scarf in a multitude of blues. Out of the shower, she'd used Earthly Products's Sugared Pumpkin Latte lotion because it smelled warm and inviting, and that's exactly what she wanted to exude to Theresa. With as much subtlety as she could.

Kelsey had barely gotten the car shifted into Park when Theresa came out her front door, down the steps, and across the front lawn. She pulled the passenger side door open, sat down, blew out a breath, and turned those gorgeous blue eyes on Kelsey.

"Hey," she said quietly and with a smile.

"Hey." Kelsey did her best to rein in the goofy grin that wanted to bust out across her face. She only half-succeeded. "You look great." She did. Her blond hair was a little longer than Kelsey remembered, the waves turning gently on themselves as they reached past Theresa's shoulders. Her jeans were faded and looked super soft. She wore a puffy down jacket in a muted eggplant color with with white gloves and a white scarf.

"Thank you," Theresa said with a grin and a very light blush. "So do you. And you smell amazing."

Kelsey's turn to blush. "Thanks. It's my job."

"But, yeah, that jacket will never get you through a Chicago winter." She fingered the sleeve of Kelsey's lightweight nylon jacket with the thin flannel lining. "You'll have pneumonia before Thanksgiving."

Something about the combination of Theresa's touch and the concern in her voice made Kelsey feel...very content. Too content. Like this was how it should be. Trying not to let that thought run away with her, she cleared her throat. "You're the boss. Where are we headed?"

Theresa quietly directed her as they drove, pointing here and telling her to turn there, until they pulled into the parking lot of Jig's Sporting Goods. It was surprisingly large and designed to look like a giant log cabin from the outside.

"Wow," Kelsey said as they exited the car. "How have I never heard of this place? It's enormous."

"You have to know a local," Theresa said with a wink. "Come on."

Kelsey decided walking slightly behind Theresa was a very smart choice, though she did her best not to openly stare at her behind, but man, it was hard.

When they reached the front door, Theresa pulled it open and waved Kelsey in. “After you, ma’am.”

“Oh, I’m ‘ma’am’ now. Terrific.”

Theresa chuckled and followed Kelsey in. “Okay, I’m going to tell you what I’m thinking and then you can correct me or add things or whatever. Okay?”

Kelsey nodded, enjoying the animation in Theresa’s voice, in the way she used her hands to talk. She had a plan for the route they’d take around the store, which items she’d need (coat, boots, gloves, hat, scarf), how long it should take.

“So...you’ve thought this through.” Kelsey said it lightly, jokingly, but Theresa’s face stayed fairly serious.

“I have,” she said, with one sharp nod.

Interesting.

Part of Kelsey wanted to talk, to discuss things, to dive right in. But another larger and louder part kept her from doing that. Instead, she decided to simply enjoy this time with Theresa. Laugh, joke, have fun, and wherever things went, they went.

Not nearly as easy as it sounded.

They took care of boots first. As they stood in front of the display wall that showed them twenty-five styles, easily, Kelsey made a point.

“I live in an apartment. I don’t need to shovel or anything, so I probably only need something basic. Nothing big and fancy.” She glanced at the price tag on a pair of boots with built-in foot warmers, extra traction soles, and zip-tie laces.

"What if I want you to shovel my driveway?" Theresa asked.

Kelsey just stared for a beat. "I would," she said honestly, then turned the tag over. The number caused her to mutter, "Holy shit," before she could stop herself, and Theresa laughed. "But not in these. Are they serious? Are these made of Corinthian leather and also gold? Because that's the only way I'd justify this price."

Theresa laughed some more before taking the overpriced boot and placing it back on the shelf. Then she tugged Kelsey by the arm down the wall a bit. "You don't need top-of-the-line. You need warm, functional, and affordable."

"Exactly." Kelsey stayed close, hoping to keep Theresa's warm hand on her arm for as long as possible.

Once they'd chosen a pair of boots that fit Kelsey's needs (and wallet), they moved on to coats. Theresa pulled three off the rack immediately, and Kelsey felt that familiar tightening in her lower abdomen. There was something inarguably sexy about Theresa picking out clothes for her, even if it was bulky outerwear and not sleek and sexy lingerie.

"Try this." Theresa handed her a navy blue Columbia with a hideaway hood and a zip-out lining.

Kelsey slipped her arms in and Theresa stepped right into her space, pulling the sides of the coat to zip it up, tugging on the arms and around the shoulders. When she grasped each side of the collar, her thumbs brushed Kelsey's jaw on both sides, and the contact made her swallow. Theresa caught her eye and they stood like that for a long moment, close enough to kiss.

Theresa cleared her throat and took a small step back. "Warm?"

Kelsey nodded, not trusting her voice.

"You like it?" Theresa gestured to the full-length mirror behind them and Kelsey took a long look.

"I do." She gave a nod and Theresa handed her a second coat.

"Try this one."

They did this same dance for six different coats. Kelsey would have tried on a hundred if it meant Theresa would continue to dress her, to stand close and touch her. By the time she decided on light blue coat with faux fur trimming the hood, she felt slightly worn out, as if it had taken most of her energy simply to keep calm and outwardly unmoved by Theresa's proximity. The reality was that her insides were burning. Completely ablaze. In a good way. She wasn't sure how she hadn't just incinerated into a pile of ash, and she was so ridiculously turned on that, if they hadn't been standing in a store full of other people, Kelsey might actually have thrown herself at Theresa and said, "Please. Just take me. Now. Right now."

Instead, they moved on to accessories. As they rifled through different gloves and hats to find some that matched the coat Kelsey had chosen, they grew quieter and quieter. Yet they still seemed to stay, by unspoken agreement, remarkably close to each other. Kelsey could feel Theresa's body heat, wondered if she felt as warm as it seemed she should. When Kelsey glanced at Theresa, she was staring off into space and her cheeks were tinted a very rosy pink. Could she be as affected as Kelsey?

They went through the checkout line in silence. Kelsey handed over her credit card and tried not to wince at the total. It was all necessary. She was buying nothing frivolous, and that helped ease the anxiety. A little.

"This stuff will last you at least a couple years," Theresa said quietly, startlingly close to Kelsey's ear. "It's worth the money. I promise."

Kelsey nodded, signed, and took her bags. As they exited Jig's, she asked, "Now what?"

"Hungry?" Theresa didn't look at her when she asked.

Kelsey hit her key fob and her car beeped itself unlocked. "As a matter of fact, I am. You?"

"Starving. I didn't eat any breakfast."

The weather was chilly and as the breeze kicked up, slicing right through her nylon jacket as Theresa had predicted, Kelsey was suddenly grateful for the purchases in her trunk. "Okay. Late lunch/early dinner it is. Where to?"

They ended up at a cute little café called Root 66 that specialized in local, organic, fresh-made foods, and their salads were huge. Kelsey ordered a Cobb salad, grateful for all the greens and tomatoes to balance out the chunks of chicken, turkey, ham and cheddar that would suddenly appear in the salad as she moved her fork, like hidden icebergs in the Arctic Ocean.

Theresa's grilled cheese sandwich looked heavenly, though.

"So...what if I asked for a bite of your sandwich?" Kelsey asked. "Is that allowed?"

"It is if I can have a chunk of that chicken," was Theresa's reply. "And maybe a bite of cucumber?"

They were more than halfway done with their meals before Kelsey finally decided she needed to bring up the subject, the enormous gorilla that had been tagging along with them all day.

She sipped her soda, wiped her mouth with her napkin, then leaned her forearms on the table and waited for Theresa to give her eye contact.

"So." Kelsey wet her lips, paused to choose the right words. "What made you suggest today?"

Theresa stopped chewing for a second, then began again. "Well," she said, setting down the crust of her sandwich and dabbing at her own mouth with a napkin. "Several things, really."

Kelsey propped her chin in her hand and made a show of being all ears.

"It's getting cold. Winter's almost here, and I promised I'd help you prepare." Theresa toyed with the straw in her Diet Pepsi as she gazed somewhere over Kelsey's shoulder.

"Uh-huh." Kelsey watched her face, was pretty sure she saw flashes of uncertainty. Of nervousness.

"And I thought, after all the texts and e-mails and messages and your visit, maybe it was a good idea to be face-to-face for a change. You know?" Those gorgeous blue eyes shifted so Theresa looked at her for no more than a second or two before darting off again. This was hard for her, Kelsey realized.

"I do know," Kelsey said, and sipped her 7UP.

"And..." Theresa hesitated and Kelsey could see her swallow. Then she cleared her throat and finally settled her gaze directly on Kelsey. And held it for a long stretch before finally saying, very softly, "And I missed you."

Kelsey wasn't sure how to respond to that. All she knew was that her heart rate picked up speed and a warmth began to spread from inside her body outward to her head, her limbs, her fingers and toes. She could feel the smile form, feel the corners of her mouth turn upward before it even registered in her brain that she was about to smile. It was that instantaneous, and it was that effective. And poor Theresa looked so anxious, like she'd let something slip she hadn't meant to and was now awaiting her horrible fate. Kelsey let her off the hook.

"I've missed you, too."

They basked in that for a long moment, and the relief was like a vapor surrounding their table and then gently lifting away. Kelsey could tell by Theresa's expression that she felt it, too, though it was also obvious there was more she wanted to say. She reached across the small table and covered Kelsey's hand with her own. "I mean, I can't figure out why," she said with a grin, obviously trying to lighten the mood.

"Right?" Kelsey laughed along with her before they both grew serious again and Theresa spoke softly.

"So...I'm just going to say this and if you think I'm way off base, I need you to tell me. Okay?" Her voice was still quiet, and now there was a new earnest quality to it that told Kelsey she needed to listen and be honest. She nodded once. Theresa wet her lips, studied the remnants of her sandwich for several seconds before looking back up at Kelsey. "I've touched on this before, but I think it bears repeating. I feel like we have something, you and I. Something good. Call it potential. Call it possibility. Call it whatever. But I think it's there. It's the reason I haven't been able to just blow you off, chalk us up to a fun romp and let it go. Even after...everything else."

She had the grace not to mention Kelsey's horrid behavior, and for that, Kelsey was grateful. Kelsey also knew she needed to address it herself. "I was such an asshole," she said, barely above a whisper.

"No," Theresa said with conviction and squeezed Kelsey's hand. "You weren't. You were upset."

"I was. I was in a really bad head space. In my mind, I was losing a dream I'd worked hard to build, but now I know that maybe I was looking at the wrong thing, that maybe it was my move alone that was the big dream, the big lifestyle change, not the actual shop. I really like my new job, there's much less stress, and I'm making more money. So, yes, I was upset at the situation, but that was no excuse to take it out on you for simply doing your job." Theresa's expression seemed slightly skeptical, so Kelsey added, "I know you had yourself removed from the account."

Theresa's eyes snapped to hers. "You do? How?"

"Liz. She's very mama bear—or stepmama bear, rather—with you, you know that?"

A half-grin tugged up one side of Theresa's mouth as she gave a gentle nod. "I know."

"You didn't have to do that," Kelsey said quietly.

Theresa's gaze became a bit more intense as she said, "Yeah. I did."

Kelsey cocked her head, curious, so Theresa went on.

"I saw how much your store meant to you that day when I popped in. I hadn't realized it until I saw the pride on your face, how happy you were there. I knew I couldn't stop what my company was going to do, but I could fix it so I didn't actually take part."

"But...you jeopardized your position there."

Theresa merely shrugged. "You meant more."

Kelsey sat back in her chair, just a little bit stunned at the revelation, and stared. Had Theresa really just said that? Did the gorgeous, intelligent, successful woman sitting across from her really just tell Kelsey that she meant more to her than her very high-powered, well-paying, lots-of-room-for-advancement job she'd worked hard at for many years? For a moment, she let herself revel in the glow of that feeling, the feeling that somebody put her above so much else. An instant later, she felt her heart sink and her eyes well with tears.

"Okay," Theresa said with a grimace as she, too, sat back. "I said more than I should have. I'm sorry..."

"No!" Kelsey cried as she sat forward and grabbed Theresa's hand before she pulled it from the table completely. "No, that's not why I'm upset. I'm upset with *myself*." She snatched a napkin from the table and wiped her nose, even as the tears began to flow freely. "I was so selfish, so unwilling to even have a discussion." She shook her head in real, solid self-deprecation. She fingered the napkin, crumpled it in her palm. When she finally looked up, Theresa was watching her with a surprisingly open expression. "I was horrible to you, Theresa, and I am so very sorry."

The two of them sat in silence for what felt like a long time. Out the café window, the wind had picked up, and clouds the color of old ductwork were rolling in. It looked cold, hard, unforgiving outside. *How apropos*, Kelsey thought, sure that Theresa was going to get up and leave at any moment, despite not having a car. Instead, she turned her hand over so she could grip Kelsey's as firmly as Kelsey gripped hers.

"What if we started over?" she asked quietly.

Kelsey furrowed her brow. "What do you mean?"

"I know it's a bit cliché, but..." Theresa looked down at their hands, brought her other one up so she could play with Kelsey's ring. "What if we let everything that happened go? I don't feel like I handled it well. You don't feel like you handled it well. I don't feel like you handled it well. You don't feel like I handled it well..."

With a squint, Kelsey said, "Okay, now you're just rearranging the same sentence."

Theresa laughed for the first time in a long while. "I just mean, let's start with a clean slate."

Kelsey liked it. She liked it a lot. But was it possible? "I think we can give it a shot. Do you?"

Theresa pressed her lips together, rolled them in as she seemed to contemplate her next words. "I've been thinking a lot lately. Like, a lot. Trying to figure out what it was about our situation that made it so not cut and dried, which was how I expected it would be. And what I came up with was this: I asked myself what matters most. You know? Is it my job? Is it my pride? Or is it this profound connection I felt with this woman—in bed and out—that won't let me shake her out of my head? What matters most?"

"It's a good question," Kelsey told her, and it was. "I'm not sure I've asked myself that in quite some time."

"Maybe you should."

"Maybe I should."

They sat there, grinning at each other, still holding hands. As Theresa spun Kelsey's ring, Kelsey studied her. This beautiful, amazing woman wanted to try again. If Kelsey was going to be honest, she wasn't sure she'd give herself another chance if she were in Theresa's shoes. She wasn't proud of her behavior, and that was something she was going to have to accept and move on from. Not an easy feat.

But I want to.

And that was key. Looking at Theresa now, she still felt the same flutter, the same intense arousal, the desire to be around her, to spend time with her, to have in-depth conversations about anything and everything. None of that had changed. She still wanted to be with Theresa, to give them a shot, and Theresa wanted the same thing.

Wasn't that what mattered most?

CHAPTER TWENTY

THE KNOCKING SEEMED MUFFLED, like it was coming from underwater. Or maybe Kelsey was the one underwater. Which couldn't be the case because she was too comfortable. Too warm. Too not drowning.

Without opening her eyes, Kelsey took stock of her surroundings. She was toasty and cozy, and it wasn't hard to identify the feel of her own bed beneath her back, her favorite pillow cushioning her head. She could tell it wasn't quite dark yet, both by the color of the insides of her lids and the fact that she wasn't sleeping deeply. It wasn't the heavy, comatose sleep that came at two in the morning. It was a catnap-type sleep. Light. Temporary.

Next, she took stock of her body, and the most important detail was that she was naked. Gloriously naked and sated, her thighs doing a gentle throbbing of muscles that would be sore tomorrow. The best part, though? The other warm, naked body that was wound around her like ivy taking over a tree, wrapping its branches, its trunk. The smell of cinnamon and honey and sex permeated the air, the sheets, and, still with her eyes closed, Kelsey pressed a gentle kiss to Theresa's forehead, which was very near her lips. In response, Theresa snuggled closer as she let out a little breathy sigh in her sleep.

The knocking came again, and this time it was accompanied by a voice.

"Kelsey?" It was Chris. "K-Pete. You in there? I see your car, but you're not answering your phone. Is everything all right?"

Shit. Kelsey had turned her phone to silent when she and Theresa had ventured into her bedroom after their late lunch. They had joked a bit about how prominent sex was apparently going to be in their relationship, and then Theresa was kissing her with that gorgeous mouth. Touching her with those hands that seemed to know her better than she knew herself. And then they'd gotten lost. In the touches and the murmurs and the gentle words...and then things moved far away from gentle. Thus, Kelsey's sore thighs. She grinned at the memory even as her body flooded her with a new wave of arousal (again?).

Kelsey shook herself free of the thoughts of sex and opened her eyes. Chris was worried, so she needed to reassure her favorite cousin that she was, in fact, alive. Extricating herself from Theresa's body as gently and quietly as she could, she donned a fleecy red robe and padded out to the front door.

Chris blew into the small apartment like a tornado, forcing Kelsey to step out of her way or be run over.

"Jesus Christ, Kels. Where have you been? You never don't answer your phone. You had me worried sick. Are you okay?" She took in the robe. "Are you sick? Do you not feel well?"

"No, no, I'm fine. I forgot I turned my phone to silent. I'm so sorry."

Chris pushed out a breath, obviously relieved. "Well, good. Don't do that again, okay? I didn't know what to think."

Kelsey grimaced. "Sorry," she said again. "I'll be better."

Chris flopped down onto the couch. "I was calling because we're having a game night at Hannah's tonight and I want you to come. Relax and have fun. You in?"

"Game night, huh?" Kelsey stood so Chris was facing her and unable to see the gorgeous woman with the sleepy eyes and tousled blond hair leaning on the doorframe of the bedroom. She wore Kelsey's green-and-white-striped pajama bottoms and the matching green V-neck T-shirt, and Kelsey wanted nothing more than to back her into the bedroom again. She smiled at her, then said to Chris, "Can I bring a date?"

Chris flinched as if Kelsey had poked her with a stick. "A date? You want to bring somebody?" Her surprise was apparent.

Kelsey nodded, her eyes on Theresa, and Chris turned to follow her gaze.

"Oh," Chris said, drawing the word out so it had three long syllables. "A date. I see."

"Wanna go?" Kelsey asked, her eyes on Theresa. "Game night at Hannah's?" She raised her eyebrows, waiting. "Totally your call." She did her best not to let her eyes wander, not to let them roam over Theresa's body, down those long, shapely legs, not to flash back to an hour ago when that body was under hers, fingers digging into Kelsey's back, hips moving to Kelsey's rhythm...

"I think it sounds fun." Theresa gave one nod of agreement, and Kelsey's grin grew wide.

"Awesome," Chris said as she slapped her jeans-clad thighs and stood. "Eight o'clock. Bring beer." She glanced at her watch. "That should leave you time to get another round in..." She winked at Kelsey and dodged the playful slap, and then she was out the door, her chuckle echoing in the hall even after Kelsey had closed the door after her.

Kelsey felt the heat from Theresa's body before she felt her press against her back. Her arms came around the front and crossed at Kelsey's stomach, her lips near Kelsey's ear, and they stood that way for a long moment, Theresa holding Kelsey, Kelsey basking in the warmth and joy of being held so tenderly.

"You ready for this?" Theresa asked quietly. "Hannah might be less than receptive."

Kelsey shrugged. "I think she'll be fine. She and Chris seem to be moving forward. Slowly."

"So slowly," Theresa said with a gentle laugh.

"I think it's working for them."

"It's not like we can be critical. We obviously have no idea what slowly means."

"We so do not."

They laughed together, and Kelsey wrapped her arms over Theresa's, pulling her even more tightly against her back.

"You know what we do know, though?" she asked.

"Tell me." Theresa set her chin on Kelsey's shoulder.

"We know what matters most."

She could feel Theresa's smile against her skin as she responded, "We do."

Kelsey squeezed, then turned in Theresa's arms, kissed her tenderly. "Now, let's get dressed. I feel a win in Taboo coming on."

Unable to dodge the slap to her behind from Theresa, Kelsey giggled as she padded back to the bedroom feeling happier and more content than she could ever remember feeling in her life.

Not with Janice. Not at Common Scents. But here. Now. With Theresa.

This *is what matters most.*

THE END

By Georgia Beers

Novels

Finding Home

Mine

Fresh Tracks

Too Close to Touch

Thy Neighbor's Wife

Turning the Page

Starting From Scratch

96 Hours

Slices of Life

Snow Globe

Olive Oil and White Bread

Zero Visibility

A Little Bit of Spice

Rescued Heart

Run to You

Dare to Stay

What Matters Most

Anthologies

Outsiders

www.georgiabeers.com